Riot

D1255108

By Jamie Shaw

Riot
Mayhem

JAMIE SHAW

AVONIMPULSE
An Imprint of HarperCollinsPublishers

Excerpt from *Chaos* copyright © 2015 by Jamie Shaw.
Excerpt from *Various States of Undress: Georgia* copyright © 2015 by Laura Simcox.
Excerpt from *Make It Last* copyright © 2015 by Megan Erickson.
Excerpt from *Hero By Night* copyright © 2015 by Sara Jane Stone.
Excerpt from *Mayhem* copyright © 2015 by Jamie Shaw.
Excerpt from *Sinful Rewards 1* copyright © 2014 by Cynthia Sax.
Excerpt from *Forbidden* copyright © 2015 by Charlotte Stein.
Excerpt from *Her Highland Fling* copyright © 2015 by Jennifer McQuiston.

EPub Edition FEBRUARY 2015 ISBN: 9780062379689
Print Edition ISBN: 9780062379672

10 9 8 7 6 5 4 3 2

For every reader who falls in love with Joel.

Chapter One

"Kiss me," I order the luckiest guy in Mayhem tonight. When he sat next to me at the bar earlier with his "Leave It to Beaver" haircut, I made sure to avoid eye contact and cross my legs in the opposite direction. I didn't think I'd end up making out with him, but now I have no choice.

A dumb expression washes over his face. He might be cute if he didn't look so. freaking. dumb. "Huh?"

"Oh for God's sake."

I curl my fingers behind his neck and yank him to my mouth, tilting my head to the side and hoping he's a quick learner. My lips part, my tongue comes out to play, and after a moment, he finally catches on. His greedy fingers thread into my chocolate brown curls—which I spent *hours* on this morning.

UGH.

Peeking out of the corner of my eye, I spot Joel Gibbon stroll past me, a bleach-blonde groupie tucked under his arm. He's too busy whispering in her ear to notice me, and my fingers itch to punch him in the back of his stupid mohawked head to get his attention.

I'm preparing to push Leave It to Beaver off me when Joel's gaze finally lifts to meet mine. I bite Beaver's bottom lip between my teeth and give it a little tug, and the corner of Joel's mouth lifts up into an infuriating smirk that is *so* not the reaction I wanted. He continues walking, and when he's finally out of sight, I break my lips from Beaver's and nudge him back toward his own stool, immediately spinning in the opposite direction to scowl at my giggling best friend.

"I can't BELIEVE him!" I shout at a far-too-amused-looking Rowan. How does she not recognize the gravity of this situation?!

I'm about to shake some sense into her when Beaver taps me on the shoulder. "Um—"

"You're welcome," I say with a flick of my wrist, not wanting to waste another minute on a guy who can't appreciate how long it took me to get my hair to curl like this—or at least make messing it up worth my while.

Rowan gives him an apologetic half smile, and I let out a deep sigh.

I don't feel bad about Beaver. I feel bad about the dickhead bass guitarist for The Last Ones to Know.

"That boy is making me insane," I growl.

Rowan turns a bright smile on me, her blue eyes sparkling with humor. "You were already insane."

"He's making me homicidal," I clarify, and she laughs.

"Why don't you just tell him you like him?" She twirls

two tiny straws in her cocktail, her eyes periodically flitting up to the stage. She's waiting for Adam, and I'd probably be jealous of her if those two weren't so disgustingly perfect for each other.

Last semester, I nearly got kicked out of my dorm when I let Rowan move in with me and my roommate. But Rowan's asshole live-in boyfriend had cheated on her, and she had nowhere to go, and she's been my *best* friend since kindergarten. I ignored the written warnings from my RA, and Rowan ultimately ended up moving in with Adam before I got kicked out. Fast-forward to one too many "overnight visitors" later, I still ended up getting reported, and Rowan and I got a two-bedroom in an apartment complex near campus. Her name is on the lease right next to mine, but really, the apartment is just a decoy she uses to avoid telling her parents that she's actually living with three ungodly hot rock stars. She sleeps in Adam's bed, his bandmate Shawn is in the second bedroom, and Joel sleeps on their couch most nights because he's a hot, stupid, infuriating freaking nomad.

"Because I *don't* like him," I answer. When I realize my drink is gone, I steal Rowan's, down the last of it, and flag the bartender.

"Then why is he making you insane?"

"Because *he* doesn't like *me*."

Rowan lifts a sandy blonde eyebrow at me, but I don't expect her to understand. Hell, *I* don't understand. I've never wanted a boy to like me so badly in my entire life. I don't even want Joel to just *like* me—I want him to worship the ground I walk on and throw himself at my feet. I want him to beg me to be with him and then cry his eyes out when I tell him I'm not a relationship kind of girl.

When the bartender arrives to take our orders, I order shots for both of us. At eighteen, Rowan and I are far from being old enough to drink, but our fake IDs and the stamps on our hands say otherwise.

"Make hers a double," Rowan says, pointing a thumb in my direction.

I finally stop scowling long enough to smile. "See? This is why I love you."

We've just gulped down our shots and slammed our glasses on the bar top when something heavy lands on my shoulder. Leti rests his left elbow on me and his right elbow on Rowan. He's been dancing his butt off on the dance floor with some tattooed beefcake, but he smells like he just stepped out of the shower, fresh and sexy clean.

"What are we celebrating?"

I groan, and Rowan shakes her head in warning.

"Oh," Leti says. "Joel?"

"He's such an ass," I complain.

"Didn't you just spend the night with him this past weekend?"

"Yes!" I shout. "God, what is his problem?!"

Leti laughs and massages my shoulders. "If you like him, just tell him."

Okay, number one, in what freaking universe do they think that would ever work? Joel is a serial player. He lures girls in with his bad-boy hair and his panty-dropping smile, and then he chews them up and spits them out. "Liking" him would be like "liking" ice cream. Sure, it's great when you're stuffing your face with it, but then it's gone and you're just left with this all-consuming emptiness. Yeah, you can go to the store and get more, but what if they don't have the flavor you want? What then?!

And number two, have these two ever met me? Boys chase after ME, not the other way around.

"I don't like him!" I protest.

Rowan and Leti share a look and speak at the same time. "She likes him."

"I hate you bitches."

I hop off of my stool and head toward the crowd. Mayhem is the biggest club in town, and tonight, The Last Ones to Know are opening for a band even bigger than they are, so *mayhem* is an understatement for the vibe on the floor. Before the bands take the stage, the club pulses with house music that makes the floors throb and the walls shiver. I have every intention of dancing my ass off until my brain overheats and shuts down from mind-numbing exhaustion.

"Aw, come on, Dee!" Rowan pleads before I get too far.

"Don't be mad!" Leti adds.

I turn around and prop my hands on my hips. "Are you two coming or what?"

After four songs of me being the meat in a Rowan-and-Leti sandwich, the house music fades out and the roadies begin the sound check. The crowd splits in half—half surging toward the stage to get good spots, and half retreating to the bar to catch their breath and drown themselves in liquor. Rowan, Leti, and I join the latter half, grabbing the best seats at the bar and spinning around to face the stage.

Every time Adam is about to perform, Rowan gets antsy, her feet dancing and her fingers curling. She picks at the pretty pink polish I painted her nails in this morning, and I tell her to stop, but I'm pretty sure she'd self-combust if she ever actually listened to me.

Adam is the first to walk onstage, and the crowd goes insane. He's followed by Shawn, the lead guitarist and backup vocalist. Then Cody, the annoying rhythm guitarist who had the nerve to ask me for my number; Mike, the adorable drummer who has grown on me these past couple months; and Joel, the bane of my existence.

His eyes rove over the front row, and I know what he's looking at: eager faces and barely-covered boobs. Those girls are just eye shadow and tits on legs, which is just how Joel likes them. And now, with Adam making it widely known that he's off the market, Joel and Shawn have their pick of the litter. Cody gets the leftovers, and Mike avoids them like the plague—which each of those girls probably has, along with a million other communicable diseases that health teachers lecture horny freshman about in high school.

"Let's go backstage," I tell Rowan, already hopping off my stool. I have one thing those girls don't—a best friend with a permanent backstage pass I intend to use to my advantage.

"I thought you wanted to stay out here?" Rowan asks. Adam wanted to drag her backstage before he left to perform—since Rowan's dirty-blonde hair, big blue eyes, and tight little figure aren't exactly dick repellant, in *any* sense of the word—but I insisted I wanted to stay at the bar so we could drink.

"I did want to. Now I don't."

She and Leti follow me to the backstage door, where Rowan doesn't even need to tell security her nickname to get them to let us in. Most of the guys know her as Peach, which Adam took to calling her back before he bothered learning girls' names or remembering their faces. Now, she has him wrapped around her little finger.

"What?" she asks when she catches me studying her. Sure, she's gorgeous, but so are lots of other girls who throw themselves at Adam. Something about her won him over . . . maybe her innocence. Maybe I should give it a try. Stop being so forward, wear flats more often, keep my mouth shut once in a while.

I laugh when I realize I can't even imagine that. "Nothing."

I lead Rowan and Leti past the side of the stage where Shawn stands, circling around the back to get to the side where Joel stands. My heels click against the stage stairs, and once we're at the top, I pull my long chocolate hair over my shoulders, hike my skintight dress up a little higher, and freshen my lip gloss.

It's hard not to scream like a groupie while I watch the guys command the stage, especially from this vantage point. The way Joel's blond spikes shine deadly under the foggy blue glow of the spotlights above him. The way he doesn't even need to look down at his guitar while he plucks the strings. The way his blue eyes periodically find mine and his mouth tips up at the corners. His presence on the stage is magnetic. It turns my blood to lava and makes it impossible to think. Part of me wants to play hard to get, but the other part of me knows all too well the rewards of letting him have me.

When Joel's impossibly blue eyes capture mine and hold them long enough to make me melt under their heat, my skin flushes and I know I need to do something to put myself back in control. With a devilish smile, I say, "Ro, you might want to close your eyes for this."

Without lifting my dress up, I wiggle out of my lacy black thong and dangle it from a manicured pointer finger. Joel's hands are busy playing his guitar, but his eyes remain fixed on me, and when I toss my panties at him, he snatches them out of the air. He finishes the song with them dangling from his wrist, and then he stuffs them in his back pocket, giving me a wink that would make any other girl weak in her knees.

"I can't believe you just did that!" Leti shouts over the music.

"I can!" Rowan shouts back, making me laugh.

"I'm heading back to the bar," I tell them, and Rowan questions me with a look.

"Why?"

The truth is, I want to see if he'll come after me. And if he doesn't, I need to have enough distance to pretend that I don't care.

At the bottom of the stairs, I turn around to stop Rowan from following me. "I want another drink. You stay here. Wait for Adam."

She frowns at me, but I give her a smile and walk backward toward the door. "I'll see you after."

At the bar, I sit next to the hottest guy I can find and flash a smile in his direction. Two minutes later, I have a drink and a distraction.

"So do you like the band?" he asks, nodding toward the stage.

I shrug. "They're alright." They're also the last thing I want to talk about right now, since I desperately need to stop agonizing over what's going to happen when their set ends, but God apparently hates me.

"I went to high school with most of them," the guy brags, like he can claim some kind of residual rock-star status for having shared a zip code. I almost burst out laughing, barely managing to hide it behind the drink I'm sipping.

"Were you friends?" I ask, not caring but knowing it's my turn to say something.

He goes on and on about the classes they shared and the time he got to see them in the talent show and how he went to one of Adam's parties his senior year. I'm mentally plotting my escape when the guy's eyes flit over my shoulder and open wide, sending untamed eyebrows jumping up into his forehead. His hand latches onto my forearm like a lifeline, and I turn my head just in time for my lips to brush Joel's cheek. "Is this guy bothering you?" he questions in my ear, his blue eyes turning to read mine before narrowing on the guy's hand, which recoils from my arm even though the rest of the guy looks totally dazed. With his wide eyes and unhinged jaw, he's so starstruck that I can't help but cast a quick glance at his lap to check for a man-for-man hard-on.

"You know Joel Gibbon?" he gasps, startling me from my detective work.

"Who, him?" I ask, pointing a lazy finger at the boy

standing behind me. Inside, I'm giddy as hell that Joel came to find me. Outside, I'm mildly bored and totally unfazed.

"Oh my God," the guy says. "I'm such a huge fan!"

"You apparently went to school together," I add without turning to face Joel, who loosens up behind me even as both of his heavy arms come to wrap around my shoulders. Since no one else has popped up at my sides, I'm guessing the rest of our group stayed backstage to watch the closing band perform.

Joel's chuckle rumbles against my back. "Oh yeah? What year were you?"

The guys talk and I tune them out until the hot fanboy eventually gets a picture with Joel and leaves. And then Joel's suggestive voice is in my ear again.

"Are you ready to get out of here?"

"Are you ready to stop being a man-whore?"

He has the nerve to laugh. "Why, are you jealous?"

Insanely. "Why would I be jealous?" I peel his arms away and turn on my stool to face him. "I'm the one you always go home with."

"Isn't that interesting," he muses with an agitating glimmer in his arctic-blue eyes.

Joel usually begins the night with someone else—or a *few* someone elses—and on nights I'm not around, he goes home with them. But on nights I *am* around, I always end up winning his attention—through exhaustive efforts that I'm really getting tired of exerting.

"If I say no, what will you do? Go home with one of them instead?"

"You won't say no."

I scoff at him. "Shows what you know."

When I spin away from him, he squeezes up behind me again and presses his lips against my ear. "You won't say no because you know all the things I want to do to you."

He starts telling me exactly what those things are, and my toes curl in my peep-toe pumps. Goose bumps spread from my ankles to my ears, and I abruptly hop off my stool.

"Where are you going?" Joel calls after me.

"To see if you're a man of your word!"

Chapter Two

BY THE TIME we make it to the bus in the parking lot of Mayhem, Joel's groping hands have my blood rushing. If he slid them over the curve of my ass and squeezed one more time, I was pretty sure I was going to strip naked wherever we happened to be standing.

I reach for the bus door but don't even have time to open it before he steps against me, pressing me into it. I brace myself against the cold black metal, and his palms cover the backs of my hands. He clasps our fingers together and raises our hands higher, working his jeans against me and kissing the back of my neck. I reward him by rocking my hips, rubbing my ass firmly over his attentive length, and he quickly spins me around, claiming my mouth in a way that makes everything dark. The moon and stars go black. Oxygen leaves my lungs. My heart stops beating and all I can feel are Joel's teeth nipping at my lip and the cold metal of the bus biting against my bare skin.

I reach down and rub him outside of his jeans, which probably gets me even more turned on than it gets him. He moans low in his throat and impatiently tugs me away from the door so he can pull it open.

"Fuck," he complains when it doesn't budge. He yanks on it again, but still it doesn't move.

I'm so frustrated, I want to scream. Instead, I manage to simply say, "You don't have a key?"

"Not on me." He looks around the deserted parking lot until he spots something that makes the corner of his mouth tug up, and then he grabs my hand and tows me across the lot. There are tons of cars, but everyone is inside for the headlining band, so I'm not worried when Joel pulls down the tailgate of a random black truck that I'm sure doesn't belong to anyone he knows.

I barely have time to squeal in surprise when he wraps his hands around my waist and effortlessly lifts me onto it. He steps between my knees, buries his fingers in my hair, and pulls me to his mouth again, kissing me like I've wanted to be kissed all night. My hands are fumbling with the button of his jeans before my mind even processes what they're doing, and his are sliding up my thighs to push my dress up to my hips. Before I can finish with his button, he finishes the job for me and reaches into his zipper, pulling himself out. A second later, his hard length is begging entry between my legs, and I want him so badly that I'm surprised I manage to say what I say next.

"Condom," I pant, my breath leaving in a wintery swirl.

"Lie back," he breathlessly orders, fishing a condom from his pocket and tearing it open. I watch him roll the rubber on, involuntarily tightening my thighs around his hips in anticipation of what's to come. His fingers lift to smooth over the thin fabric covering my pert nipples, and then he applies pressure, urging me to lie down.

I can't believe we're doing this here, in the middle of a damn parking lot, on some stranger's truck, but if I don't get him inside me soon, I'm pretty sure I'm going to do something humiliating like cry and beg for him to fuck me.

And wouldn't he just love that.

I lie back against the hard metal, fisting Joel's crisp T-shirt in my hand and tugging him closer. With my hand in his shirt, my legs curled around his hips, and his fingers gripping my waist, he eases inside me in a single long thrust. I feel every inch of him drive its way inside me as the moan that escapes my lips penetrates the night sky.

He's thrusting in and out of me at an overwhelming pace when I hear a group of people talking. I quickly push myself up to search for the sound, and Joel stops moving, but the group continues walking and never sees us. He starts moving inside me again, slower now, but my mind remains elsewhere until he tugs the top of my strapless dress down under my breasts, exposing my already firm nipples to the icy air. They're extra pink from the cold, and when he caresses them with the warm pads of his thumbs, I have to bite my lip between my teeth to keep from whimpering. It feels so good that, when he removes one of his hands, I almost beg him to keep touching me. Instead, he circles his arm behind my back to hold me in place as he leans forward and closes his burning hot lips around a chilled pink tip. My head falls back and my fingers weave into his stiff hair, silently demanding that he never stop what he's doing with his tongue regardless of who might see us.

His hips never break pace as he teases one nipple and then the other, frying every neuron in my brain. With his spikes and stubble pricking my palm, I urge him to take his fill, pulsing around him and feeling like I'm about to shatter into pieces. His tongue flicks over the pink peak he's holding between his lips, and I reflexively squeeze tighter all around him. It's like my body is trying to draw him in and force him out all at once, which means it's just as confused as the rest of me.

"Joel," I moan, tightening and untightening and bursting apart and coming back together. I haven't tumbled over the edge yet, but God, I'm close. I'm so, so, so close.

Joel stands up straight and strokes my swollen clit with the rough pad of his thumb. I'm playing with my still-moist nipples when he lifts his thumb to his mouth and runs his tongue over it.

"I'm already soaked," I pant, frustration cutting into my voice because I'm teetering on the precipice and desperately need him to just push me over. If sex in public was more my thing, I'd already be there, but it's hard to relax when the sane part of me—no matter how small that part may be—is nervous about getting caught and possibly arrested.

"I know" is all he says. With his ice-blue eyes locked on mine, he lowers his thumb and circles it over my moist nub again. One . . . two . . . *oh* . . . *God* . . . three . . . four times. My hips jerk, and he lifts his hand to his mouth again. He slowly curls his tongue around his damp thumbprint and licks every bit of me off of it.

The sight of him—this unbelievably hot fucking rock star who could have had any girl he wanted tonight—savoring the taste of me . . . it ignites a white-hot fire that erupts from my core and floods every cell in my body. My eyes roll back, my fingers tunnel into my own hair since there's nothing else to hold on to, and my legs tremble violently. Joel suddenly thrusts every inch of himself into me, pinning my knees against his hips and pushing into me like he wants to make me fit him, only him, and no other man ever again.

"You feel so fucking good," he growls, his husky voice making the fire inside me blaze hotter until I'm melting all around him.

A white cloud of gasped curse words swirls from my lips toward a blanket of burning stars, and Joel throbs inside me as he sends up a cloud to match. He pumps into me until he has nothing left to give, and then he rests both hands on the truck bed to hold himself up, his head hanging and his shoulders rising and falling with each panting breath he takes. When he's gathered enough strength, he lifts his chin to give me a self-satisfied smile that makes me tighten around him all over again. His eyes close and he makes a sound that makes me do it yet again. Each time I tighten, he moves inside me involuntarily, and if he doesn't pull out soon, I'm hoping he has a second condom in his pocket, because we're definitely going to need it.

I'm not sure if I'm disappointed or relieved when he slowly pulls out of me and slides onto the truck bed, but when he collapses onto his back beside me, his arm pressed tight against mine, I'm nothing but content.

"That was fucking hot," he says, and I smile to myself, somehow summoning the strength to pull the top of my dress back up and the skirt of my dress back down. He sits up far enough to take off his jacket, and then he lays it over top of me and lies back down.

"Can I have my panties back?" I ask.

"No."

"Why not?"

"I'm keeping them."

I smile even wider and stare up at the night sky with him, feeling cold on the outside and molten on the inside. I know I should get up and walk away, try to pretend I'm not as affected as he is by what we just did, but I'm far too satisfied to move. Too satisfied to *not* smile and stay put beside him.

Even when the show inside ends and the guy who owns the truck starts shouting curses and death threats as he jogs toward us, I can't do anything but laugh. Joel grabs my hand, leaves a sticky souvenir behind for the truck driver, and races back through the parking lot with me until we burst through the doors to Mayhem.

Inside, we part ways so I can go to the bathroom and put myself back together. I run my fingers through my thoroughly tangled curls as best I can, and then I freshen my makeup and try to wipe the stupid smile off my face.

Yes, sex with Joel is amazing. Always amazing. Like mind-blowingly, life-alteringly, really freaking amazing. But it's still just sex, and I don't want him or anyone else thinking otherwise. I don't ever want to catch myself looking at him like those other girls look at him—with a dumb smile on my face and desperate hope in my eyes.

When I get backstage, he's hanging with the rest of the guys from both bands, along with Rowan and Leti.

My best friend immediately narrows her gaze on me. "Did you just have *sex*?"

My eyes widen and I smack Joel's stomach, but he just laughs. "I didn't say anything!"

"Then how does she know?!"

"Girl," Leti says, circling his hand in front of me, "you are looking *thoroughly* sexed."

The guys all laugh hard, and when Adam raises his hand in the air for a high five from Joel, I'm thankful that Rowan elbows him in the ribs.

I shrug and grab a water bottle from a nearby table, untwisting the cap and trying to play it cool. "Whatever. I was just trying to prove something."

"What's that?" Joel asks as I take a sip. I lower the bottle and smirk at him.

"You aren't a man of your word."

Chapter Three

WHEN ROWAN WARNED me about Joel's snoring, she described it as a polar bear in need of an exorcism. But the sound I wake up to the morning after the concert is more like a demonic Rottweiler trying to chew its way through cement.

I kick my foot behind me to wake the Rottweiler up. He's on his back, and I'm on my side facing away from him.

He startles, but then the demon-dog starts chewing again.

"Joel." I reach my hand back and fumble it over his stubbly face to wake him up. "Get up."

He bats at my arm and whines for me to stop.

"Get up," I groan, rolling toward him and trying with my hands and feet to push him out of my bed. "It's time for your walk of shame."

He rolls on top of me to get me to stop pushing him,

putting all of his weight on me and squishing me into the mattress.

Wide awake and *not* happy about it, I fist my hand into his hair and slowly tug his head away from where it's planted next to my face. Nose to nose, he gives me a smile full of wicked intentions, and then he resists my grip to press his lips against mine in a kiss that causes my fingers to loosen and my skin to flush.

Last night, he came home with me and lived up to every single promise he had whispered in my ear at the bar earlier that night. He's like a drug in my veins, one I need to quit before I lose myself completely. I try to muster the willpower to turn him down, but his name is a weak protest on my lips. Just a breathless word that I manage to say before he drops those lips to my neck and steals any resolution I had.

Half an hour later, he's still in my room and I'm walking to the bathroom down the hall, every step I take reminding me of just how many hours over the past twenty-four he's been inside me. I've left him stretched out on my bed so I can take a cold shower and try to get my head straight—which is nearly impossible when I imagine him sprawled naked on top of my covers with his hair a mess and my fingernail scratches marring his skin.

After a quick shower, I get dressed and do my makeup in front of a mirror in the bathroom, and then I walk back to my room with a towel wrapped around my head and a mask of impatience on my face. It works to hide the smile permanently threatening to bloom anytime Joel so much as glances in my direction.

"You're still here?" I ask, barely giving him a sideways glance before I plant myself in front of my vanity to comb out my wet hair.

He chuckles and stands up, stretching his arms over his head. He's slipped into his soft-worn jeans from the night before, but they're barely clinging to his hips, held up by a too-loose studded belt. There's just something about a guy with tattoos—something about Joel, with the neck of a guitar inked on his forearm and black script curling up his ribs—that makes brain function impossible. I'm drooling over the reflection of his toned, tattooed torso when my eyes drift up and I realize he's caught me staring. The corner of his mouth quirks into a cocky smile that makes my cheeks redden, and I quickly turn my eyes away, wishing he'd put his damn shirt on so I could stop wanting to tackle him back onto my covers.

"Can you give me a ride to Adam's?" he asks.

Most nights, Joel crashes on the couch in the living room of the apartment that Adam, Shawn, and Rowan share. Some nights, he stays with me. And other nights, he stays with airheaded groupies who should really punch themselves in the face.

I knew he'd ask for a ride, which is why I've already texted Rowan and Leti to tell them I'm dragging them out for breakfast, but I give Joel a hard time anyway because it's too tempting to resist. "I think I've given you enough rides this morning, don't you?"

He laughs and steps up behind me, giving me a sweet smile in the mirror. "You look beautiful this morning."

He's so shameless about his ass kissing, it's hard not to

smile back at him. With a barely managed straight face, I say, "Are you saying I don't look beautiful other mornings?"

"You look *especially* radiant this morning," he says, dipping his chin onto my shoulder and giving my reflection a cheesy smile that makes me laugh in spite of myself.

"Whatever. Put your shirt on and I'll think about it."

I give Joel a ride and curse myself for doing it. Mind-blowing sex is a mutual exchange, but since when did I also become a free hotel room and complimentary taxi service? Next time, I'm kicking him out right after—I don't care *how* toe curling the morning extracurriculars are.

After picking up Leti, I drop Joel off and trade him for Rowan, and then I drive myself and my two best friends to IHOP. Thanks to my driving and ability to tune out Rowan's pleas for me to slow down, we beat the church rush and don't have to wait to be seated.

"So I suppose you're all wondering why I called you here today," Leti announces once we're settled in a booth. He clasps his fingers on top of the table, and I share a look with Rowan. She's sitting next to him, looking just as confused as me.

"Uh, I called *you* here," I argue.

Leti reaches across the table to take my hands in his. In a lavender My Little Pony T-shirt, with his wavy ombre hair pulled back by the bright rainbow sunglasses on top of his head, he says, "Sweetie, we're staging an intervention."

"We are?" Rowan asks.

Thanks to Joel, I got next to no sleep last night, so I really don't have the patience for this. Pulling my hands away, I say, "What the hell are you talking about?"

My eyebrows are scrunched tightly in Leti's direction when our server, an elderly woman with more than her fair share of pancakes collected around her middle, pops by to take our drink orders. As soon as she's gone, Leti gives me another teasing smile. "The first step is admitting you have a problem."

I lift my eyebrow at him. "And what's my problem, pony-boy?"

"You're an addict. We're here to help you."

My gaze swings to Rowan, but she just shrugs and shakes her head.

"Okay. I'll bite." I dramatically take Leti's hands in mine again and drape myself across the table to meet him halfway. "What am I addicted to? High heels? Hair spray?"

He grins and says, "Oh, something much more dire."

"Lip gloss? Glitter nail polish?"

He smirks at me. "You're addicted to whatever is causing you to have those ghastly purple bags under your eyes, and my guess is that the culprit is hot and spiky and rhymes with *bowl*."

I can't help chuckling before I release Leti's hands. "Jealous?"

"Incurably." He turns his pouting face to Rowan. "Are you sure none of the other guys are gay?"

"Positive."

"Bi?"

Rowan shakes her head, long blonde strands tumbling from her messy bun. "Sorry, don't think so."

"Curious? Confused? Impressionable?"

Rowan and I both laugh, and Leti sighs and deflates in the seat.

Our drinks arrive, and I'm tearing open three sugar packets at once when he asks, "So what exactly *are* you and mohawk-boy anyway?"

He and Rowan stare at me expectantly while I finish stirring the sugar into my coffee and answer, "Why do we have to *be* anything?"

I don't expect them to get it. Rowan hopped from being in a three-year relationship to living with a guy she's head over heels in love with. And Leti flirts around a lot, but he seems to be holding out for the right guy. If we weren't friends, I have no doubt these two would think I'm a slut. And technically, I guess the shoe fits, but so what? I like boys. I like sex. And if I'm safe about it and no one gets hurt, what's it matter what I spend my nights doing or who I do those things with?

Leti takes his sunglasses off his head and points them at me. "Well you two aren't *nothing*. You've been hooking up for months now. How many times is that? Like a thousand?"

"What's it matter?" I ask defensively. "I just haven't gotten bored with him yet."

Rowan gives me a look. "Do you remember when you told me I liked Adam, and I kept insisting we were just friends?"

I hold up my hands to derail that crazy train before it picks up steam. "Joel and I are NOT you and Adam."

"Aren't you?" Leti asks.

I swing my sparkly purple fingernail back and forth

between the Tweedle sisters. "Look, ladies, this isn't some cheesy Disney movie where Rowan gets a boyfriend and their two best friends end up together too and it's like one big happy weird little freaky family. This is *me* we're talking about. And *Joel*."

"Okay, first off," Rowan says, stirring her orange juice with a straw, "*Shawn* is Adam's best friend, not Joel. Joel is more like . . . a mascot." She grins to herself and stops stirring. "And second, you're different lately."

"Am not," I argue, casting an exaggerated smile at our server when she interrupts our conversation to set down our food. Rowan immediately snatches up the syrup and soaks her pancakes. Then she hands it to me and I do the same.

"Are too," she insists. "You care what Joel thinks of you. You never care what *anyone* thinks of you." She pours a second coat of syrup on.

"Joel is a game."

"And what's the prize if you win?"

I'm about to say something smart when my mouth clamps shut and my eyes get wide. Rowan starts to turn around, but I jerk her arms forward. "Don't look."

"Why?" she says, and I struggle to think up a believable lie.

"Jimmy just walked in," I say, pulling a name out of thin air.

"Who's Jimmy?" She starts to turn around again, and I jerk her forward again. Leti is turned all the way around in his seat, but he's not the one I'm worried about.

"A guy I screwed around with a few weeks ago," I lie.

"He won't stop calling me. I need you to get me out of here." My foot knocks at Leti like a woodpecker under the table, and the expression on his face slowly turns to one of realization. I toss my purse on top of the table. "Leti, can you get our pancakes in boxes and pay with my card?"

He nods and slides out of the booth to let Rowan out, and I wrap my arm around her shoulder, spinning around like a seasoned body guard shielding her from paparazzi. I keep her pinned against my side until we've emerged through the double doors into the bright morning sunlight, and then I start telling her all about the fictitious Jimmy.

When we pass a silver Cobalt on the way to my car, I amp up the story to distract Rowan from noticing. "And THEN," I say, throwing my hands in the air, "he had the NERVE to tell me I'd never forget him! Like HELLO, if you stopped calling me every two minutes, maybe I could!"

Rowan chuckles and continues walking, oblivious to the car or the way my heart is pounding in my chest. "Sounds like he really likes you."

"Him and a million other guys. He had his chance, but he was all *hands*, Ro. And not like Joel's hands, because those are just . . . well, Adam plays the guitar, so you know." She blushes, and I continue rambling. "But this guy's hands . . . God, it was like making out with the Hamburger Helper guy!"

She laughs hysterically, and my heart slows just a little. When we get to my car, I unlock the doors and she gets in. I open the driver's side but pause before sliding in next to her. "Shit," I say, "I forgot to tell Leti which card to use. My Visa is maxed out."

She reaches for the handle to get out. "I'll tell him."

"No!" I force a smile at the startled look she gives me and add, "I'll do it. In and out, real quick. Don't move. I'll be right back."

I jog back to IHOP, slip just inside the front doors to wait for Leti, and take my purse from him when he hands it to me.

"Her ex?" he asks, and I nod while flipping through my keys to find the sharpest one. Brady broke Rowan's heart into a million pieces when he cheated on her—and ground those pieces into dust when he did it *again*—and I've been itching for payback ever since. He's here with a girl, and he's lucky Rowan was with me or I would have scratched his eyes out right in the middle of IHOP.

With a jagged key pinched between my knuckles, I smile at Leti and say, "Smile and pretend you don't hear this." As we pass by Brady's Cobalt, my key digs a deep, screeching gash into the silver paint, all the way from front to back, and Leti and I smile like lunatics. By the time we hop into my car, we're both laughing hysterically.

"What?" Rowan asks, her eyebrow raised as she stares back and forth between us.

"Nothing," I say, starting the car and shooting Leti a smile in the rearview mirror. I begin backing out of the spot and add, "Thanks for getting me out of there, Ro. Love you."

I smile at the confused look she gives me but lose it less than a half-minute later, when Leti abruptly recalls what we had been talking about back in IHOP.

"So," he says, his big head popping between my seat and Rowan's, "Bowl."

"I could crash this car right now, you know."

My warning just makes him laugh. "Really? That'd be better than just admitting your feelings?"

My head snaps in his direction with a look that should make him flinch. Instead, his smile widens and I'm the one who looks away. "What feelings?"

"Mushy ones. Probably feels like butterflies. Or mashed potatoes."

There's a chirp at my right as Rowan barely contains a giggle, but I ignore it and let my foot weigh heavier on the gas so I can limit the amount of time Leti has to annoy me. "Yeeeah, I don't have any of those," I say, but I can feel his bright-as-ever smile burrowing into the side of my head.

"What about Joel? I bet his stomach is fuuull of mashed potatoes."

"Joel has never had mashed potatoes in his life," I counter, immediately cursing myself for going along with Leti's stupid mashed-potatoes analogy.

I'm going forty in a twenty-five when Rowan says, "He said you're special."

Leti and I both look at her, and it's only by the terri-fied look in her eyes that I manage to slam my foot on the brake to avoid running a red light. "He said *what*?"

She has one hand glued to the dashboard and the other clinging to the armrest at her right. "Can you please not kill us?"

"Tell me what he said and I'll think about it."

Rowan's fingers unpeel from the dashboard one by one, and she takes a deep breath when the light turns green and

I ease onto the gas again. "I asked him why he keeps going back to you when he doesn't really do that with anyone else, and he said you were special."

"What's that supposed to mean?"

Rowan shakes her head. "I asked, but he just smiled and shrugged."

Typical Joel. My brow furrows at the road ahead of me, and Leti singsongs, "See! Mashed po-tat-oes!"

"He's full of something," I say, "but it isn't mashed po-tatoes. If he thinks I'm so special, why was he slumming it with that groupie last night?"

"He picks you every time he gets a kiss card during Kings," Rowan counters, and I scoff.

"He doesn't mind when other girls pick *him*." The last time we played, one groupie bitch lucked out and picked all three remaining kiss cards. She picked Joel every. single. time.

Leti chuckles. "He held your hair back when you got so mad about it that you scarfed down margaritas and ended up puking your guts out."

"See?" I argue. "Joel fills my stomach with margaritas, not mashed potatoes."

"And puke," Rowan adds, and I chuckle as I manage to stop at the next stoplight without my tires screeching.

"And puke."

Chapter Four

"I'LL CALL YOU."

Those were the last words Joel said to me the day I dropped him off at Adam's. It's what he *always* says. And he always does—when it suits him.

Sometimes, I answer, and sometimes, I don't.

For the past week and a half, I would have answered. But for the past week and half, he hasn't called.

So on Wednesday night, it's his fault that I'm making out with someone who was obviously in some horrific farm accident as a child and had to have an emergency tongue transplant with only cows to serve as donors. I swear to God, I've never had so much tongue in my mouth in my entire life. It's like this guy decided on quantity over quality and has dedicated himself to giving that method his all. And by *his all*, I mean his entire. freaking. tongue.

I turn my head to the side, and Cow Tongue thankfully drops his lips to my neck. I'm on my back, on his bed, in his bedroom. Classes this week were annoying. Work at the restaurant this week was annoying. Not hearing from Joel at all was annoying. Wanting to hear from him was annoying. I spent my entire serving shift tonight thinking of him—constantly checking my phone for texts even though I knew damn well he was probably already breathing heavy in some other girl's bed—and I realized I had to do something about it.

Leti was right: Joel is a problem. He makes me feel . . . lonely. Crazy. Desperate.

Cow Tongue, who told me his name was Aiden even though I hadn't wanted to know, was the next guy to smile at me after I decided a one-night stand was exactly what the doctor ordered, so he was who I opted to go home with. I figured if I started acting like my old self again, maybe I'd start feeling like my old self again. The only reason Joel felt like the only guy that mattered was because I *made* him the only guy that mattered.

I want to forget him, and yet, when I gaze up into Aiden's brown eyes, I can't help wishing they were blue. I can't help wishing his soft brown hair was spiked and blond. I can't help wishing the smile he gave me made my insides molten hot instead of old bathwater warm.

"Take off your pants," I tell him, and he wastes no time following orders. I strip mine off too and tell him to get a condom.

"Shit," he breathes, giving me a panicked look. "I don't have one."

"My purse," I say, nudging him toward the dresser it's

sitting on. I lie there patiently while he grabs it and proceeds to spill half its contents onto the floor.

"Sorry," he stammers, and then he spills the other half while he's trying to pick up the first half.

"Worry about that *later*," I hiss, trying to keep the frustration out of my tone. I'd hoped to be in the throes of mind-numbing ecstasy by now, not lying alone and frustrated on sheets that smell like dog hair—which is just disturbing considering I've seen no sign of a dog.

Aiden grabs the condom off the floor and rips it open, sliding it on and climbing back over top of me. I spread my legs around him and he settles between them, immediately trying to push into me. But I'm bone dry, and my body isn't having it.

"Kiss me or something," I order, instantly regretting the suggestion when his tongue fills my mouth again. I break away as soon as possible and change my strategy. "Just use spit." I'd suggest lubricant, but if this guy didn't even have condoms, I'm guessing a good lube might as well be the Holy Grail.

Aiden gives me a boyish smile, and then he starts to crawl his way down my body.

"Oh, no, that's not what I—"

He spreads my legs wider and laps at me like an over-anxious puppy, but instead of moaning or wriggling or *liking* it in any way, my legs just kind of close a little tighter and I'm left casting a weird look at the ceiling, my nose scrunched and my eyebrows drawn.

When he drills his tongue into me like an aggressive anteater, I yelp, and he apparently takes this as encouragement. More drilling. More weird looks at the ceiling. I close my eyes and try to enjoy it, but my thoughts are instantly on Joel. When Joel does this, it's slow and teasing and he savors every bit of me.

I'm just beginning to get turned on when Aiden says, "Do you like that?"

I ignore him and try to bring the image of Joel back into my mind. The way his hands capture mine when I'm so out of my mind with lust I don't know what to do with them. How strong his arms feel when he wraps them around my middle and refuses to let me wiggle away from him.

"Mm, do you like that?" Aiden asks again. If he had any decency at all, he would STOP TALKING.

"Yeah," I lie, wishing he would shut up. He laps away, and I imagine the way Joel's tongue does tiny little flicks against the most sensitive parts of me.

The drilling starts again, and Aiden asks me for the third freaking time if I "like that."

"YES!" I shout, realizing he's not going to be quiet long enough to let me get myself anywhere near orgasm.

Which means I'll have to fake it or suffer through more cow-tonguing, puppy-lapping, and anteater-drilling.

"Oh," I say, bucking my hips and rolling my eyes simultaneously. "Oh God." I put on a porno-worthy performance and pull him to my face. When he starts to lean down to kiss me again, I hastily push against his shoulders and roll him onto his back. If he shoves that tongue inside my mouth one more time, I'm pretty sure I'll choke and die. And with the way this night has been going, that doesn't sound too terrible.

I straddle his hips and lower myself onto him, and he moans loud enough to wake up the entire neighborhood. Great. I can already tell that if I don't hurry, he's going to climax before I do and then I'll be on my own.

I brace my hands on his chest so I can start moving up and down on him, but whereas Joel's body is lean and toned, Aiden's is mushy-soft. I slide my hands to the sides of his neck and hold there instead, but he's sweaty and it feels like petting a buttered porpoise, so I wipe my palms on his pillow and sit back. With nowhere to put my hands, I thread them into my own hair. I manage to move up and down only one and a half more times before Aiden moans and releases into me and I realize the mistake I've made. I lower my hands, not sure if I should feel flattered that the sight of me was enough to make him orgasm, or so outraged that I need to strangle him before packing up my things and going on the run.

"That was awesome," he pants, and I unstraddle him to roll onto my side. He wraps his arm around me, which I tolerate only because I really don't want to be alone tonight.

"You're amazing," he tells me, and I wish I could manage a smile or at least believe him, but I can't.

I WAKE WHEN it's still dark outside, to nothing but utter silence. There's a heavy arm around me and there's a face buried in my hair, but there's no snoring in my ear, and that disappointing realization makes me squeeze my eyes shut and gnaw on the inside of my lip. With a heavy sigh,

I sneak out from beneath the arm, gather my clothes off the floor, and slip them back on. I don't bother casting a second glance at the stranger passed out on the bed before tiptoeing across his room. I learned the art of sneaking out the first time my dad tried to ground me when I was thirteen years old. By the time I got my license, I was an expert.

I turn the knob to Aiden's apartment as carefully as if I were disarming a bomb. Then I gently push the door open, escape onto the front porch, and close the door behind me. I don't release the knob until the door is all the way closed, when I very slowly allow it to turn back to its normal position.

In the parking lot, I rest my forehead on my steering wheel, wishing I had picked a guy up from a bar instead of from work. At least then I could've gotten sloppy drunk and still be passed out right now. Instead, I'm sober and awake with too much on my mind.

Against my better judgment, I drive home, shower and change, pick up coffee, and drive to Adam's. I'm dressed in a killer top, skirt, and heels combo with all intentions of making Joel sorry he didn't call me last night, but sitting in the parking lot staring at my reflection in my rearview mirror, all I can see is the purple exhaustion under my eyes and the pale hue of my skin. I look just like my mother. With a disgusted grunt, I text Rowan instead of going up.

Driving you to school today. In parking lot. Hurry up.

While waiting, I cake on more makeup and contort my face in the mirror, trying to distinguish myself from the woman who cheated on my dad and left him a blubbering mess. I have her brown eyes, her dark hair, her olive skin. It's an arsenal of weaponry. She used hers to capture my father's heart and then destroy it. I use mine to ensure that no one ever does the same to me. I'll never have to rely on one person for love or affection because I can get it from anyone.

Well, *almost* anyone.

Fifteen minutes later, my head is resting against the window and I'm singing a girl-power song when Rowan slides into my passenger seat. I turn down the music, and she gives me a questioning look I have no desire to answer.

"Want to talk about it?" she asks, buckling her seat belt as I back my car out of its spot.

"Talk about what?"

"Why you're picking me up on a Thursday morning?"

"Because I woke up early."

"Then let's talk about why you didn't come up to the apartment."

I look her in the eyes, leaving no room for confusion. "No."

Rowan sighs and leans back in her seat. She keeps quiet and stares out the window as I drive, but I don't even make it a full minute before I say, "Was he even there?"

Not needing to ask who I'm talking about, she shakes her head without looking at me. "I haven't seen him much this week." She casts a glance in my direction, catches the frown on my face, and quickly adds, "He asked about you yesterday though."

"What did he say?"

"He wanted to know what you were doing last night. I told him you were working."

Working? More like narrowly resisting the urge to choke out customers with complimentary breadsticks.

"Do you want me to tell him he should call you?" Rowan asks, and I nearly jerk the car into a ditch.

"NO!" I stare at her like she's lost her damn mind. "No freaking way, are you nuts?!"

She frowns and grips her seat belt. "Well, then you should call him. Call him or forget about him, Dee, because you're going a little crazy."

Understatement of the century. I feel like some crazy hormonal girl invades my body anytime Joel's swoon-worthy face pops into my mind, and she makes me want to punch myself in the head until she leaves or I knock myself unconscious.

"Did you even turn in the proposal for your marketing project that was due yesterday?" Rowan asks, her tone revealing she already guessed the answer.

The short answer is no. The long answer is the excuse I gave my professor, which involved a dead grandparent and an orphaned cat.

"I told my professor I'd turn it in late."

Rowan frowns at me. "That project is worth most of your grade, Dee. You can't keep blowing stuff like this off or you're going to fail. Maybe if you spent your energy obsessing over school instead of obsessing over Joel—"

I give her a warning look, and she immediately silences her lecture.

"I'll do it this weekend," I say.

"Mayhem is this weekend." The guys are performing again, and we've never missed even one of their local shows.

"I'll do it Sunday."

After classes, I drop Rowan off at Adam's and head back to my apartment to change into my work clothes. I arrive late, bitch out my boss for trying to reprimand me, and spend most of my five-hour shift thinking about what the hell I want to do with my life.

I definitely don't want to be working in a place like this when I'm in my thirties, having to deal with customers like Miss Gable, who thinks *server* is just another word for slave.

Tonight, she seriously asked me to get her a salad with only hearts of romaine instead of our usual mix. When I complained to a coworker about it, he said that he usually picks all the other stuff out for her. I gaped at him until he walked away from me, and then I proceeded to pick Miss Gable's salad apart—and give her nothing but the leafy parts. I told her we were all out of the hearts and promised her extra after-dinner chocolates as a consolation, fucking over the customer and the establishment with one fell swoop. I still landed an awesome tip, but that hardly made up for the old men who tried to hit on me or the insecure girls who forced their boyfriends to give me low tips because they stared a little too long.

No one would ever accuse me of being cut out for customer service. But the problem is, I'm not really cut out for college either. When I thought about college, I thought about boys and parties and more boys and more parties. I didn't think about studying and homework and tests and actual *learning*. Last semester, I barely passed my classes with low Cs. This semester, I'm pretty sure I'm already failing. Midterms are next week, and my dad is *not* going to be happy when I tell him what my mid-semester grades are.

I doubt he'd ever stop supporting me financially, but I hate disappointing him. Not that that's stopped me from doing it in the past . . . but I always feel like crap afterward.

My dad just loves too much. He loved my mom even after she left him, and I think he still loves her now. He blames himself for her leaving, and that makes me want to bash her head in with a rock. When I was eleven, she had an affair with some loser she went to high school with and she eventually ran off with him to Vegas. The most contact she's had with me since then is a Facebook friend request I promptly declined before blocking her.

She didn't love my dad enough, but that's not what makes me hate her. What makes me hate her is that she pretended she did. She made vows she didn't keep and left my dad to raise me alone. Sometimes, I wonder if the reason he loves me so much is that I'm a part of her, and every day, I'm worried I'll turn out just like her.

Which is why I'm never saying those three toxic words to anyone. Ever.

Joel would never want me to say them, which is part of why I can't get him out of my head. After five grueling hours of half-assed customer service and another twenty minutes of nightmare traffic, I flick on the switch of my room, kick my work shoes off, and fall face-first onto my bed. I've wiggled my phone out of my back pocket so many times tonight that I'm surprised I don't have brush-burn on my ass, but that doesn't stop me from wiggling it out one more time and groaning when I don't see any missed texts or calls from the idiot guitarist who's apparently lost my number.

With my cheek smushed against my comforter, I pull his name up on my screen and hover my thumb over his number, fighting the urge to call him and ask him to come over. With an irritated growl, I let the phone fall back to the bed and close my eyes.

I'm having a weird dream about my phone ringing when I hear, "Hello?"

I'm still half-sleeping when I open my eyes. I'm still fully clothed. I'm on top of my covers instead of under them.

"Hellooo?" the familiar voice asks again.

I push myself away from my mattress and stare at my phone. Joel's name is on my screen, along with a timer that ticks from 12 seconds to 13, 14, 15.

"Anyone there?"

OH. MY. GOD. I fucking face-dialed him! In my sleep! WHO DOES THAT?!

I hit the button to end the call as quickly as humanly possible, but my phone starts ringing a few seconds later and I end up just sitting there staring at it like it's possessed by the devil. After three rings, I realize I need to pick it up or risk having this situation get even more awkward than it already is.

"Hello?" I answer as nonchalantly as possible, trying not to sound like a complete spaz who face-dials people in her sleep.

"Did you just call me and hang up?" Joel asks, and I wish there was a wall within head-banging distance because face-palming really just isn't going to cut it this time.

"Why the hell would I call you and hang up?"

"Because you secretly love me and wanted to hear my voice?"

He's joking, but I bristle anyway. "I must have butt-dialed you. Don't flatter yourself."

Joel chuckles. "So your *butt* is secretly in love with me. Interesting."

"Hanging up now."

"I'm glad your butt called," he continues, ignoring my idle threat. "I was actually just thinking about it."

I'm not sure whether to giggle or roll my eyes, so instead I say nothing.

"Come pick me up."

I want to. I sincerely, desperately want to. Instead, I counter with, "Get a car."

"Come on. I miss you."

The crazy part of me wants to ask him why he hasn't called then, but the rational part knows he's just saying whatever he needs to say to get what he wants tonight. And Joel only ever wants one thing. "I'm tired. I didn't get any sleep last night."

"Hot date?" he jokes, but he has no idea how happy I am he just asked that.

"I guess you could call it that." I grin as I steal the upper hand in our conversation.

"I thought you had to work?"

"I did."

There's an awkward moment of silence, and then I brave teasing, "You're not jealous, are you?"

"Why would I be jealous?" he counters. "I had a 'hot

date' myself last night." When I can't even muster a response to that, he says, "Are *you* jealous?"

"Oh, *insanely*," I counter, hoping he doesn't realize how honest I'm being. I feel like I need a padded room and ice cream. A shit-ton of ice cream with sedative sprinkles.

"Seriously . . . come pick me up."

"Seriously, why don't you have a car?"

"Don't need one."

"You need one right now, don't you? Because I'm not coming to get you."

"Why not?"

"To prove that you need a car. You have money, Joel. Why don't you get a car or an apartment? You make no sense." I hug my covers tight, relieved that I'm finally hearing the sound of his voice after a full week and a half of wanting nothing else.

"Life is more fun when you don't have those things," he insists.

"How?"

"You don't have to worry about car payments or bills. You have an excuse to hang out with your friends every day. You never know where you're going to end up at night, so you get to go wherever you want and do whatever you want."

"Well I guarantee you'd be having a lot more fun right now if you had a car," I argue.

"So I can come over as long as you don't have to come get me?"

Unable to resist the temptation, I tell him he can. But an hour later, when he still hasn't knocked on my front door, I realize he probably found a girl who *was* willing to pick him up and he's probably forgotten all about me. I change out of the sexy nighty I put on, dressing in an over-sized pair of cotton boxers and a worn-thin cami instead, and then I crawl under my covers and turn out the light, regretting my decision to not go to him when every single piece of me—sane and not so sane—was screaming at me to get in my car.

My room is pitch-dark and I'm deep in a dreamless sleep when my light turns on and I open my eyes to see Joel standing in my bedroom doorway. His hair is always the first thing that catches my attention—buzzed on the sides and pulled up into a spiky blond line that crawls down the middle of his head. And then, those eyes. The brightest blue I've ever seen. He's wearing a black canvas jacket over a long neon-green band T-shirt and faded blue jeans. The loose T-shirt hides his hard muscles, but my fingers remember their lines.

"How did you get in?" I ask, and Joel jingles Rowan's keys from his finger.

"Peach leaves these just lying around."

"Turn off the light," I groan, squeezing my eyes closed and turning my face into the pillow to hide my smile.

Joel turns off the light and walks to the other side of my bed.

"What time is it?" I ask.

"Two o'clock." I hear his shoes thump onto the floor before the rustle of more clothes. He usually sleeps in just his boxers, but I know he came here to do more than just sleep.

"Why is it two o'clock?" I ask, still not completely awake.

"Because I walked." He lifts the covers and crawls in next to me.

I can't believe he walked all the way to my place. It's less than a ten-minute drive, but that means it probably took him at least an hour to walk here. I'm trying to make sense of that in my head when his chilled hand sneaks under the hem of my top, making me squeal and jerk out of his grasp.

Joel laughs. "My hands are cold!"

"YOU THINK?" I smack him away and slide my body to the edge of the bed. "I'm tired now. You should've come earlier." I have no idea why I'm turning him down, other than that I'm trying to prove I won't be at his beck and call, no matter how much I want to be.

When he presses up close, there's no more room for me to inch away from him. His cold hand circles around my stomach again, but since he keeps it over my clothes, I don't bat it away. "You're really going to be like this after you made me walk all the way over here?" His hand slides up my stomach to cup my breast, and an aching starts between my legs and tightens in my core. I don't pull his hand away.

"I didn't *make* you do anything."

Joel caresses his thumb over my soft nipple, and it perks under his touch. "Was the guy from last night better than me?"

When he pinches my nipple with icy cold fingers, my back arches, pressing my ass into his groin. His hips press forward against me, and I nearly flip over right then to lose myself in the way his lips can conquer mine and make everything else cease to exist. "I don't remember."

"Don't remember how good he was, or don't remember how good I am?"

"Don't remember how good you are," I lie, trying to knock Joel's confidence down a peg because he definitely has all the control right now. I'm warm putty in his hands just waiting to be played with.

My strategy backfires when he leans forward and traces the tip of his satin tongue along my neck, bringing his lips to my ear and speaking to me in a voice that makes my skin shiver. "Then let me remind you."

Chapter Five

EMPTY BED. QUIET APARTMENT. The only signs Joel was here last night are his scent on my sheets and the ache in my muscles. I roll onto my stomach and pull my pillow tight over the back of my head, trying to convince myself I'm content to wake alone—that I *prefer* to wake alone.

"You realize all you have in your fridge is butter and pickles, right?"

I push the pillow away and stare at Joel like he's an apparition. He's standing in my doorway with a tub of butter in one hand, a half-empty jar of pickles in the other, and one sandy blond eyebrow firmly raised.

"What am I supposed to make you for breakfast?" he complains, making me feel so warm and fuzzy inside that I'm pretty sure I need to giggle rainbows or explode into glitter. How many butterflies does a girl need to feel in her belly before she turns into a butterfly herself?

"There's a coffee shop down the street," I offer.

"How do you *live*?" He lifts the yellow tub in front of his face and narrows his eyes. His mohawk is spiked firmly in place, and I wonder how many of my hair products he had to mix to get it to stand up like that. "This butter isn't even any good. It expired two months ago."

"There's ice cream in the freezer . . ."

I giggle at the look he gives me, and he shakes his head. "We need to go grocery shopping."

"*We?*"

"Yes, we." A smirk taunts me from the corner of his gorgeous mouth. "Are you going to drive me, or are you going to make me walk again?"

DESPITE HOW TEMPTING it is to see if Joel would actually walk if I refused to drive him, I take him to the grocery store, feeling awkwardly domestic. I've never grocery shopped with a guy before. I keep stealing glances at him as we cross the parking lot, and he smiles at me when I grab a grocery cart and start pushing.

"So is this your thing?" I ask, casting him a sidelong glance as we walk down the cereal aisle and he tosses boxes in my cart—all of them featuring cartoon characters and colored marshmallows. When he looks at me for clarification, I quietly explain, "Your shtick or something. Having sex with girls and then taking them grocery shopping."

Joel doesn't try to keep his voice quiet when he says, "I've fucked you like a million times and I've never taken *you* grocery shopping."

The old woman walking past us, who definitely heard

every foul word out of Joel's mouth, gives us a reproachful look from behind her oversized spectacles. I smile sweetly at her and nudge my elbow into Joel's side, but he just chuckles. I tilt my chin up to give him a look, and he tucks his hand into my back pocket and gives my butt a tight squeeze.

"You're horrible," I say, not removing his fingers from my pocket.

"You love it," he counters, and I can't even pretend to disagree. He fondles my ass until I step out of his reach, and when I glance back at him, he's enjoying the view. I turn back around, enjoying giving it to him.

"Can you get me that creamer?" I ask when we get to the dairy section. Normally, I get coffee at school or at the place down the street from my apartment building, but if we're seriously making breakfast at my place this morning, I need something to put in my coffee, and the crème brulée creamer I want is all the way at the back of the top rack.

Joel crosses his arms and leans against the whitewashed wall, smirking and shaking his head.

I glare at him, but then I do exactly what he wants: I stand on my tippy-toes and reach up as high as I can. My ass curves out, my shirt pulls up, and my breasts push into the icy air of the refrigeration. My cold nipples strain against my top as I turn my face to Joel and make my eyes big and my lips pouty. "I still can't reach it," I say.

"Do you need my help?"

"Please?"

His lips pull into a satisfied smile, and he comes up behind me, pushing his hard-on tight against my ass as he reaches up to get the creamer for me. "This one?" he asks, intentionally pointing to the wrong one to torture me.

"The one next to it," I say, and he curls his fingers around my hips with his left hand to tug me even tighter against him as he reaches for the creamer with his right.

"This one?" he asks, pointing to the one on the wrong side.

"The other one," I say, standing on my tippy-toes again to create friction between us. I point to the one I want, my shirt lifting up to reveal my taut stomach again.

"Oh, you mean this one." While Joel reaches for it with his right hand, his left snakes around my waist. His fingers trail lightly over my stomach and sneak under my raised top, giving me goose bumps all over and making me shiver. His lips press near my ear and he says, "I can't wait to get you back to your place."

I don't think he means it literally, but I sure as hell *feel* it literally. I'm about to pull him into a dirty bathroom so he can fuck me against a wall.

"Split up so we can get this done faster?" I suggest, and we speed-walk in opposite directions.

I don't even know what the hell I'm shopping for, so I throw a few things in the cart—bacon, eggs, bread, whipped cream, extra-large condoms—and then I walk back through the grocery store searching for Joel.

I find him in Aisle 6 with two girls who barely look legal.

I take a step back to be better hidden from view, watching as he flirts with them. They smile and giggle, flip their hair and bat their eyelashes. Then they mold themselves to his sides for a picture.

They must be fans, and fans, I'm fine with. Pictures, I'm fine with. I'm even fine with one of them writing what I'm assuming is her number on a piece of paper and handing it to him. What I'm *not* fine with is him tucking it into his pocket and reaching forward to play with her necklace.

Part of me wants to march right up to them and stake my claim, wants to let the girls know that Joel is *mine* and if they don't want to get their eyeballs clawed out, they'd better stop looking at him. But I'm not going to give him the satisfaction of turning me into that kind of girl, especially not when he'd just continue being a man-whore and driving me crazy. Instead, I grit my teeth and abandon my cart right where it's parked, walking from the grocery store with my head held high but my molars threatening to grind each other into dust. I climb into my car, back out of the spot, and drive all the way home. When my phone beeps along the way, I don't bother looking at it. I don't check it until seven beeps and two missed calls later, after I've slammed my apartment door behind me and have grounded myself on the couch.

Where the fuck are you?

Joel's latest in a long line of texts—which went from being confused, to concerned, to angry—just pisses me off. My phone receives the brunt of my temper as I type back, *Home. Looked like you got another ride, so I figured I was off the hook.*

What the fuck are you talking about?

I don't bother responding. Anything I say will just make me sound jealous—because I *am* jealous. I hope Joel fucks those girls and makes them a breakfast they all choke on.

Did you seriously leave me at the fucking grocery store?

Not responding.

This is so fucked up!

Not responding.

You're fucking crazy!

I text him a GIF image of Marilyn Monroe blowing a kiss at the camera before I turn my phone on silent and toss it on the coffee table.

When Rowan calls me, I'm angrily biting into an unlucky pickle.

"Did you really have sex with Joel and then leave him at the grocery store?"

"He brought it on himself," I insist, and she starts laughing.

I hear Joel yell in the background, "I TOLD YOU!"

"What did he do?" she asks.

"He dragged me to the grocery store, and I left him alone for two minutes—two freaking minutes, Rowan—and he goes and gets some other girl's number."

She yells at Joel, "You took her grocery shopping and got some other girl's number?!"

"She just gave it to me!" he yells back.

"And you took it?!"

"He's an asshole," I say, biting off more of my pickle.

"It's not like I was going to go home with her right then or something!" Joel insists, like that makes a difference. I can practically hear Rowan's eye-roll.

"Joel, you should probably stop talking," she orders.

"Why?"

"Because if you don't, I'm going to smack you and it's going to hurt."

"Whatever," I hear him say. "Dee is crazy."

I hear a loud *WHAP!* and then an "OW! WHAT THE HELL!" Loud laughter follows—I'm guessing from Adam and Shawn.

"One more word, Joel!" Rowan warns, and I smile around a mouthful of pickle. "Hold on," she tells me, "I'm going outside."

A door opens and closes. Footsteps. "He's such an ass," she finally says. "I'm sorry he did that."

"Don't be."

"You seem okay."

"I'm always okay."

A short pause, and then, "Are you over him now?"

"I was never under him." Unless last night counts . . . and the dozens of times before that.

"You know what I mean. Are you two done?"

"For now."

A longer pause, and then, "Are you still coming to Mayhem tomorrow?"

"Wouldn't miss it," I say, already planning what I'm going to wear to make Joel sorry he ever even *considered* calling another girl.

Rowan sighs heavily into the phone. "You're so not done."

Chapter Six

IN A WAR of social combat, there is one key to victory: Act like you've already won. In high school, it worked on bitch cheerleaders who were angry about their jock boyfriends calling me after school. Now, it's going to work on the one guy who is too stupid to realize he should never try to do better than me because I'm the best there is.

In my shortest skirt and skimpiest top, I walk into Mayhem like a general prepared to accept the surrender of his enemy. I have my armor—the sequins shining on my top and the black boots stretching up to my knees. I have my weapons—the cleavage squeezed into my plunging neckline, the miles of skin shimmering between boots and my skirt, and the smooth black nail polish glimmering under Mayhem's muted lighting. And I have my war paint—my shadowy eye makeup, my thick black lashes, and my moist pink lips. I'm dressed for the kill, and I'm prepared to draw first blood when I spot Joel at the bar and nearly stop dead in my tracks. Rowan and Leti stop walking to glance back at me, but I only hesitate for half a step before resuming my march.

He's standing at the end with hot girls under each arm—like seriously *hot* girls, with big boobs, long legs, and commercial-ready hair. By the way his eyes lift to meet mine and the corner of his mouth quirks up, I can tell this is the equivalent of him taking the first shot.

I ignore him and squeeze into a spot between Shawn and Adam with Leti at my back. Adam gives up his stool so that Rowan can sit there, preferring to stand behind her with his arms draped around her shoulders.

"You're prettier than them," Leti assures me in my ear.

Rowan must not have heard, because she leans over to tell me the exact same thing, and the fact that they're both insisting on it makes me worried that I'm not. Defensive, I open my mouth and throw down the gauntlet. "Did you enjoy your long walk home, Joel?"

When I turn my gaze to him, he's grinning at me, his sparkling blue eyes welcoming my challenge. "I didn't need to walk. That girl's number came in handy."

I'm trying to prevent hurt from flashing across my face when Shawn shouts, "How are you going to stand there lying like that?"

"I had to come pick your sorry ass up!" Adam adds, and I laugh along with the people around me while Joel bristles.

"You know what *I'd* like to talk about?" Mike says from the other side of Shawn, and all eyes turn to him. "Literally *anything* else."

Mike is the only member of the band who doesn't constantly have groupies trying to shove their hands down his pants, but that's only because he has no interest in them. He's a bit shorter than Joel, Adam, and Shawn, but he's taller than Cody and has more meat on his bones. His eyes are a warm brown, and he has a thick mop of chestnut hair I wouldn't mind tugging my fingers through . . . It's only too bad he'd rather drink beer and play video games than have a good time.

Shawn laughs and clinks his beer bottle to Mike's. I roll my eyes and flag the bartender, ordering a vodka cranberry and telling him to make it a good one. I down it quickly, listening to the guys' banter and contemplating separating myself from them completely so I don't have to buy my next drink. I'm scanning the other side of the bar when I see Cody, the band's third guitarist, appear in the crowd.

The first time we met was the same night Adam made a public spectacle of asking Rowan to be his girlfriend. I was sitting next to Joel on the bus after the show when Cody slid into the seat next to me.

"Want the grand tour?" he asked. His leer made it clear he was already assuming my answer would be yes, and I knew which room he wanted to show me—the black-satin bedroom Rowan had told me about, which I had no interest in seeing with anyone other than Joel. Or Shawn. Or even Mike. But definitely not fucking Cody. There was just something about the way he looked at me that made me want to knee him in the crotch.

"I was hoping Joel would show me," I suggested loudly

enough for Joel to overhear, and he removed himself from the conversation everyone else was having to turn his head in my direction and give me that smile that made my clothes feel too small and the space between us feel too big. I had just met him the night before, but we'd already had sex all over every inch of my dorm room, trashing it in true rock-star fashion.

Cody's hand slid across my back and curled around my waist. "I want my turn."

My eyes snapped back to him. "Excuse me?"

"You look like fun. Joel's already had his turn."

"Are you fucking serious right now?" I wasn't some fucking toy to be passed around, and I also wasn't going to sit there and let him assume I was.

Joel burst out laughing. "Code, is that really the best line you've got?"

"Didn't think she was the type of girl I'd need to drop lines on," Cody said, still giving me a shit-eating smile that I itched to slap off his face.

Joel tugged me onto his lap to get me away from Cody, but I was full-on seething. I was contemplating planting my stiletto heel between Cody's legs when Joel buried his face in my hair and slid his rough fingertips up my bare thigh. "Ignore him. I don't plan on sharing you."

I finally stopped glaring at Cody long enough to gaze at Joel, and he gave me a warm smile that defused me.

"I'm ready to give you that tour now," he continued, and then he kissed me and Cody disappeared.

Now, Joel is the one I want to disappear, and I need Cody to help make that happen. Every night since demanding his turn, he's taken every available opportunity to let me know he still wants it. Winks behind Joel's back. Comments whispered in my ear when Joel isn't around. Tonight, when he spots me at the bar and rakes his greedy eyes over me inch by deliberate inch, I don't scowl or flash him my middle finger. I let him take his fill, and when his eyes finally meet mine, his lips curl with satisfaction and I push away from the bar. He walks toward me, I walk toward him, and when we meet at the edge of the dance floor, I take his hand and pull him deep into the crowd. We're in the middle of a clash of dancing bodies when I spin around and drape my arms around his neck, pushing up close to him and getting pulled even closer when he tightens his hold around my waist.

"Finally done with Joel?" he asks, smirking at me. With my heels, we're eye level, a comfort I don't have when I'm staring doe-eyed up at Joel. Maybe short guys aren't so bad after all.

I place my finger over his lips. "Stop talking."

Cody removes my finger, his smile gone. He opens his mouth to say something, but I really, *really* don't want to talk.

So I kiss him.

I let the floor-vibrating music swallow me whole, and Cody and I make out and grind against each other until I'm pretty sure my brain is starving for oxygen. But even then, I refuse to let it have any. I dance until my muscles burn, and then I push past the fire until they go completely numb. I close my eyes and pretend that Cody's hands are just hands. Just me dancing with a thousand hands all over me under flashing blue lights in a sea of warm bodies.

His hands are on my stomach, my legs, my ass, my breasts. I let them touch and squeeze and keep me in a serotonin-induced fog. He catches all the right curves, lavishes all my best features—because he appreciates me in a way that Joel never will. Because he's never had a girl like me, and Joel has had me way too much.

When he pulls away and says he has to take a piss, I nearly beg him to keep touching me. Instead, I tell him to bring me a drink.

I'm dancing alone, eyes closed and hands raised toward the ceiling, when someone presses up behind me and a strong arm wraps around my middle. Not caring who it is, I wrap my arms around the back of his neck and continue dancing.

"Using Cody isn't going to make me jealous," Joel's low voice warns in my ear. One of his hands is pressed firmly over my sequined stomach and the other is sliding up the burning hot underside of my raised arm. He takes my hand and spins me around.

Face-to-face with him, I stop dancing and glare. "Not everything is about you, Joel."

He tugs me flush against him and glowers down at me. "You shouldn't let him touch you like that."

"Why not?" I argue, bracing my hands on his hard biceps.

"Because he's not me."

"Thank God for that," I snap. I push at him, but since Joel is immovable, I end up stumbling back a step.

He snaps right back at me. "You don't even like him."

I laugh in his face, and he stiffens. "Sorry to break it to

you, sweetie," I cup his cheek in my palm, giving him my sweetest smile, "but I never actually care about *any* of the guys who touch me." His eyes harden, and I'm not sure if they're burning with jealousy or if it's just plain anger, but either way, I'm feeling reckless and plan to throw fuel on the fire.

Joel walks away from me just before Cody returns with drinks in his hands, oblivious to what just happened. I take mine and gulp it down. Then I toss the plastic cup to the floor and spin around, pressing my ass against Cody's groin and grinding my way down his body to the beat of the music. Now that I know Joel is watching, I plan to give him a show.

By the time the lights cut and Cody has to head backstage, I'm pretty sure I could audition at any strip club in town and instantly be hired as their star attraction. I don't even need to buy stripper clothes, because I already have a whole closet full of them at home.

I'm slowly making my way back to the bar when Leti materializes at my side and falls in step with my boots. "What the hell was *that* about?"

I chuckle and give him a big smile, hooking my arm in his. His skin is as hot as mine, so I'm guessing we've been sharing the dance floor. "Just having some fun."

"You don't even *like* Cody."

"But he likes me," I reason. "And besides, Joel was watching."

Leti frowns. "I hope you know what you're doing . . ."

Really, I have no fucking clue, but I smile like I do and Leti drops the lecture. When we get to the bar, he has a hot guy waiting for him, so I release his arm and slide onto a stool next to Rowan.

"*Cody*, Dee?" she says, her nose scrunched like his name leaves a bad taste in her mouth. She's wearing one of my dresses—a slinky dark blue number that flatters her every curve—but she insisted on wearing flats with it and all my energy had already been expended persuading her not to wear leggings.

I shrug. "He wasn't a half-bad dancer."

"I think you mean 'molester.' " Her brows are pinched tight over blue eyes flooded with judgment. "That was just disturbing."

"Joel was jealous," I explain, smiling as I take a sip of my drink.

My reasoning does nothing to wash the disapproval from her face. "Was it worth it?"

I nod emphatically. "So worth it."

After three more drinks, I'm sitting at the bar swooning over Mark, the volunteer firefighter Leti is flirting with. "You two are perfect for each other," I insist, feeling the alcohol pumping through my veins like caffeinated cocoa. "You should make gorgeous babies together."

Leti and Mark laugh, and Leti takes a sip of Mark's drink. They're both shamefully gorgeous. Leti, with his golden ombre hair and his stunning golden eyes. Mark, with his dimpled cheeks and thick lashes.

"You're pretty fantastic, you know that?" Mark says, and I fall for him a little more.

"I *do* know!" I insist, motioning with my hand and nearly spilling my drink. "Thank you!"

Rowan takes my cup so I don't splash everyone. "Let's head backstage."

"Do you see that guy up there?" I ask Mark, ignoring Rowan and pointing to the stage with my entire arm.

"You mean the one you were dancing with?"

"No. The douchiest one up there. The one with the douchey hair and the douchey smile. The one that thinks he's sooo hot."

Leti laughs, and Mark scans the stage.

"She means the guy with the mohawk," Leti clarifies, but I fail to see why any clarification was needed.

"Yeah. What about him?" Mark asks.

"*He* doesn't realize how fantastic I am."

"Well then *he* doesn't deserve you," Mark says, pulling a long curl over my shoulder.

"You really think so?"

"That's what we've been saying this whole freaking time!" Rowan objects.

I glare up at the stage, my hazy vision locking on Joel. He's smiling down at the front row, his blond spikes and white teeth shining under the bright spotlight showering golden rays all over his golden body. "*He* needs to realize that," I explain.

If Joel knew he didn't deserve me, there wouldn't be a problem. The problem is that he thinks I don't deserve him. He thinks I'm just another girl.

I tear my gaze away and give my attention back to Leti and his firefighter. "Do you guys want to come backstage?"

Mark smiles at Leti. "I think I'd rather get another drink. What about you?"

"See you tomorrow," Leti tells me, and I giggle when I receive his message loud and clear—I was going to be his ride home, but it looks like he no longer plans to go home tonight. I wink at him before hooking my arm in Rowan's and using her for support as we make our way away from the bar.

Backstage, I watch the band while dutifully keeping my eyes off of Joel. I can feel him watching me, and Rowan tells me he keeps looking my way, but I won't give him the satisfaction of even glancing in his direction. Instead, I watch Mike beat life into his drums, I watch Shawn shred his guitar, I watch Cody compete for attention, and I watch Adam play up the crowd. He has an amazing voice, but he's an even better performer than he is a singer. He knows exactly what to do to get the crowd riled up, building the energy in the room until it's buzzing like a shaken-up Coke bottle. With his shaggy brown hair, his braceleted wrists, and his black fingernails, he looks every bit the bad boy—and every bit the type of guy I never would have imagined my best friend playing house with.

The way he looks at her every time their eyes meet . . . I've never been looked at by a guy like that. It's like he's showing her his heart, like he's telling her it belongs to her and no one else.

The way Cody looks at me only tells me that his dick belongs to me, and even then, only for the next few hours.

But he's not the one I wish would look at me like that anyway.

When the guys exit the stage, I let Cody approach me, knowing he will.

"Did you like the show?" he asks in that smug way of his. His eyes are such a muted blue, it's hard to tell if they're even blue at all. His nose is too wide and his lips are too thin.

"Always," I tell him with a come-hither smirk. "Do you have to do one more song?"

"Yeah, but then I'm all yours."

Lucky me.

When the guys go back onstage, Rowan turns to me. "You're not seriously planning to hook up with him to-night, are you?"

"With Cody?" I scoff. "Never in a million years."

"Thank God." She sighs. "You had me worried." She studies me for a moment, and then her eyes narrow. "So what *are* you planning to do?"

"Besides get Joel to confess his undying love?" I laugh, but she doesn't, so I roll my eyes and say, "Actually, that's the plan. Get Joel to confess his undying love."

"Why can't you just go for a normal guy?" Rowan asks, and I bristle.

"You mean like you did?"

"That's different."

"How is it different?"

"Because I wasn't *trying* to get Adam to fall for me."

Leave it to Rowan to cut to the bone without even meaning to.

"Well I'm sorry not everyone is as perfect as you, Rowan," I snap. "I'm sorry not everyone has rock stars fall-ing at their feet."

"That's not what I meant . . ."

"Sure, whatever," I say, brushing her off. I turn away to watch the band, sweeping over Joel before my eyes accidentally gravitate right to him.

"Dee . . ."

"I don't want to fight with you," I warn her.

"I don't want to fight with you either . . ."

"Good. Then let it go."

When the show ends for real, the guys head back into the crowd to take pictures with fans. In the swarm, I find Cody and whisper in his ear, "Let's go to the bus." When my lips finish brushing over the sensitive parts of his ear, I pull away, and the look in my eyes tells him everything he needs to know to drop everything he's doing and sprint with me to the bus.

Chapter Seven

MAKING OUT WITH Cody isn't very different from dancing with him. He knows what he's doing, and even though the logical part of my brain remembers that he's skeezy as hell, the serotonin-drowned part is wearing him like a life vest. His hands are everywhere, and my closed eyes reveal only darkness. The only differences between being here and being back inside Mayhem are that I'm beside him on a bench seat instead of in front of him on a club floor, and instead of music, my ears are filled with the sound of his labored breathing.

It's quiet. Too quiet. I hate when it's this quiet. There's too much room to think.

"Hold on," I say when Cody's hand jams beneath my top and squeezes my breast. Kissing aside, I have no intentions of letting this go anywhere. Joel will arrive any minute now, which is why I insisted Cody and I stay on the lower level of the bus instead of going upstairs. I'm hoping that seeing me with Cody will push Joel over the edge. I'm hoping it will turn him all caveman-possessive and that he'll throw me over his shoulder, take me upstairs, and claim me in a way that makes it impossible for him to let me go.

Cody doesn't listen. Instead, he pushes my top up over my bra.

"Cody, stop," I huff, trying to pull my top back down.

"Come on, don't be a tease." He drops his lips to my cleavage and runs his tongue between my breasts.

"CODY." My fingers scramble for his hair, but there's not enough to grab. "Seriously, stop!"

He grips my wrists and pins them at my sides as he slides over top of me, his tongue slithering up to my neck. "God, I've wanted to have you like this since the first time I saw you."

His pelvis grinds against mine, shoving my body into the stiff gray leather, and blind panic steals the voice from my lips. Fear burns through my veins, making my attempts to wrench my wrists away from Cody's iron fingers useless. Between his weight and my sweat-glazed skin sticking to the leather, it's impossible to move. With tears searing my eyes and the breath stolen from my lungs, I'm drowning.

"Cody," I finally manage to say, my voice just as desperate and frightened as I feel. I'm squirming and kicking and my wrists feel like they're going to snap in half. "Please!"

He moans and rocks against me. "You're so hot."

A sob pushes out of my throat, and Cody releases one of my wrists to squeeze his arm between our bodies and touch me between my legs.

I hate myself for dressing like this. For wearing a skirt that allows him to touch me without effort. What was I thinking? I never think.

I latch on to his shoulder and try with all my might to push him off me, but his weight is impossible and he doesn't move an inch.

"Cody, stop," I plead, attempting to kick against the seat to squirm away from his rubbing hand. I turn my head to the side and start crying, words like *no* and *stop* being sobbed without any effect.

And then the door to the bus opens and Joel steps inside first, a girl under his arm and a stunned look on his face as he takes in the view of Cody on top of me. I think he must hate me, but then his eyes meet mine. They fill with rage that turns on Cody, and a second later, Cody's body is flying off of me and landing on the floor.

I'm weightless as I find my feet and rush off the bus. Adam and Rowan are behind Joel and the girl he was with, and they saw everything. Shawn and Mike see only the view of me racing past them with my skirt bunched up, my hair a mess, and mascara streaming down my cheeks.

I nearly trip down the bus stairs, gulping in air and trying to quiet my sobbing. I pull my skirt as low as I can get it as I speed-walk toward my car. I don't even have my keys, but I need to get away. I need to get far away.

"Dee!" Rowan's hand lands on my shoulder, stopping me in the middle of the parking lot. "What happened in there?"

I want to tell her, but I know that if I attempt to speak, I'll start crying again. I'll break down right here in the parking lot and I won't be able to pull myself together. I bite my lip between my teeth and shake my head, silently begging her not to ask.

When I reach my purple Civic, I drop to my knees and fumble to find the hide-a-key stashed under the carriage, the sharp asphalt in my knees proving that this isn't just a bad dream. I still feel frantic, my fight-or-flight response demanding I get home as fast as humanly possible. My shaking hands open the box, remove the key, and let the box fall to the ground instead of trying to put it back where I found it. I'm desperately trying to fit the key in my car door when Rowan's hand covers mine. She takes the key from me and wraps her arm around my shoulders, walking me to the passenger-side door and helping me climb inside. Once she slides into the driver's seat beside me, she holds me in her gaze. I can tell she wants to hug me, wants me to tell her what happened so she can assure me everything will be okay. But that's not what I need from her right now. I need her to take me home.

I stare down at my shaking hands resting on my lap until she finally starts the car. She drives me home and walks me to our apartment, which is good because I'm pretty sure I'd be terrified to walk anywhere alone right now. Inside, I don't let her get a word out before I retreat to the bathroom. I turn on the shower and climb inside without taking my clothes off. I don't want to be naked right now. I just want to cry without anyone hearing me.

And I do. As soon as the water hits my face, the tears start falling. I curl up in the corner, wrap my arms around my legs, and sob into my knees. I sob so hard that I have to throw up on my hands and knees in the drain, which only makes me cry even harder. I'm pathetic. God, I'm so fucking pathetic.

When Rowan opens the bathroom door, the water has gone cold but I'm still curled up in the corner of the shower. Fully clothed, she climbs in with me and wraps me tight in her arms. I tuck my head into her shoulder and let the last of my tears drip onto her already wet skin. She holds me tight while I pull myself together, and then she helps me from the shower and dries me off while I try to pretend I'm fine.

She pulls two T-shirts and two pairs of yoga pants from my dresser, and we both change into the pajamas and climb onto my bed. She settles behind me, running a brush through my wet hair and not saying anything. The silence in the room is thick, creeping down my throat and making me nauseous, so I say the only thing I can say. "I didn't mean to snap on you at the concert."

Rowan stops brushing and wraps her arms around my shoulders, pressing her cheek against the back of my head. "I want to kill him, Dee." When I don't respond, she adds, "He can't get away with this. You have to press charges."

I wrap my hands around her slender arm and shake my head.

"Why?"

"It's not like he raped me," I say, and that word makes me want to throw up all over again. My stomach rolls, and I close my eyes to keep from retching. He came close. He came too close.

"But he . . ." Rowan trails off.

He touched me. He hurt me. He forced himself on me, and if Joel had been just a few minutes later . . .

"He went too fucking far," Rowan finishes. "He had no right, Dee. That was *assault*."

"I kissed him first," I say. I came on to him, and even on the bus, I enjoyed myself. Cody was a good kisser. I liked kissing him.

I close my eyes and blow a long breath from my nose when my stomach churns again.

Rowan turns my shoulders to stare at me, her brow furrowed. "That doesn't matter . . . You know that, right?" When I don't answer, she squeezes my shoulders and says, "Did you tell him no?"

Not at first. I should have said it sooner. "Yeah, but—"

"But nothing. If you said no, that's the only thing you needed to fucking say."

She doesn't get it, but I don't expect her to. Rowan never would have put herself in a position like that. She never would have lowered herself to making out with a guy like Cody. She never would have hooked up with that guy from work I went home with the other night. She never would have fucked nearly every guy on the football team in high school.

Because she's not a slut. But I am.

When someone knocks on my front door, I panic and tell her not to answer. I don't want to see anyone. I don't want anyone to see *me*. When Joel and his arm candy and Rowan and Adam and, God, *everyone* saw me bawling my eyes out on the bus, I wasn't sure if I was relieved they showed up or so humiliated I just wanted to die.

Rowan and I both wait for the person to go away, but instead, they knock again. "I'm just going to see who it is," she says, and then she leaves my bedroom. I stay on the bed, out of view of the front door, and listen to her walk to the peephole. Then she opens the door.

"Is she okay?" Joel's voice asks as soon as it opens. I pull my pillow onto my lap, wishing it was big enough to hide under.

"Yeah," Rowan says. "I mean, she will be."

"Where is she?" His voice echoes from the hallway outside my apartment door, and I pray Rowan doesn't let him inside. I don't want to know how he'll look at me— With pity? With disgust? With anger? I don't want to see any of it.

God, please just go away. I don't want to see his face.

"She's sleeping," Rowan lies for me, and I bury my nose in the overstuffed pillow, wishing I could live inside it where no one would ever find me. "I'll have her call you, okay?"

Adam's voice asks, "Are you staying here tonight?"

"Yeah," Rowan answers.

"Here's her purse," Joel says, almost too quietly for me to hear, and Rowan gasps.

"Oh my God, what happened to your hands?!"

"He shouldn't have touched her," he answers in a voice that gives me chills, dangerous and unapologetic.

I'm curious about his hands, but the door clicks closed. I pad to my cracked bedroom door, peeking out and seeing that Rowan has stepped into the hall and closed the door behind her. If I wasn't so physically and emotionally exhausted, I might care enough to put my ear to the door and eavesdrop on the rest of their conversation. Instead, I climb into bed and pull the covers up to my neck, pretending that today was just a bad dream and that I didn't invite Cody to put his hands all over me.

That I didn't deserve what happened.

Chapter Eight

THE NEXT MORNING, the sound of my own pained groaning wakes me from a restless sleep. Every muscle in my body aches like it's been run over while I slept, and when I put pressure on my hands to lift myself off the bed, I inhale a sharp gasp and fall back against the mattress. Tears sting my eyes when I lift my wrists in front of my face and see the angry red and purple bruising marring my olive skin.

"Dee?" Rowan calls from the other side of my closed door. "Are you alright?"

Last night, she tried to crawl in next to me because she thought I needed the comfort, but what I really needed was to be alone. I told her I wanted to sleep by myself, and she reluctantly left my room to sleep in her own bed. I'm not sure which was worse about last night—having Cody put his hands all over me or breaking down in the shower afterward like some kind of helpless victim.

Rowan jiggles the knob. "Dee, are you okay?"

I clear the gravel from my throat. "Yeah. I'm fine."

A long moment of silence passes, and I know she's still lingering behind the door. "I'm going to make breakfast. You want anything?"

She's in for a surprise when she opens the fridge and finds nothing but expired butter and a jar full of pickle juice. "No," I answer, "I'm going back to bed." I hesitate and then add, "You should go back to Adam's. I might be out for a while."

Rowan's voice is sad and careful when she says, "Dee . . . can I come in for a minute?"

I attempt to run my fingers through my hair in a nervous gesture, but end up hissing through my teeth when lightning pain reminds me of the bruising. "I'm tired, Ro. I'll call you, okay?"

I think I hear her sigh against the crack in my door; then she says with stubborn insistence, "I'll be here when you wake up."

I ignore her when she knocks on the door later to offer me lunch. I ignore her when she recruits Leti to try to talk me out of my room. I ignore her when she whines, threatens, and tries to bribe me with strawberry pancakes and chocolate ice cream. And I fall asleep ignoring the near constant texts and calls I receive from Joel.

The next morning, his voice is the one that wakes me.

"Dee, open up." His pounding on my door causes me to bolt upright, putting all of my weight on my bruised-to-hell wrists.

"Fuck!" I cradle my arms in my lap and grit my teeth.

"I'm not playing games, Dee! Peach says you haven't

eaten anything. I brought you IHOP and you're going to come out here and eat it."

"Go away," I growl. Joel is the last person in the world I want to see right now. Making a fucking fool of myself wasn't what I wanted to do to win his attention.

"Are you seriously going to sit in there feeling sorry for yourself?"

"Fuck you."

"That's not the girl I know!"

"YOU DON'T KNOW ME."

"Last chance," he says.

"Or what?" I challenge.

I hear muffled voices and then Joel saying, "Fuck yes I'm going to break this door down. What's she going to do, starve herself?" Speaking to me, he threatens, "One."

I glare at my closed door, not falling for his bullshit.

"Two."

"Get bent, Joel!"

"Three."

A satisfied smile tugs at my lips when nothing happens, but then Joel bursts through my door in a flurry of limbs and splintered wood.

"What the hell!" I shriek, eyes wide as he falls to the floor yowling in pain. I launch off my bed and hover over all six-foot-one of him writhing on the floor. He's cradling his shoulder in his hand and stringing curse words together in arrangements I've never heard before. His knuckles are wrapped in bandages and his face is a mask of pain.

"I fucking dislocated my shoulder, goddamn it!" he curses. Rowan sidles next to me and Leti next to her.

"Did you seriously dislocate your shoulder?" Rowan asks.

Leti shakes his head with pity. "I told you not to do it."

"No," Joel snaps, "I'm joking, Peach. I just like rolling around on the floor for no fucking reason!"

She kicks him in the shin, and I burst out laughing. I'm still pissed as hell at him, but I can't help laughing when he's lying on the floor, bandaged and bruised with a dislocated shoulder, and my best friend is kicking him while he's down. He's a hot mess.

"I'm glad you find this so funny," he growls up at me.

"I didn't ask you to come over here."

"Or to break down the door," Leti adds.

"OR to break down the door."

Joel sits up and glares at me until he sees my wrists. "Shit . . . Dee . . ."

Rowan and Leti follow his gaze and inhale sharp breaths, and I throw my hands behind my back to hide them from view. "It's not a big deal. Stop staring at me like that."

"Is that why you wouldn't come out?" Rowan asks. Since there's a half bathroom attached to my room, I didn't have to see her at all yesterday, despite her multiple attempts to lure me out. And this morning, I vaguely remember her trying to wake me up to go to school, but I'm pretty sure I told her that my professors could go eat dicks.

"I just didn't feel like it. God."

Rowan steps toward me like she wants to hug me, pauses, and finishes her assault by throwing her arms around my neck. Since my wrists are out of commission, I don't attempt to push her away.

"I'm fine," I insist, and Leti's hand lands on my shoulder, his gaze full of pity that makes me roll my eyes.

"You know who's not fine?" Joel asks. "The guy on the floor with the dislocated shoulder. Is anyone going to help me up and take me to the hospital?"

"Why would we do that when there's IHOP waiting to be eaten?" I ask, and Rowan chuckles before releasing me and teaming with Leti to lift him up.

IN THE WAITING room of the hospital, I'm sitting between Joel and Rowan with Leti on Rowan's other side. My legs are crossed and there's a plate of pancakes on my lap that is very quickly turning into a plate of just syrup. I offered Rowan a bite, but she said the scent of antiseptic stole her appetite. It probably would have stolen mine too if my stomach didn't feel like it was trying to eat itself.

"What happened to your hands?" I ask Joel, too curious to keep my thoughts to myself.

He glances at Rowan, and I catch her staring at the floor. She already knows, but whatever happened, she's kept it from me.

"Cody's face," Joel answers, his tone loaded with latent aggression I'm finally beginning to feel.

"Did you make him sorry?" I ask, and Leti answers before anyone else has a chance to.

"He nearly killed him." When I lean forward to search Leti's expression, he adds, "I went out to show Mark the bus . . . Shawn and Mike had to carry Cody out. He looked like Rocky Balboa decided to use his face as a punching bag."

"He wouldn't stop talking," Joel explains unapologetically.

I find myself gently unwrapping the bandages from his hands, and Joel watches me do it, not pulling away from me. I frown when I see the angry red scratches and taped stitches. "You didn't have to do that . . ."

"Yeah, I did," he says matter-of-factly.

I release my tender hold on his hands and withdraw my attention, not sure how to feel about what Joel did for me. I carve off more pancakes and push them into my mouth, trying to make sense of it. What could he possibly have to gain from getting involved?

A nurse comes to retrieve Joel with her eyes buried in a clipboard, but when they lift, the friendly smile falls from her face. With his mohawk, torn jeans, and battered knuckles, he's a disheveled mess. He's also the epitome of a bad boy, and I'm trying to ignore the fact that he's hot as hell.

She clears her throat. "Joel Gibbon?"

Joel nods his head in my direction. "Take her first."

I cough around a throatful of pancakes. The nurse eyes me until her gaze lands on my wrists, and an embarrassed flame ignites beneath my skin.

"I'm fine," I growl at Joel under my breath.

"Yeah, whatever," he says, standing up and waiting for me with agitated impatience. "Waiting on you, Deandra."

I narrow my eyes and stand up, and Rowan and Leti are quick to follow my lead, with Joel taking up the rear. The four of us enter a curtained ER cubicle, where I'm prescribed pain medication for my bruised wrists and given a handful of domestic abuse pamphlets, and Joel is lectured about busting through doors with his shoulders and breaking faces with his fists. He's taken for X-rays that determine his shoulder is just badly bruised, and then he's prescribed his own pain medication, which we pick up on our way back to my apartment.

I ignore him as we climb the stairs of my apartment building and navigate the hallways to my front door. Once inside, I attempt to head straight to my room, but he's right on my heels.

"Go away, Joel," I order as I turn a glare on him.

"Not until you talk to me."

Rowan clears her throat and begins backing toward the front door. "I'm going to go pick up some groceries." She grabs Leti's sleeve and drags him out with her, and I scowl at them even after the door closes between us.

With my arms crossed over my chest, I shoot Joel a look of impatience and wait for him to say whatever the hell he needs to say. But he just stares right back at me, engaging me in a silent standoff that I don't stand a chance of winning.

"What do you want from me?" I snap.

His trained expression reveals nothing. "Why do you think I want something from you?"

Because that's what boys do. They pretend to give a shit about you, but only because they want something. And then when they don't get it, they try to take it anyway.

My fingertips are absent-mindedly nursing my wrists when Joel gently draws my hands toward him. His thumbs caress my pulse points while he studies my bruises, and he wears a look of such sincere sympathy that I almost choke up. "He shouldn't have done this to you."

I pull my hands away and try to slam the lid back on my emotions, resenting Joel for bringing them to the surface. I spent all yesterday nearing tears and choking them back down, and if he makes me break down now, all of that effort will have been for nothing. "I shouldn't have led him on."

It's the truth, but Joel's brows pull down in a picture of contempt that makes me look away from him. "Are you seriously standing there excusing what he did to you?"

I shrug my shoulders. I'm not sure what the hell I'm doing, but fighting and lying seems easier than telling the truth and crying.

"Dee," Joel pleads, his slender fingers coming to rest on my shoulder, "you know nothing that happened was your fault, right? Cody is a piece of shit. The entire band voted him out. It was unanimous. It wasn't even a fucking question."

"You voted him out of the band?" I ask, dread churning in my stomach.

Joel nods, pushing my thick chocolate hair behind my shoulder.

"You shouldn't have done that." I hate that the band is now going to suffer because I was too stupid to know better than to play games I couldn't win.

"Why? You'll never have to see him again . . ."

God, he just doesn't get it. "Maybe I *wanted* to see him again!" I shout, needing him to know how upset I am but not wanting to explain why. If I was pouring my heart out,

I'd tell him how stupid I am, how crazy he made me, how many regrets I have. But instead, I add more regrets to the list by shouting things I don't mean.

Joel drops his hand from my shoulder like I just slapped him in the face. "Are you serious right now?"

"Who knows!" I snap, throwing my hands in the air. "Maybe I would've fucked around with him the next time you were busy fucking one of those girls from the grocery store!" His face falls, and I point an angry finger at him. "You know what, I don't need to explain myself to you. You never cared about me before, why the fuck are you pretending to now?"

"No one's pretending!" he shouts back at me, making me flinch. "I *do* fucking care about you, Dee, or I wouldn't be here! The only one pretending right now is you."

My humorless chuckle cuts the space between us. "Okay, Joel. Since you apparently think you know me all of a sudden, what am I pretending?"

"You're pretending to be okay."

The truth of his words pierce my heart, and I throw my defenses up, praying they don't let me down. "I'm *always* okay. I don't need you to be my knight in shining fucking armor."

"Good, because I'm not your Prince fucking Charming. I'm just a guy who fucking cares about you, and I'm going to keep caring about you whether you want me to or not." He turns away from me and tosses a dismissive hand in the air before swinging open the door to my apartment and slamming it behind him.

I'm left standing stunned in my living room, trying to

make sense of his words through the haze of frustration in my head. He cares about me? Since fucking *when*?

Furious, I sprint to the door and swing it open, emerging into the hall and yelling at the back of his spiky head. "Where the hell are you going?"

"What do you care?" he shouts back without bothering to slow down.

"JOEL!"

His shoulders tense before he whirls around and shouts back, "To get shit to fix your stupid door! Is that a problem?"

When he walks away from me again, I chase after him. A million questions are warring for priority on my tongue, but the one I shout at him is, "Why?! Why do you care all of a sudden, Joel? You never cared about me before!"

In a second, his body spins and pushes me against the wall. His eyes blaze the color of butane flame, and my chin tilts high to hold their heated gaze. His bandaged hands lift from my shoulders to cradle my cheeks, and then he says in a voice so serious it gives me chills, "Because I saw what he did to you and I almost fucking *killed him*, Dee."

The fire in his eyes steals the oxygen from my lungs as he searches my face for a fleeting moment. I want to kiss him. I want to rise on my toes and kiss him for doing everything I just yelled at him for, but before I can, his lips smash against mine.

My fingers claw over the thin fabric covering Joel's hard shoulders, which flex under my touch when he wraps his uninjured arm behind my back and lifts me off my feet. Using that single arm, he carries me back to my apartment, and I cling to him the entire way. We tumble onto the couch, our need for each other desperate and consuming, a blur of kissing and touching that overwhelms me until I'm launching myself off his lap.

Out of breath, I toss a hand up when he begins rising to his feet to reclaim me. I want to tell him I'm not ready. I'm not ready to give him or anyone else what Cody wanted from me. And I'm especially not ready to give it to Joel when something has obviously changed between us, and whatever that is feels terrifying.

He sits back down, waiting for me to explain. When I don't, he simply reaches out to take my fingers in his, gently coaxing me forward until I crawl sideways onto his lap. I tuck my cheek against his chest, and he holds me tight against his heartbeat.

"I've *always* cared about you, Dee."

"Stop saying that," I demand, but my heart isn't in it.

"Why?"

Because you don't mean it. Because I need someone to mean it. Because I hate that I need that. "Just stop."

"No."

"Please."

"No."

Frustrated, I pull away from him and slide to the opposite end of the couch. "You can't really care about someone you don't even know, Joel."

He glares at me and says, "I'm willing to bet you know my favorite color, food, and band."

Green, mozzarella sticks, and the Dropkick Murphys. I bristle and say, "So what? That would only prove I know you, not the other way around."

"Purple, ice cream, and Paramore," he says, and my anger bubbles to the surface when he gives all the right answers.

Crossing my arms over my chest, I nod my chin at him defiantly and say, "Big deal. You act like any of that shit *means* anything."

Joel shifts to face off with me. "What it means is that we've spent enough time with each other to know those things, Dee. How are you going to sit there and seriously act like we don't know each other? We spent Valentine's Day together, for God's sake."

"All we did was have sex!" I protest.

"What about after that?"

I throw my hands in the air because he's clearly insane. "Had more sex!"

Undeterred, Joel growls and says, "BETWEEN ALL THE SEX, DEANDRA!"

I glare at him while I think back, and then I remember, "We ordered pizza."

"And?"

"And watched Lifetime movies." That night, *between* all the sex, we'd sat shoulder to shoulder on the couch, with a box of pizza half on Joel's lap and half on mine, criticizing the movie characters. We gave them horrible relationship advice that made us both laugh until Joel had a stitch in his side and I had tears in my eyes.

When the corners of my mouth slowly tip up at the memory, Joel returns my smile, his eyes brightening like he's remembering too. "How many girls do you think I've sat around watching Lifetime movies with?"

When I don't answer, he tugs my legs over his lap and says, "Look. It's not like you ever really wanted me to be your boyfriend, so stop acting like you're pissed off I didn't want a girlfriend." I open my mouth to say something I haven't quite figured out yet, but he cuts me off. "You just wanted me to chase after you like every other guy who ever lays eyes on you, and then you would have dropped me just like the rest of them." I would argue if I could, but I can't, so I don't. When I try to pull my legs away, he tightens his hold on them. "I'm not going to do that. I'm *never* going to do that."

"Great."

Ignoring my sarcasm, he says, "But I am going to care about you. Because you're more than this bitchy person you pretend to be. You're also the girl who watched shitty movies with me on Valentine's Day and force-fed me crackers when I got shit-faced on New Year's."

I'm stunned into utter silence, a heat creeping into my cheeks as he becomes more real to me than he's ever been.

"You can say I'm pretending all you want," he continues, "but I'm not and there's nothing either of us can do about that."

"So you're asking me to be your girlfriend?" I ask, attempting to sound flippant while a million nervous butterflies flutter in my belly. I don't know what I want his answer to be. If it's no, it's going to hurt me. If it's yes, it's going to hurt him.

"What, just so you can turn me down?" he says with a half smile. "No, I'm not asking."

Chapter Nine

"So HOW DID things go with Joel?" Rowan asks from the couch as soon as we're alone. We spent the evening watching three rocker boys who had no clue what they were doing try to fix my door. Adam and Shawn noticed my bruised wrists but pretended not to, and I drowned my discomfort in a blender full of frozen margarita mix and tequila. I probably should have studied for the big test I have tomorrow, but there was no way I was going to miss the spectacle in my apartment. By the time the guys left, all they succeeded at doing was taking the old door off its hinges and suggesting that I buy one of those beaded privacy curtains to take its place.

I shrug and stand in the open doorway of my room, shaking my head at the open space. "He thinks he cares about me." Since our talk, I've stopped doubting that Joel *thinks* he cares about me. The only question now is how long it's going to last.

"So do I," Rowan says, and when my surprised eyes fix on her, she explains, "He busted his knuckles open and broke your door down."

I flop onto the cushion next to her. "Yeah, because he's an idiot."

She chuckles. "Yeah, he is, but he's an idiot who likes you."

"Lucky me."

She frowns and says, "Isn't this what you wanted?"

Rubbing my eyes, I confess, "Yeah, but not just because he feels like he has to."

"What do you mean?"

I sigh and let my hand fall to my lap. "He wouldn't have done this before." I don't have to specify before what, because my entire life will now be measured by the before and the after of that single event.

"Maybe that was just his wake-up call . . ."

"Yeah maybe," I say, too tired to burst her bubble. Rowan wants me to be happy, and I want that too, but the kind of happiness I find with guys is fleeting, and the kind I'd find with Joel would be crushing.

After washing my face and telling Rowan goodnight, I curl up under warm covers, careful to place my wrists on top of my pillow instead of under it. My eyes close to the present, and a dream drags me into the past.

"Dee, come down here," my mother says, just like she had the last time I ever saw her.

I was eleven years old, standing at the top of the stairs, staring down at her bags packed by the front door. "Where are you going?" I asked.

"Come down here so I can give you a kiss."

I reluctantly went to the bottom of the stairs and into her arms without hugging her back. She kissed the top of my head. "Be good for your dad, okay?"

I stared up at her when she released me, and she gave me a saccharine smile I didn't try to mirror. I knew she was leaving us. I just had no idea I'd never see her again. She cast one last look at my father, who was sitting on the couch with his head in his hands, before she turned around and stepped onto the porch, closing the door between us.

When the door clicks shut, I wake with my face covered in tears. I angrily wipe them away and knock my tear-soaked pillow into a thin ray of morning sunlight cutting a line across my hardwood floor, cursing my subconscious for making me dream of *her*. I haven't cried over her since that year, after I cried every last tear out with Rowan's arms around me. My dad cried too, when he thought I wasn't listening, and I'll never forgive her for that.

Seconds later, I have the phone to my ear and him on the line.

"Hey, sweetheart."

I almost break down as soon I hear his soft voice.

"Dee?"

"Hey, Dad. How are you?"

"Is something wrong?" he asks, his concern for me making me stronger.

"No, I just woke up. I had a dream about you."

"Oh? What was it?"

"I dreamt I was at home and still had to eat your pork chops and green beans," I lie.

My dad breaks into big belly laughter that dries my tears and makes me smile. Even though he was the one who raised me, he never mastered the art of cooking, and he never met a pork chop he couldn't burn. "Keep it up and that's what we'll have every holiday you come home," he teases.

I wipe the last of my tears away with the heel of my palm. "I miss you, Dad."

"I miss you too. Now are you going to tell me what's wrong or am I going to have to call Rowan?"

God, so many things are wrong, I wouldn't even know where to start. But I can't tell my dad about any of them or he'd want me to quit school and go somewhere closer to home. It was hard enough leaving him on his own as it was. And he'd also want me to press charges against Cody, but Rowan and I already had that argument, and I'm not going to change my mind. I want to put what happened with Cody in the past and leave it there, and I know that's selfish, but it is what it is. I'm also guessing the only reason Cody didn't press charges against Joel was because of the leverage I have.

"I think I want to quit my job," I tell my dad. It's at least part of the truth, and it's as much as I can share. I blew off a shift last night that I may or may not get fired for, and I have no desire to deal with annoying customers this week or to potentially run into Aiden after what I did with him a few nights ago. Now, the memory just makes me sick.

"Did something happen?"

"No. I just hate people."

My dad laughs again, eliciting another smile. "You

know you never needed to get that job in the first place. I just want you to concentrate on school. How are your classes going?"

I sit up and crisscross my legs, propping my elbows on my knees and tugging on my tangled hair. "Midterm grades are going to be posted soon . . . and mine aren't going to be pretty BUT," I say before he can interrupt me, "I'm going to do better, I swear."

A pause, and then, "How 'not pretty' are they going to be?"

Another pause, and I admit, "I probably shouldn't even tell you."

My dad sighs. "But you're going to make them prettier?"

"Starting today."

"You swear?"

"Pinky swear."

"And you're going to come home some weekend soon to see your dear old dad?"

I chuckle into the phone. "Of course. Easter's right around the corner. I'll even cook the whole time I'm home."

"I think I'd rather take you out to celebrate the good grades you're going to get."

Oh, daddy guilt—he sure knows how to lay it on thick. "It's a deal."

As soon as I get off the phone, I launch my plan into action. Step one: skip my history class because I didn't study for the big midterm we have today. Step two: go to the doctor's with a fake cough so I have an excuse for missing the big midterm we have today.

I go to my first two classes but skip the last. I'm sitting in the waiting room of the student health center when my phone dings and I read a text from Joel.

Come over after school.

Why?

Do I need a reason?

Actually, now you need 10 or I'm not coming over.

I smile wide when the texts start coming through one at a time.

1. I miss your hot body.

2. I miss your hot face.

3. I want to see what you're wearing.

4. I'm bored and hungry so we should go eat.

5. Adam is busy writing and won't let me help.

6. Shawn won't let me borrow his car b/c he's lame.

7. Have I mentioned you're hot?

8. You're smiling right now.

9. I care about you. ;)

When a shadow falls over me, I look up into the scowling face of an angry Mrs. Doubtfire. "Didn't you see the sign?"

Of course I saw the sign. The stupid one about turning your phone off in the building. The one no one pays attention to. "What sign?"

"You need to turn your phone off," she orders.

I turn it on silent and shove it back in my purse, killing her with an oversweet smile. My name is called a few minutes later and I'm taken to a patient room where a rookie doctor buys my sob story. He writes me a note—and a prescription, which I toss into the trash on my way out—and then I'm walking to my car and rooting my phone back out of my purse.

10. I have a surprise for you.

Oh, that boy likes to play dirty.

What kind of surprise?

The kind you'll need to come here to get.

When I find myself glaring and smiling at the same time, I growl at my phone and bury it back in my purse.

Twenty minutes later, my car is parked in front of Adam's apartment building and my heels are clicking down the fourth-floor hall.

I knock on the door to apartment 4E and immediately hear Rowan yell, "NO! You stay in the kitchen!" A few seconds later, she swings the door open, her face twisted with exasperation. I reach forward to wipe a smudge of flour off her nose before following her into the living room.

Adam is sitting at the breakfast bar, his foot swinging back and forth as he picks a cluster of chocolate chips out of a glass bowl and tilts his head back to eat them. Rowan launches forward and captures his wrist before he can, dragging his hand back over the bowl and smacking at it until he drops the chips back in with the rest.

Shawn, leaning against a kitchen wall, laughs and reaches his hand into the bag of chocolate chips he's holding, tossing a whopping handful into his mouth.

"How come he gets to eat them?" Adam whines as he eyes Shawn.

"Because *he* went to the store and bought extra," Rowan answers. On the kitchen side of the breakfast bar, she sidles up next to Joel, who is smiling at me like he has a secret he can barely contain.

"Share with me," Adam orders Shawn, and Shawn pops another choking-hazard-sized handful into his mouth before directing a shit-eating grin at Adam.

"Share with yourself," he teases with his mouth full.

"Shawn," Rowan barks, "give Adam some damn chocolate or I'm going to beat you with a wooden spoon." She waves her weapon of choice at him. "And you know I will!"

Shawn and Adam both laugh, and Shawn sets a single chocolate chip on the counter in front of Adam. Adam glares at it and then at Shawn before popping it in his mouth.

"Cookies?" I ask, hoisting myself up onto the stool next to Adam.

"Joel wouldn't stop whining about how bored he was and how much he wanted them," Rowan explains, "so he's going to learn how to make them."

"I changed my mind . . ." Joel says, dipping his finger into the cookie batter.

"YOU'RE GOING TO LEARN," Rowan barks, and I bite back a laugh. I know that living with three guys grinds on her nerves sometimes, but today they must have really sent her overboard.

"You realize you guys are rock stars, right?" I swing my gaze between the three of them. Sometimes, it's hard to reconcile the performers I've watched command the stage with the guys who hang around doing Disney-appropriate things like baking chocolate-chip cookies.

They stare back at me like it just occurred to them, and Joel smiles wide. "She's right. I'm too cool for this shit."

Rowan whacks him on the arm with the wooden spoon, and Joel yelps and resumes stirring the cookie batter.

Trying not to laugh, I say, "Is this my surprise?"

Joel's blue eyes swing to mine, his expression bright with excitement. "Come on, Peach," he begs, "I need to give her the surprise!"

Rowan sighs and dismisses him with a wave of her hand before pulling out a roll of parchment paper. "Whatever. Go, but I'm not giving you any cookies."

Joel's face falls in a pout. "Seriously?"

"Fine," Rowan growls, "you can have some. Just go before I stick my head in the oven."

Adam and Shawn chuckle, and Joel swoops down to plant a kiss on my best friend's cheek. "Love you, Peach!"

He breezes past me into the living room, and I hop off of my stool to join Rowan on the other side of the counter. She lines the pan while I start rolling the cookie dough into balls. We've fallen into a wordless rhythm when Joel finishes rooting something out of a backpack by the couch. He stands next to Adam and smiles at me, holding something behind his back.

"You ready?"

"This had better be the best surprise ever," I warn. He's built this up to epic proportions.

"Remember how you said you wanted to go to Mani-Fest?"

"You didn't . . ." I say. My hands stop balling the dough as I gape at him. ManiFest is a huge music festival that's held each year, but the where and when is as unpredictable as the entertainers who perform. A few weeks ago, the festival was announced, but tickets sold out within twenty-four hours.

Joel sweeps his hand out from behind his back in a dramatic gesture, and I stare at the tickets in his hand.

"Oh my God!" I squeal, grabbing his hand over the bar and pulling it close to my face. Six tickets. Six freaking tickets to a sold-out freaking show! "Oh my GOD!"

I'm frozen, and Joel says, "What? I don't even get a kiss?"

I rush around the bar and launch myself into his arms. "How did you get them?"

He squeezes me tight and sets me back on my feet, smiling like I just gave him the surprise instead of the other way around. "We have a ton of friends performing."

Adam and Shawn start rattling off the names of bands they know, and I just stare at the tickets while feeling overwhelmed and kind of nauseous.

"I don't think I can go," I mutter.

"What?!" Joel says. "Next week is Spring Break! Why can't you go?"

I *know* he's doing this to prove he cares about me. If I accept it, what will that mean? "I have a project."

"Since when do you care about projects?" Rowan asks, her brow furrowed with suspicion.

"Since I promised my dad I'd pull my grades up." I do have a project, and I did make a promise.

Shawn pushes off the wall and hands Adam the bag of chocolate chips. "What kind of project?"

"For my marketing class," I explain. "I have to find a local company and come up with some advertising materials for them, and then research how the materials affect the business. It's a semester-long project and our proposal was due last week, but I never turned mine in." I avoid Rowan's frown. I had promised her I'd do it last weekend, but . . . things came up. "It's worth most of our grade," I finish.

There's a long moment of silence, and then Adam pipes in with his mouth full of chocolate chips, "What about a band?"

"Huh?"

"What about doing the project for a band instead of a company?" His chocolate chips struggle to get down his throat, and he seems cautious when he adds, "We need to find a new guitarist . . ."

Right. Because I ruined things with the last one.

Resisting the guilt wrapping its icy fingers around my throat, I say, "Why not just bring Cody back?"

All three guys stare at me like I just suggested we lick cookie dough off the floor.

The clang of the oven slamming startles me, and Rowan whirls around with an exaggerated smile on her face. She wipes her hands on her jeans and says, "I think doing a band project sounds like a great idea. You could come up with flyers and advertise online and stuff. And researching how well it works would be simple, because if they find a guitarist, it worked." The corners of her mouth tip up in a triumph, and I begin envisioning the flyers in my head.

"I could advertise at the festival," I muse. This project would be easy, and it's the least I could do for the guys after what they did for me.

"So you're coming?" Joel asks, spinning me around by my shoulders to give me a hopeful smile that's impossible to resist.

I pluck a ticket from his hand, steal Adam's chocolate chips, and plop down on the couch to write an overdue proposal.

Chapter Ten

THE WEEK BEFORE the festival passes in a blur of quitting my job, attending classes, getting the guys to finally fix my door, and dreaming of Cody. Every night since Saturday—with the exception of the one night I dreamt of my mom—I've woken in a cold sweat with Cody's face fading from the backs of my eyelids. He always looks at me like he wants to eat me alive, telling me how hot I am and how much he wants me. Each morning when I've gotten ready for school, I've been tempted to wear yoga pants and hoodies—baggy clothes to hide my curves and prevent anyone from getting the wrong idea.

So instead, I've worn my shortest skirts, my highest heels, and my fiercest smile. I refuse to let him make me hide, even if my clothes are fitting looser against my frame because I can't eat, can't sleep, and feel smaller than I am. The fading bruises on my wrists are a constant reminder that he was more than just a nightmare, and I've decorated them with bracelets and bangles and cute fingerless gloves. Every day, I've treated life like a runway, strutting with a confidence I hope to someday feel again.

On Friday, I'm standing with Rowan in the only private room of the band's tour bus staring down at the clothes she's dressed me in. The oversized purple tank top, I can deal with. The cut-off jean shorts, those are okay too. But the black-and-white Chuck Taylors on my feet? "You've got to be kidding me."

Rowan giggles. We're parked at the music festival, preparing for our first day of shows and general mayhem, and she's enjoying this way too much. Normally, I'm the one dressing her, not the other way around.

She's made me into her personal scene-kid Barbie.

This has got to be what hell feels like.

"Do I need to put my hair up into a messy bun, too?" I scoff, wiggling my toes in the world's flattest shoes. They might be cute if they had a wedge heel or something, but the guys insisted that if I didn't wear flats, my feet would fall off—which led to a long, disturbing conversation about amputation that I'll probably have nightmares about for weeks to come.

"Actually, you probably should," Rowan says, offering me a hair tie. "It's hot as hell out there."

I point a manicured fingernail at her like I'm warding off the hounds of hell. Even though we're in the middle of some ungodly hot, middle-of-March heat-wave in crocodile-country Georgia, I have no intention of rocking Rowan's college-bum hairstyle. "No freaking way. If I'm going to wear these grungy shoes, I'm at least keeping my hair down."

A few hours later, my chocolate locks are melted against the back of my neck and my feet are dragging as I walk with my best friend and four sizzling-hot rock stars along a row of tents. When the guys emphasized that the festival was 'down South' and that it was going to be 'warm', I had no idea it would feel like sunbathing on the equator. Distant music drifts to my sweat-sprinkled ears from the area where the stages are, but right now we're searching for food. "Can I borrow your hair tie?" I beg Rowan. "Just for like . . . an hour."

She shakes her head. "I told you to wear one. You should've brought one along."

I throw both arms in the air. "And put it where? I'm wearing like fifty billion wristbands!" I've purchased one at almost every band merchandise tent we've stopped at because they cover my faded bruises, help me fit in, and are way cuter than I'd ever willingly admit.

Without warning, Joel steps in front of me and scoops me over his good shoulder. His other is still healing, but the stitches in his knuckles were removed yesterday, so he's looking like less of a mess. "There," he says while I hang upside down like a soggy noodle, "now your hair is off your neck and your feet don't hurt. Stop whining."

Adam, Shawn, and Mike all laugh, but I'm too busy enjoying the reprieve from walking to mind. "Thank God."

Joel chuckles and carries me all the way to the barbecue pit, where he sets me back on my feet and we all get in line. I insist I don't want anything, but Joel orders a sandwich for me anyway, and the band covers the tab before we commandeer a long picnic table.

Today, I taped neon-green flyers *everywhere*. Between the handouts and the ads I posted online, I'm hoping we'll have a good turnout for auditions next weekend. I'm taking this project and my debt to the band as seriously as I've ever taken anything—I'm going to sit in on auditions and make sure to see this through. The sooner Cody is replaced, the sooner I can feel like he's not *missing*, like he's not going to pop back up and finish what he started.

"So are you having fun?" Adam asks Rowan and me as he puffs on a freshly lit cigarette, and I pull a smile back onto my face as I watch his free hand distractedly tug strands of hair from Rowan's messy bun.

"Aside from the stalking, yeah," she grumbles, batting Adam's hand away while I chuckle. At home, most people are used to having the guys around. Fans ask for pictures and try to hang out, but they usually don't lose their minds or do weird things like follow us around. Here, the guys are one of the smaller bands, but there have been a few diehard fans who have been hard to get rid of, including one weird little girl wearing a The Last Ones to Know T-shirt who screamed so loudly I thought she was going to pass out.

Adam smiles and leans in to kiss the corner of Rowan's mouth, slow in a way that makes my cheeks just as red as it makes hers. I look away and add, "I just wish we knew where and when all the bands are playing."

ManiFest is like Mayhem in that it's organized chaos. Part of the gimmick is that they don't reveal the performance schedule ahead of time. The philosophy is that attendees should pick stages at random and experience new music and become fans of new bands—which is awesome up until you miss your favorite band because you had no clue where or when they'd be performing.

"What band do you want to see?" Joel asks, gazing over at me from behind black shades. He's dressed in long black jean shorts and a royal-blue tank top with extra long armholes. It hangs loosely over his fit body, revealing the tattooed script running down his side and making him look deliciously rocker. Even girls who had no idea he's a rock star have stared at him like he's a rock star, and I've pretended not to notice.

"Cutting the Line," I say without needing to think about it, "and maybe the Lost Keys." Both bands are huge right now—so huge that I'd recognize most of the members if I saw them walking around. I've kept an eye out, but so far, no luck.

"Alright," Joel says, pulling out his phone, "I have Phil's number. Who has Van's?"

My eyes widen when I realize he's in the process of texting one of the guitarists of the Lost Keys and has just asked the guys who has the number for the lead singer of Cutting the Line. Van Erickson is a God right now, and Cutting the Line is the main reason I wanted to come to the festival.

"Are you serious?" I breathe.

Joel's black sunglasses are staring down at his phone, but the corner of his lips tugs into an amused smirk.

"I have Van's," Adam says, already texting a message.

Rowan and I share a look, and a minute later, Joel tells me where and when the Lost Keys are performing and

Adam tells us where and when Cutting the Line is set to play.

"I can't believe you *know* them," I say, too stunned to bother eating the pulled-pork sandwich on the slip of foil in front of me. Joel lifts his up and takes a big bite.

"We opened for the Lost Keys a few times last summer," Shawn explains from down the table. "And Cutting the Line came to one of our shows out near where they live."

I'm still gaping when Adam blows a string of smoke downwind from Rowan and says, "They'll all be at the bonfire tonight."

Our bus is parked in the designated campsite for the headlining bands since the guys were given special permission to park there. The organizers of the festival did the guys the favor since they want them to perform next year, and I was reminded once again that no matter how well I get to know Joel, Adam, Shawn, and Mike, they're are all freaking rock stars. One day, they might even be as big as Van Erickson.

After lunch, we all part ways—Ro and Adam go back to the bus to, I assume, screw each other's brains out; Shawn and Mike head to the main offices to thank the organizers for the parking spot; and Joel volunteers to take me wherever I want to go.

With the sun casting pink ribbons all around us, I point to a random stage area. "That one's huge. I bet a big band is playing there."

Joel follows my finger and smiles. His shades are hanging from the loose neck of his tank, his skin absorbing a golden tan despite the sunscreen we've kept applying.

"Sometimes they put small bands on big stages to throw people off."

"Only one way to find out!" I tug him deep into the crowd, weaving through the growing crush of bodies until we're snug in the middle of it. Between the all-nighters I've spent trying to pull my grades up and the nightmares I've had almost every night about Cody, this week has been a haze of sleep deprivation. My body is running on caffeine and manic excitement, and I plan to ride the wave until it crashes.

"Have you ever been right in the pit before?" Joel asks, gazing around us like we're swimming in a fishbowl of piranhas. "I could see who's playing and see if we could go in the cage . . ."

Each stage is surrounded by a chainlink fence, and while it would be awesome to be that close, I'm excited about getting the full experience. A beach ball floats down from the sky, and my hands reach up with dozens of others to bat it back into the air. "No way. This is going to be awesome."

"If anyone tries to pick you up in the air," Joel warns, "kick them in the nuts, okay?"

I laugh. "But crowd surfing looks so fun!"

He shakes his head and shifts me in front of him, locking his arms around my shoulders. "The guys in this crowd would eat you alive . . ." His arms hug me tighter. "And I really don't want to have to go to jail tonight."

My giggle is drowned out by the collective scream of the crowd when the banner at the back of the stage unrolls to reveal the name of a huge, hardcore rock band. Joel's arms unwrap from around me so we can both throw our hands into the air and cheer along with everyone else, and a second later, the band comes out and people lose their damn minds. The pushing begins even before the music does, and Joel and I surge toward the stage along with hundreds of other people. The music starts, blaring from stacks of speakers bigger than I am, and I'm laughing but can't even hear the sound. I jump in time with everyone around me, singing familiar lyrics at the top of my lungs but hearing only the collective voice of the crowd and the roar of the lead singer onstage.

Crashing waves of people knock me from side to side and forward and back with each and every jump I take, but Joel manages to stay fixed at my back. His strong hands periodically wrap around my waist to steady me or tug me this way or that while I lose myself in the music, the jumping, the crush of everyone around me. I'm part of a living, breathing ocean, surfing waves that flood my body with chemicals that make me feel like I could sing at the top of my lungs every second of every day for the rest of my entire life.

By the time the band finishes its set, my throat is raw and my muscles are spent. Joel takes my hand and leads me out of the dispersing crowd, and once I have the room, I launch myself onto his back. With my arms wrapped tightly around his neck, I press my face against his shoulder and smile against his fire-hot skin.

"Joel?" I say as he hoists me up and carries me through the shallow pools of people that the performance left in its wake.

"Yeah?"

"Thanks." I squeeze him tighter, earning envious stares from every girl who had her eyes on him.

"For what?" he asks.

For everything. For the tickets, for the fun, for making me forget real life for a few hours. For catching me when I need to be caught and carrying me when I need to be carried. "For today."

He glances over his shoulder at me, and I resist the urge to kiss him.

Smiling, he says, "I think the sun is getting to you."

He walks me to the outskirts of the festival and drops me in the shade of a big oak tree, and we sprawl out next to each other on the dry grass, listening to the distant sounds of music being carried on the wind.

"What's it like?" I ask, focusing on the leaves rustling in the branches above us. A kaleidoscope of green and yellow shifts in the canopy, dropping patterns of light and shadow all over our skin.

"What's what like?"

"Being onstage. Performing in front of all those people." When I glance over at him, Joel is staring up toward the sky, his face bathed in a glowing patch of sunlight. His blond mohawk cuts a line into the grass, his skin still flushed from the heat and exertion.

He takes a moment, and then his voice drifts toward the leaves. "Have you ever done something, and in that moment, you know you're doing exactly what you're meant to be doing?"

He says it with a surety I've never felt before, and in that moment, I ache for it. "Not really."

"When we go onstage," he continues, "and the kids sing our songs back to us . . . that's what it's like. That's when I know I'm doing exactly what I was put on this Earth to do, because there's no better feeling than that."

I close my eyes, wishing for that kind of moment, wondering how it would feel, and doubting I'll ever know. Rowan, my dad, guidance counselors, my academic advisor—they've all tried to help me discover what I want to do with my life, but maybe there's nothing to find.

"Sorry," Joel says after a while, "that was corny as shit. Adam can probably explain it better."

My eyes are still closed when I shake my head. "That was perfect."

When I sense him shift beside me, my eyes open and I find him propped on his elbow next to me. My gaze drifts to his lips, and mine begin to tingle with memories: him, kissing me inside Mayhem, outside Mayhem, in my car, on a truck, in a hallway.

He hasn't made a move on me since Monday, and even though I've loved hanging out with him, I miss when we couldn't be together for more than an hour or two before sneaking off somewhere to fool around. Now, it's like the heat between us is gone, and all that's left is his friendly smile and adorable laugh, which should be enough but isn't.

I want to ask him why he isn't kissing me, why he's just hovering over me with his gorgeous lips and beautiful eyes, but then those lips open and he says, "Have you ever performed in front of a crowd before?"

"I had a few dance recitals," I reluctantly answer, looking back to the leaves above us while remembering my dad with a video camera in his hand and my mom with a proud smile on her face. I only ever saw those smiles when I was dressed up like a plastic doll for recitals or parties or pictures. I never realized I was just a plaything to her until the year that she outgrew me.

"You dance?" Joel asks, and I shove my emotions back into the catacombs of my heart.

"Used to."

"Why'd you stop?"

When my mom left, I grew to hate everything that reminded me of her. To this day, I still can't stand the smell of coconut perfume or the taste of lemon meringue pie. She's the reason I haven't danced ballet since I was eleven years old, the reason I can't bring myself to wear ballet flats even when they're the height of college-girl fashion.

"Just grew out of it," I say, rising to my feet to escape further interrogation. "You ready to head back to the bus?"

Joel doesn't move to stand. Instead, his blue eyes track me from where he's lying in the grass and he says, "Why do you do that?"

"Do what?"

"Shut me down every time I ask you something personal."

"I don't know anything personal about you," I argue, citing it as evidence that it's better this way. Instead, he takes it as a challenge.

"I used to draw," he offers, and a line forms in my forehead.

"Huh?"

"I used to draw." He pushes off the ground and rises

to his feet, wiping the grass from his shorts. "Not many people know that about me. I used to paint a little too, but not as much. Music classes and art classes were pretty much the only reasons I stayed in school."

"Why'd you quit doing it if you loved it so much?"

He straightens and says, "I'll tell you if you tell me."

After a moment, I offer a trade. "Tell me *and* draw me something, and we'll call it a deal."

Joel assesses me for a moment, and then he counters with, "When's your birthday?"

"May thirtieth."

"I'll draw you something for your birthday. How's that?"

I don't know why I want him to draw me something, but I do. I want him to draw me something meant just for me, something I can keep. "Promise," I demand, and he doesn't hesitate.

"I promise." The sincerity in his blue eyes tells me he means it.

"You first then," I say.

"I quit because it just stopped mattering so much."

"Why?"

He shrugs. "I used to draw mostly when I was alone, and I'm never alone anymore."

I stare at him for a long moment before sighing and knowing it's my turn. "I quit dancing because it was my mom's dream, not mine."

It's not the entire truth, but it's the closest I've ever told anyone.

Chapter Eleven

"I'M JUST SAYING we should look at the evidence," Rowan says as I toss clothes from my suitcase in a tornado of not-skirts and not-dresses. There's a festival's worth of rock stars outside—including one in particular who seems dead set on not noticing how hot I still am—and I'm stuck on the bus with a consignment shop wardrobe and a fashion-challenged best friend.

"I'm never going to forgive you," I complain, cursing myself for letting her pack for me.

Ignoring me as if I said nothing at all, she begins counting on her fingers. "One, Joel got you these tickets."

"I mean, what the hell is this?" I hold up an oversized T-shirt that looks like it could swallow me whole. "Do I *look* like I weigh five hundred pounds?"

"Two, he fixed your door."

"And this!" I present a pair of ridiculously long shorts.

"Even if I was a forty-year-old mother of five, I still wouldn't be caught *dead* in these."

"Three, he spent all day following you around."

"I should just go to this party naked," I grumble.

"Four, he ignored every other girl who tried to get his attention—"

"ROWAN," I interrupt, huffing and turning on my haunches to scowl at her, "do you know what all that evidence says? He wants to be *friends*."

Not even two hours ago, I was lying on my back beside him, and instead of crawling over top of me or even just *kissing* me like he wouldn't have been able to resist doing a few weeks ago, he insisted on talking about dancing. And drawing. And anything except why he's no longer interested in me, which, as far as I'm concerned, is the only thing that really needs to be talked about.

Rowan lifts her eyebrow at me. "Do you remember when I thought Adam just wanted to be friends, and you told me I was an idiot?"

I turn my attention back to the suitcase, taking my frustration out on clothes that get thrown across the room.

"I hate to tell you this," she continues, "but you're an idiot."

"He hasn't even tried to kiss me at *all* this week," I growl, standing up and dumping the suitcase on the bed. An avalanche of clothes tumbles from the mountain I create, none of them the kind I'm looking for. "We hang out, we have fun. He says he cares about me, but all he ever wants to do is *talk*. He doesn't even want to have sex with me anymore!"

I'm so frustrated by what happened at the tree, I could scream, but I'm trying to put a cap on my crazy. I'm not going to try to make him jealous. I'm not going to beg. If he wants to be friends, I'll be his friend.

But that doesn't mean I can't look hot doing it. He should be fully aware of what he's missing.

"Maybe he wants *more* than sex," Rowan counters, and I give her a look that says, *Are you freaking kidding me?*

"Dee, I *live* with Joel, okay? *I'm* his friend, and trust me, he'd never carry my stuff around for me all day or let me drink the last of his water."

"It's different when you go from being fuck-friends to just-friends," I reason. Yes, Joel was sweet today. No, it doesn't mean anything. "Maybe he thinks he has to do those things." Or maybe he still feels like he owes me for what happened with Cody. One day, maybe he'll consider us even and then we'll be nothing at all.

Rowan sighs and flops flat on her back on the black-satin bed. I kick her foot and say, "I need scissors."

"For what?"

"To murder you for convincing me to take your packing advice." When she glares at me, I roll my eyes and say, "I need to go all fairy-godmother on one of these T-shirts."

After she finds me a pair from downstairs, I spread one of my new band shirts flat on the bed and cut one of the sleeves off to make the shirt one-shouldered. Then I cut the other sleeve into a thin strap and tie the top of it into a cute knot. I continue cutting slits all the way down that side of the shirt, and then I cut a straight line through them and tie the ends of fabric together into more cute knots. With knots and peek-a-boo slits laddering the side of the shirt, I carefully pull the now fitted top over my head and ask Rowan how I look.

Even though she's shaking her head, a smile sneaks onto her face. "You look like a freaking rock star."

Outside, the air is thick with unshed rain, and in the open lot next to the buses, there are people *everywhere*, laughing and drinking and chasing each other with squirt guns. Singers and guitarists and drummers. Roadies and festival volunteers and girls. Sooo many girls.

Shadows intrude on the massive bonfire from all sides, and in the darkness, cigarette cherries twinkle like fireflies. Girls with dyed hair and piercings are prancing around with sparklers or draping themselves over guys who spent the day performing onstage. When a topless girl with big fake boobs skips up to us, I'm too busy staring at her bouncing tits to notice she's trying to hand me a sparkler. Rowan takes it instead, and the girl frolics away. Some guys are gawking, some are drooling, and yet others are barely glancing in her direction. Rowan and I are both staring after her with our mouths hanging open.

"Oh . . ." I say.

"My . . ." Rowan adds.

"God."

We look at each other, mirroring wide-eyed, open-mouthed expressions.

"What the hell was *that*?" Rowan asks, and I shake my head.

"A sparkler fairy?"

She lets that sink in for a moment, and then we both burst out laughing.

"Oh my GOD," she says mid-laugh, grabbing my shoulders with a look of absolute horror on her face. "My *boyfriend* is here somewhere!"

When we find Adam, he's already unsteady on his feet, standing in a group of around a dozen people while warding off a pair of groupies with two sparklers crossed like a crucifix. When he spots Rowan, he shouts, "Peach! Did you bring the holy water?"

Joel, Shawn, and Mike are standing nearby laughing their asses off with a bunch of other guys, and the girls in front of Adam are pouting.

"Do you need something?" Rowan asks the girls, fully accustomed by now to putting groupie bitches in their place. She sidles next to Adam and gives them a look that could kill.

"Who the hell are you?" one of them asks.

"Are you deaf?" I taunt from behind them. "She's Peach!"

"And who the hell are *you*?" the girl snarls, turning her scowl on me.

Rowan smiles my way and says, "She's Sparkler Fairy's understudy!"

I crack a wide smile and take a flourished bow, and the girls huff and walk away with confused looks on their sour faces.

"Sparkler Fairy?" Joel asks. His shirt is off, flaunting toned muscles shadowed under golden skin, and a pair of cargo shorts is slung low on his hips, barely held up by a mesh belt. My tongue curls against the back of my teeth, missing the cold bite of his nipple ring.

"Oh, you know the one," I say, snapping myself from my ogling and holding my hand up a little higher than my head. "About this tall. Hasn't eaten a cheeseburger in her entire life. Boobs out to here." I hold my palms a foot away from my chest, and Joel laughs while Shawn grins into his red Solo cup. His arm is slung around a cute brunette—this one with her top on, thank God—and I'm surprised Joel hasn't picked up some arm candy of his own.

As if on cue, he moves to my side and wraps his arm around my waist. "You must mean Izzy."

I lift an eyebrow at him but don't bother asking how he knows her name. There are some things I just do *not* want to know.

The guys introduce Rowan and me to the rest of the people in the circle, punctuating some of the names with inside jokes I'm not paying attention to—because I'm too busy trying not to notice Joel's bare skin pressed against my side or the way his fingers are finding the side-slits in my shirt and teasing my goose-bumped skin.

"You should've done this to one of our shirts," he whispers in my ear, his fingers sliding deep into the slits. If he wants to be nothing but friends, he's doing a fucking terrible job, because my brain is flash firing with all sorts of not-just-friendly ideas.

"Why?" I manage to ask, my voice miraculously steady.

"Because I'm never going to hear the end of it."

"What do you mean?" I ask, my brow furrowing up at him.

He points his chin toward the other side of the circle, and I look across it just in time to see the lead singer of Cutting the Line join our group. Van Erickson claps hands and gives hugs to people he's apparently friends with, including Adam, Mike, and Shawn, and his eyes travel around the circle. They land on me, they stick, and my brain sputters. Joel's fingers tighten around my side.

"I like your shirt," Van says, a confident smirk curling his wide lips. With messy black hair bleached at the ends, and barbells in his ears and eyebrow, he looks like he just walked off of the cover of a rock magazine.

I gaze down at my shirt, understanding what Joel meant. I'm wearing the name of Van's band, and he's definitely flirting with me. I've seen enough guys use that look and that voice to know what he's doing. And Joel must know too because he squeezes me even tighter against his side, and that small gesture gives me a million more butterflies than seeing Van Erickson did.

"Thanks," I say, unable to prevent the smile that consumes my whole face.

"Why didn't you wear one of theirs?" Van asks, nodding toward Joel. It's obvious he's doing that thing guys do where they fuck with each other, so even though he's Van freaking Erickson, I decide to pay Joel back for all the favors he did me this week.

"Oh, I didn't want to cut one of theirs up," I say, pinching the hem of my black Cutting the Line T-shirt and staring down at the design. "I've never heard of these guys. Are they any good?"

When I glance back up at Van, he's staring at me like I just told him I was born with a split tongue. I maintain a straight, innocent face, but Joel doesn't last more than a few seconds before he breaks into a guy-giggle that makes the corners of my mouth twitch.

"She's kidding, man," Joel says, and I break into a wide smile. "She knows who you are. She's a big fan."

To my relief, Van laughs too. "You had me going," he tells me as he takes a beer from a girl he doesn't bother to acknowledge. "What's your name?"

"Dee," I answer, and he walks across the circle to shake my hand.

"I'm Van."

A million introductions and three beers later, I'm sitting on the grass between Joel's spread legs listening to Van talk about the international tour his band has been on and how crazy the shows have been. Joel's chin is cradled in the curve of my bare shoulder, his arms are coiled around my waist, and Rowan calling me an idiot is stuck on replay in my brain.

Friends don't touch each other like Joel has been touching me. His fingers have been playing with the fringes of my cut-off shorts, exploiting the open slits in the side of my shirt, and brushing through my hair. It's like he knows I haven't gotten off in over a week and is dead-set on making me explode.

"Oh!" he suddenly says, breaking me from my internal countdown. "Dee actually asked me a question today you guys should weigh in on. She wanted to know what it feels like to be onstage at a show."

A bunch of cliché answers get tossed out by random people in the circle—it's like being high, like being in a dream, like being a hero—and then Van muses, "It's like getting your dick sucked by a thousand chicks at once."

A round of laughter sounds, and I roll my eyes.

"I don't know," Joel chides. "Dee can do this thing with her tongue that—"

I shut him up with an elbow to his stomach, which makes everyone laugh even harder.

"Damn," Van says, sporting a shit-eating grin. "Now I'm curious. Dee, want to show me?"

"Sure," I say, flashing him a bright smile as Joel tenses behind me. Van's grin stretches even wider, but it falters when I wrap my fingers around Joel's wrist and bring his hand to my mouth. I shift to the side so Joel can watch me as I lick my stiff tongue up the length of his index finger and suck the tip into my mouth. I draw it out slowly, part my lips, and roll the flat of my tongue in lush waves over his fingerprint. I finish him off by sucking the entire length of his finger deep into my mouth and lavishing it with my tongue as I slowly draw it back out, gently scraping my teeth over the pad of his finger before I finally release his wrist.

When I'm finished putting on my little show, Joel is staring at me like he wants to fuck me right there in front of everyone, and I smirk with satisfaction.

"Holy shit," someone near us breathes, and Joel snaps out of his daze, shifting me off his lap and hauling me to my feet. A second later, his fingers are laced with mine and I'm being dragged toward the buses.

"Lucky bastard," someone says, initiating a chorus of catcalls that get drowned out by the sounds of my blood rushing in my ears and my heart pounding in my chest.

We don't even make it to the bus before Joel spins around and crushes his lips against mine. I wrap my arms around his neck, breathing him in like air I've desperately needed to breathe. His hands grab my ass and lift me off my feet, and I wrap my legs around him, clinging to every hard edge of his capable body as he carries me further into the dark.

My back flattens against some other band's bus, and Joel breaks his lips from mine. "Fuck," he breathes, his voice rough with need.

Suffocating without him, I grab his jaw and bring his lips back to mine, moaning when his tongue slips back into my mouth and his hips grind against me. He fries every neuron in my brain, making my closed eyes roll back in my head. "Joel," I gasp, tightening the circle of my legs around him, fitting him where I want him most.

His lips break from mine again when he pins his forehead to the bus behind me, the stubble on his jaw brushing against my cheek. "Dee, if you're not ready for this . . . you need to tell me now. And you can't be doing that fucking thing . . . with your tongue." His hips twitch forward reflexively with the memory, and he groans when the hardness in his shorts grinds between my legs. His fingers tighten around the bottoms of my thighs, and his forehead is still resting on the bus when he says, "God, I'm such an asshole."

"What are you talking about?" I ask, combing my fingers over his buzzed hair while I wait for my heart to stop pounding out of my chest.

He turns his face into my neck and kisses the spot under my ear like he can't keep his lips off me. "I wanted to get to know you." His tongue slicks over my skin and makes me hold him tighter. "I just don't think I can keep my hands off you anymore."

"So don't," I say, tilting my head back to give him better access to my neck. He kisses a trail lower and exploits the spot above my collar bone. My back arches, and he returns the pressure. "I missed you," I breathe.

Joel pulls away to study me. He searches my eyes and then my lips like he's not sure where the words came from or if I'm the person who said them. I start to feel self-conscious—like I've said too much with three quiet little words—but then he kisses me again and makes all my worries disappear. He kisses me until I'm completely, ut-terly lost.

"We need to get to the bus," he says, and I nip at his moving lips.

"Okay."

He sets me on my feet, and the whole way to the bus, he keeps turning around to kiss me and touch me and devour me with half-lidded eyes. By the time we actually get there, my bra is unclasped, the button of his shorts is undone, and my lips are tingling from his unforgiving kisses. On the bus, we fall onto the bench seat, and Joel settles between my legs. I'm moaning against his mouth when his lips drop to my neck. The leather bench is stick-ing to every inch of my exposed skin, and his hand pushes under my shirt, and he's so heavy—God he's so heavy—and the air is too thin, and my lungs are too thick, and I can't breathe, oh my God, I can't breathe—I can't breathe, I can't breathe, I can't breathe!

"Dee?" Joel asks, his voice muffled by the blood surging in my ears, threatening to make my vision go black. He yanks me into a sitting position, and I bend over while sucking in useless breaths that go straight to my head instead of my lungs.

"Breathe," he coaches, increasing the pressure of his hand on my back so I'll bend even lower and place my head between my knees.

Air enters me in a gasp and leaves in a sob. Tears sting my already watery eyes, and I stay bent over just so Joel won't see them.

"Are you okay?" he asks me, quietly like he knows I'm not.

All I can do is shake my head, hating myself for falling apart in front of him. Again. But Cody's face was in my head, and his hand was under my shirt, and—

"I'm sorry," Joel says, rubbing my back soothingly. "I didn't mean . . . I shouldn't have—"

When I sit up, he looks even more broken than I feel, which makes me hate myself even more, which shouldn't even be possible.

"We don't have to do this," he says, his hand still glued to my back. When I stand up, he lets it fall away.

"I can't believe he ruined sex for me," I say, too upset to keep my thoughts to myself. Cody has stolen sleep from me. He's stolen my appetite. He's stolen my confidence.

Last Wednesday, I saw a guy that looked like him on campus and ended up throwing up in a bathroom stall.

He's stolen everything.

"Dee, if you're not ready, we don't have to—"

"I want to!" I spin around and wipe an angry tear from my eye. Just one, and then there are no more tears to cry. "I want to, but it's like he broke me, Joel."

As I stare down into Joel's concerned eyes, my heart aches with how much I miss him. I miss being more than friends with him. I miss having him in that way that makes me feel like I know him better than anyone else could ever possibly know him.

"Do you know what I want more than sex right now?" he asks, his fingers reaching out to curl around mine. "I just want to hold you."

Another tear escapes the corner of my eye, and then another.

"Come here," he says, gently tugging me onto his lap.

I straddle him, and his arms wrap firmly around me. Our chins tuck into the crooks of each other's shoulders, and I hug him close, quiet tears dripping onto his golden skin.

"You're not broken," he assures me, and I wonder why he's still bothering to stick around. Why he's holding me closely when he should be pushing me away. There are plenty of girls outside who wouldn't end up crying when he tried to take their clothes off.

"I hate this," I confess in a whisper that sounds as defeated as I feel.

"It's not a big deal. We don't need to do anything."

I pull away and stare hard at him. "Doesn't this even matter to you? Don't you even care?"

"Of course I care—"

"Then say 'I hate this too, Dee.' Tell me how much this fucking sucks because you want to be inside me right now. Tell me how we can fix it. Don't just tell me it's not a big deal. Because it's a huge fucking deal, Joel."

His eyes slowly darken, his voice firm when he says, "Stand up."

"Huh?"

"Stand. Up."

I slide off his lap, and his big hands capture the sides of my legs, holding me in front of him. He stares up at me and says, "Are you sure you want to do this?"

It sounds like a warning, but whatever he's planning on doing—with his hands on my legs and him looking at me like that—yeah, I want him to do it. "Yes."

"Then take off your shorts."

When I hesitate, he commands me with one word. "Now."

My fingers undo the button of my shorts, and Joel releases my legs and sits back.

"Take them off. Then your shirt."

A shiver dances up my spine, and I slowly pull them down. I step out of them and pull my shirt over my head, tossing it to the side. My bra, already unclasped from our wanton walk to the bus, slips over my arms and falls to my feet, and I kick it to the side.

Joel's eyes never leave mine as his hands slide behind my thighs and his face draws closer to my stomach. His lips connect with a sensitive spot next to my navel, and he stares up at me as he licks the salt from my skin.

My eyes flutter closed, and his strong hands slide up the backs of my thighs to squeeze my ass in his palms. My fingers clutch his warm shoulders, tightening when his wet lips trace soft kisses along my panty line. The way he kisses me is sensual. Dizzying. A finger hooks into my silky waistband and tugs it down over the hollow of my pelvis. His lips connect a second later, devouring the sensitized dip in my body that drives me crazy with want.

"Joel," I pant, and he stops kissing me.

When he stands up, my eyes open, and he kisses me fiercely, breaking away only long enough to order me to take my panties off. As I wiggle out of them, he kicks out of his shorts and boxers, and then he stretches out on the bench and pulls me on top of him, lacing his fingers with mine and using them to pin his own hands next to his head.

I know what he's doing. He's giving me control, relinquishing all the power. And it's working, because I drop my lips to his and kiss him ravenously. Throbs from between my legs beg to be touched and soothed, and I pull away from his mouth, parting my lips to say something. Before I can, his mouth presses against my throat and my words get lost behind the bottom lip I have to bite between my teeth.

"Do you have a condom?" I breathlessly ask as he licks, kisses, and nibbles.

Joel's response is low and sexy, breathed against the wetness he leaves on my skin. "Upstairs."

Upstairs seems so far away. Too far away. His hands are

still pinned to the bench seat, and he's naked beneath me. All I want is to have him. To keep him.

"I'm on birth control," I offer. He already knows that, but right now, I'm suggesting it as a solution instead of a backup plan.

He parts his lips from my collarbone and stares up into my eyes, answering my unspoken question with a single word. "Okay."

With one of my hands still pinning his next to his head, I slide the other between us and wrap my fingers around him, positioning his tip firmly against me. Joel's free hand threads into my hair, and he pulls me to his lips as I lower myself onto him. I moan against his mouth, and our clasped fingers squeeze tight together.

When he's all the way inside me, I catch my breath, throbbing all around him.

"God, that feels so fucking good," he says, his eyes closed and his lips parted like all of his concentration is devoted to feeling me pulse around him.

I remove his hand from my hair and pin it back against the leather, using my weight as leverage as I lift myself off of him and lower myself back down.

Joel moans, and I chew on my lip to keep from moaning even louder. Without the condom, he feels warm and hard and so, *so* smooth. I've never had sex without one before, and I always assumed guys were lying when they said it felt so much better.

"Dee," Joel says, and I kiss my name from his lips, building a slow and steady rhythm. He kisses me back until my entire body is on fire, and then he breaks his lips from mine. My tongue curls behind his earlobe, and I nip at the soft, flushed skin. The way his fingers tighten around mine encourages me, so I'm nibbling at his neck when he pants, "You're going to need to slow down if you want me to last."

"That's not what I want," I purr against his neck.

"What do you want?"

"I want you to come in me."

A low growl rumbles deep in Joel's chest, and he stretches my arms out higher, bringing my breasts to his mouth and sucking my nipple between his lips. I gasp a moan in surprise as his tongue flicks over me, wet and firm, slicking over one pink tip and then the other. When my hips stop moving, his start, and he sinks into me over and over again as every muscle in my body coils with tension.

"Come for me first," he orders from below me. "I want to feel you do it."

His words pull a thread somewhere deep inside of me, and I unravel all around him. My white-knuckled grip on his fingers goes slack, and Joel's hands fly to my hips, holding them in place as he rockets my orgasm into uncharted territory. My fingertips dig into the gray leather beside his head, and his dig into my hips as he pours himself into me on a powerful thrust that nearly makes me collapse on top of him. I manage to stay on my hands and knees, letting him pump into me until he has nothing left to give, and then I rest my weight on top of him with my ear pressed against his chest and my fingers brushing over the damp sides of his head, the buzzed tips of his hair prickling my fingers. His heart is beating loud and fast, but his hands are the total opposite, soft and gentle as he runs them over my back.

"Why have we never done that before?" Joel asks, and I giggle against his chest, giddy with relief that I'm not completely broken, and high off of the best sex I've ever had in my entire life.

He brushes my hair away from my face, and I tilt my chin to stare up at him, a contented smile on my face.

"Do you know how many other girls have tried to convince me they were on birth control?" he asks, and my smile fades away.

"I wasn't lying," I assert in a voice devoid of all the warmth I felt just a few seconds ago. I try to push off of him, but his stubborn arms keep me from budging.

"I know. That's what I'm trying to tell you." He brushes his thumbs over my skin and says, "I've never been with anyone like that."

"Never?" I ask, studying him.

His eyes lift to the ceiling, his voice thoughtful when he says, "Never."

I should let him keep avoiding eye contact. I should keep my mouth shut. I shouldn't pretend any of this means anything.

"Neither have I," I confess, and Joel's eyes drop to mine.

He stares at me for a long moment, and I know he's wondering why him. Just like I'm wondering why me. But neither of us ask. Instead, he says, "I don't want you being with anyone else like that."

"I won't be." Sex without protection with Joel was

amazing, but with anyone else, it would be terrifying and not worth the risk.

"That's not what I meant," he says. He exhales a long breath toward the ceiling. "I don't want you being with anyone else period."

My brain flickers into static, his words lost in the noise. "Are you asking me out?"

"No."

"Then what are you saying?"

He closes his eyes, his chest rising and falling on a sigh. "Hell if I know."

I can't help it. I laugh. And eyes closed, a smile forms on his face.

"You're not making any sense."

"I know."

"If I'm not supposed to be with anyone else, who am I supposed to be with?"

"Me."

"So you *are* asking me out . . ." I say, heart pounding, palms sweating, thoughts racing. If he is, what will I say? If I turn him down, where will that leave us?

"No," he says, opening his eyes and fixing his cobalt gaze on me. My chest deflates, and I try to convince myself it's with relief. "Don't take me at more than face value, Dee. I'm not asking you out. I'm just a guy without a house or a car or anything worth offering, telling you I don't want you fucking anyone but me."

Something must be seriously wrong with me, because in that moment, I don't think I've ever wanted him more.

My eyes drift to his mouth. "Okay," I say, and then I press my lips to his.

The kiss is soft, brief, and it ends too soon when he breaks away to say, "Okay?"

"Okay, I hear you," I clarify, and then I kiss him again, unwilling to make any promises I can't keep, even if they're promises I want to.

Chapter Twelve

"WHAT THE HELL is WRONG with him?" Rowan says as we walk through the vast lot next to the buses while the guys take their morning showers. Last night, I fell asleep almost as soon as my head hit the pillow, and for the first time since Saturday, I didn't dream. I didn't have nightmares. I didn't wake thinking of Cody—I woke to Rowan hissing at me and pointing toward the stairs. She reluctantly let me shower and get dressed before dragging me outside, but then she pounced on me and made me tell her everything that happened last night, covering her ears when I tortured her with details.

"Do you know what the weird part is though?" I ask.

Rowan glances my way, stepping over a discarded beer can.

"Him refusing to ask me out was part of what made it so hot." Her face contorts with confusion, and I can't help but laugh. "Seriously. Any other guy would have told me whatever he thought I wanted to hear. He would have asked me out and then gone and cheated on me or something if I stayed with him long enough." Rowan flinches, and I rush to get her mind off her scumbag ex. "But Joel was honest with me. And he said he doesn't want me to be with other guys, and God, Ro, it was just so fucking hot."

"Wouldn't it have been better if he *did* ask you out though?" she asks, and when I don't answer, she adds, "Wouldn't you have said yes?"

I pull the length of my hair over my shoulder to detach it from the sweat beading on the back of my neck. "What would be the point? We'd just break up in a few weeks anyway. You know we would."

She can't argue, so she doesn't. Instead, she lets out a hopeless sigh and says, "I just want you to be happy, Dee. This thing with Joel . . . yeah, he makes you happy sometimes, but he also makes you miserable. What happens if we go back home and he starts messing around with other girls again?"

It's not like I haven't thought about it. When I was lying on top of him with him still hard inside me, all he said was that he didn't want me with other guys. He never said anything about him with other girls.

"I don't know," I confess. "It'll bug me, yeah, but I'll just have to get over it."

"How?"

"Bury myself in school like you do?"

She barks out a laugh, and when I push her shoulder, she nearly trips over a guy passed out on the lawn. We both end up laughing hysterically, and she chases me all the way back to the bus.

Upstairs, I root out a white The Last Ones to Know T-shirt and butcher it with scissors. The shirt I wore last night was a big hit, but I modify this one differently, cutting peek-a-boo slits in the front and slashing the shape of a heart into the back. I wear it with a lacy bright red bra that shows through the sheer material and cuts.

Joel looks me up and down when he emerges from the bathroom downstairs and spots me sitting on a bench. He's shirtless, with low-slung shorts and his hair dark with water.

"Remember what I said last night?" he asks, pulling me up by my hand and spinning me around.

"Uh-huh," I say. *I don't want you being with anyone else.* I let him ogle while I do a slow twirl.

"Yeah," he says, "*that.*"

I giggle, but he cuts it short by twirling me the rest of the way around and catching my lips with his. My fingers grip his shower-warmed biceps, and I lose myself in the scent of masculine body wash clinging to his skin. It makes my head spin, and when Rowan interrupts us by asking if we're ready to go, neither of us acknowledges her.

She clears her throat, and when that doesn't work either, Shawn punches Joel in his sore shoulder.

"Fuck," Joel barks, releasing me to rub the pain away.

Shawn shoots him an unrepentant smile. "Time to go, lover boy."

Joel quickly does his hair in the bathroom, and then he pulls on an oversized tank and big Timberland boots. He's a mismatched mess, and all I want to do is whine about how he's so fucking hot I can't stand it. All I can think about is last night, and each time the memory of his hands trickles back onto my skin, my heartbeat picks up and my cheeks flush red. I blame it on the sun, and Rowan offers me more sunscreen, but I bat it away and ignore the confused look she gives me.

After spending the morning rocking out in crowds and causing irreversible damage to our eardrums, all six of us are standing in a horizontal row at the side of the main stage. We're waiting for Cutting the Line to perform, and Joel's fingers are sneaking into the slits in the back of my T-shirt to trace the line of my bra. My breathing turns slow and steady in an attempt to keep my lungs functioning at all. I don't know what it is about his hands, calloused from years of playing the guitar, and more precise and skilled than any hands I've ever had on me. Those long fingers brush over the lacy fabric, weave over the tiny hooks . . . and my bra suddenly springs wide open. I gasp and clamp my arms to my sides to keep it in place. Everyone looks at me, but I smile and pretend Joel didn't just unclasp my bra. One-handed. In public.

He moves behind me and pulls my back to his front, and I bite the inside of my lip, getting his message loud and clear.

I'm about to turn around and drag him back to the bus when Van sprints toward us from behind the stage, and screams fly out from the crowd as soon as the fans see him. The noise stops him dead in his tracks, and he gestures for us to join him backstage before backing out of sight.

"Wade is fucking hungover," he complains when we meet him in the back. He strangles thick locks of his hair

between his fingers like he'd rather be wringing someone's neck.

"Like too hungover to play?" Adam asks.

"Like too hungover to fucking stand," Van growls,
looking back and forth between Joel and Shawn. "Can
one of you fill in? I'll give you my firstborn child, I swear
to God."

Before Shawn can respond, I nudge Joel forward. "Joel
can play."

Playing with Cutting the Line will get him more ex-
posure. Once people see and hear him, they'll want to
know who he is, who his band is. It's a good career move,
and I don't want him to miss the opportunity.

Joel glances at me before returning his attention to the
pleading look in Van's eyes. "Yeah . . . sure. Which songs
are you playing?"

"Which ones do you know?" Van asks, leading Joel to
where his two band mates are getting ready. The rest of us
go back to our vantage point beside the stage, and I buzz
with anticipation, waiting to see Joel perform with one of
the biggest bands there is.

When they appear onstage, the crowd screams just as
loudly as they would have if it would have been the original lineup. Van removes his mic from its stand. "How are
you motherfuckers doing?!"

The crowd goes wild, and Van shouts back at it, making
everyone scream even louder to be heard over the roaring
speakers. He laughs and says, "Wade isn't feeling so hot,
so we've got a special treat for you today. This sexy motherfucker over here is Joel Gibbon from The Last Ones to

Know. The rest of his band is standing right over there," Van points toward us, and the guys lift up their hands in a wave at the crowd, "and all of you are going to know who they are real soon, trust me. They're one of my favorite bands, and it's an honor to have this asshole up here on the stage with me tonight."

Joel laughs and flicks Van off, and Van grins in approval. Joel goes back to testing his pedals and getting a feel for his guitar, and Van goes back to priming the crowd.

"For real though," he says, "go to their website. Buy their album. If you're in Virginia or anywhere they're playing, go to their shows. And if you see this guy later tonight," he adds, gesturing to Joel, "suck his dick nice and good because we wouldn't have a show to put on right now if it wasn't for the huge favor he's doing us."

The crowd cheers, and some random girl in the crowd shouts, "I'll do it!"

"I bet you will," Van teases with a laugh. I'm already scanning the crowd, itching to punch her teeth out.

"Are you fuckers ready for a show?!" Van asks, and fog wraps around his ankles, lit by red and orange lights suspended around the stage.

The crowd screams, and then Joel's guitar starts the show and all I see is him. Other girls are seeing him too, screaming and reaching for him as he plays as effortlessly as he does when he's with his own band. The guitar is like an extension of him, something he'd know how to play even in his sleep.

I sing along with the lyrics, thrumming with energy that crashes through my body like rapids. When I jump up and down with the beat, I'm reminded that my bra is undone, and my laughter causes Rowan to give me a strange look.

"Can you clasp my bra?" I yell to her over the music. Her eyebrows pinch together, and still laughing, I turn away from her and lift my shirt in the back so she can re-clasp it before I turn back around.

We watch the show until the set ends, and the entire crowd screams until voices are lost and eardrums are bruised. The guys and I head backstage, and Joel barely has time to brace himself before he has to catch me in midair. My arms wrap around his neck and my knees bend as he holds me. "You were so fucking good!"

"Come back to the bus with me," he says in my ear. His voice is low, seductive, and when I pull away to look at him, his eyes are full of unspoken promises that make the rapids in my veins boil.

I drop to the ground toe by toe when the rest of our group catches up with me, and Van joins us from the other direction and claps Joel on the back. "You guys have to come with us to the meet and greet."

"Dee has a headache," Joel says without taking his eyes off me, and Van laughs and gives me a wide smile.

"Meet and greet is in fifteen minutes. Joel can take care of your headache later or you guys can find a Porta-Potty and take care of it in there, but then he needs to get his ass to our tent."

Fifteen minutes later, after Joel tries and fails to sweet-talk me into a Porta-Potty, Rowan and I are sitting at the back of Cutting the Line's merchandise tent. Van and his two non-hungover band mates are busy signing people's stuff and introducing them to Joel and the rest of The Last Ones to Know.

"Networking," I muse, swinging my pointer finger back and forth between the two bands.

Rowan nods and blows a big bubble with her gum. "Sometimes it makes me nervous." I gaze over at her, and she sighs. "Did you see how big that crowd got today?"

It was impossible not to. Once people realized Cutting the Line was playing, they abandoned other stages to join the frenzy. A mob of people manifested out of thin air, and I realized where the festival got its namesake.

"It was like the girls in the audience suddenly developed an allergy to clothes," Rowan complains, and a single chuckle escapes me. There were topless girls crowd surfing and sitting on shoulders, and it didn't escape me that one of them was probably the girl who offered to suck Joel's dick. I don't doubt that she would if given the chance, and then I'd have to kill her.

"Adam loves you," I assure Rowan, but I understand why she's worried. Relationships require a lot more than just love, and a relationship with a rock star is going to be tested. A lot.

My gaze drifts to Joel, and as if he can feel my eyes on him, he looks over his shoulder and flashes me a pearly white smile. I try to return it, but it feels weak.

When he turns back around, chatting up a group of girls clamoring for his attention, I turn back to Rowan. She's glancing back and forth between us like she's trying to figure us out. Like that isn't impossible.

"What is it about him?" she asks sincerely, and I brush off her question.

"He's hot."

"What else?"

"He's a rock star."

Rowan narrows her eyes on me. "I think you're lying."

"You also think aliens built the pyramids."

Her eyes remain narrowed, and I smirk at her. She blows another obnoxiously large bubble and pops it at me, and then we both stare out at the long line formed in front of the tent.

In our silence, I think of all the reasons I didn't give her.

I like Joel because he makes me laugh. Because he doesn't put up with my shit. Because he breaks down doors and convinces me I'm not broken. Because he tells me he cares about me. Because I'm starting to believe it.

Chapter Thirteen

THE SECOND TIME Joel and I have sex without a condom is different from the first, with lots of giggling and repositioning and knocking things over on the kitchenette counter. Afterward, I'm liquid in his hands, and it takes every ounce of strength I have left to put my clothes back on and join everyone else outside. The bonfire is relit and raging, and the entire party is rippling with an exhausted sort of excitement, the kind that makes people friendly and stupid-happy.

We find Rowan, Adam, Shawn, and Mike sitting in a circle of lawn chairs with Van, his band mates, some familiar faces from last night, and a few faces I don't recognize.

"The man of the hour!" Van shouts, and everyone cheers Joel and lifts their Solo cups in a toast. I'm looking for a spot to sit when someone taps me on the shoulder.

Two pretty girls grin at me when I turn around—one

short, one tall, both with candy-apple-red hair and milky white skin. The short one has an eyebrow piercing and a pixie haircut, and the tall one has a tiny diamond nose stud and hair down to her waist.

"I *love* your shirt," the tall one says. She's built like she was born to roll around in music videos, with long, long legs and a slim, slim waist.

"Thanks . . ."

"Did you make it yourself?" the shorter girl asks. When I nod, she beams up at her friend. "Told you!"

"Can you make me one?" the taller girl asks me.

"And me?" her friend adds.

Today, I lost count of the number of compliments I received on my shirt. A few girls asked me where I bought it and were awed when I told them I made it. But these are my first requests, and I feel an odd sense of pride getting them. "I'd need scissors . . ."

"Van!" the taller girl suddenly shouts, and Van stops flirting with a blonde sitting at his feet to look up at the girl by my side. "Do you have scissors on the bus?"

"How the fuck should I know?" he shouts back, and the tall girl rolls her eyes.

"He's useless," she says, hooking her arm in mine and walking me away from the party.

"Well, not entirely useless," the shorter one quips, and they both chuckle while leading me toward the buses. I'm too curious to resist going with them, so I follow without argument, and on the way, I learn that the taller one's name is Nikki and the shorter one's name is Molly. Nikki stops at a monstrous silver-and-red bus and roots a key out from beneath the step pad. Then she unlocks the door and leads me inside.

It's even nicer than Joel's bus, sporting slick black leather and a new car smell. The girls lead me to a kitchen in the back and root through a junk drawer until they find a pair of scissors. Then Nikki pulls off her shirt and Molly follows suit, and I'm just standing in a ridiculously extravagant tour bus with a pair of scissors in my hand and two half-naked girls practically throwing their clothes at me. This must be what Joel feels like on a daily basis.

"So you're with Joel?" Molly asks, hopping up onto the counter as I sit down at a table and stretch her T-shirt on top of it. Nikki hands me a hard lemonade, and I take a long sip, wondering who these girls are and why we're suddenly best friends.

I glance up at Molly, wondering what she's playing at, but her smile is easy and genuine, so I opt for telling the truth. "We're not really together."

"Well, *yeah*," she replies with a giggle, "but I mean, like, you're with him? You're his girl?"

Nikki is leaning against the counter next to her, studying me as they both wait for my answer. "His girl?" I ask.

"Yeah. Like Nik and me, we're with Van."

"I thought that blonde outside was with Van?"

Nikki rolls her eyes. "He probably doesn't even know that bitch's name."

"He doesn't," Molly says with a laugh. "I heard him call her Ashley, but she told me her name is Veronica."

Nikki snorts out a laugh. "That's not even close!"

"I know!" Molly says with glee, and Nikki smiles at me.

"Are you asking if I'm Joel's *groupie*?" I ask her bluntly, the situation dawning on me.

"That's such a dirty word," she says, but her tone is light and she's still smiling when Molly nods emphatically.

"Yes," the shorter girl answers.

"I'm not a groupie." I turn my attention back to cutting the sleeves off Molly's shirt, feeling more like a groupie than ever and trying to shake off the feeling.

"So what are you?" Nikki asks, and I wish I had a good answer.

"His friend." Even as the words cross my lips, I know they're a lie. Joel and I have *never* been friends. We've always been more. And less. After last night, there's no denying it, even though I fully plan on doing just that.

"Are you sleeping together?"

"Yes," I answer, hoping that ends the girls' line of questioning.

It doesn't. Instead, Nikki insists, "Then you're not friends. How long have you known each other?"

"A few months."

"Is he sleeping with anyone else?"

"Does it matter?" I ask, irritation seeping into my tone while I alter Molly's shirt.

"Oh, it matters," Nikki says. "With guys like these, you're either a groupie or a girlfriend. If he's sleeping with other people, you're a groupie. If he's not, you're a girlfriend."

"What if *I'm* sleeping with other people?" I counter.

"Then you're an idiot."

I shoot her a look, but she just shrugs and gives me a smile.

Molly swings her legs back and forth, watching me take my frustration out on her shirt. "Why would you want to sleep with anyone else when you have *Joel*?" she asks. "He's so fucking hot. Did you see him perform with Van today? He was so good. I wanted to tear his clothes off with my teeth. That mohawk?" She swoons, and Nikki laughs. "I bet he's a god in the sack."

"Confirm or deny?" Nikki asks me, and I can't help it—the ghost of a smile sweeps onto my lips.

"Oooh," Molly croons, "that's a confirm. Ugh, *I knew it*." She lets her head flop back against a cabinet, and Nikki and I both laugh.

The mood in the room lightens, and Molly suddenly perks back to life, her head flying forward and her dark eyes landing on me. "I'd *love* to join you guys . . . I mean, if you're open to that sort of thing . . . You're really pretty."

My eyes widen in surprise, and Nikki watches me with her arms crossed over her chest like she's waiting to see if I'll pass some kind of test.

"Thanks, but I don't think so," I say, and Nikki's smile widens while Molly's falls into a pout. "You're really pretty too, though," I quickly add, and her eyes light up, her shifts in mood giving me whiplash.

"You think so?" she chirps. "I'm thinking about bleaching my hair and getting blue highlights." She pulls a chunk of asymmetrical bangs in front of her face. "This red is getting so boring."

Nikki elbows her, but Molly barely seems to notice, studying her bangs like she's imagining them in a rainbow of different colors. I toss her T-shirt at her, finished with the modifications, and she holds it up and squeals.

"This is so cool!" she says, pulling it over her head and modeling for Nikki. "How do I look?"

"Totally badass," Nikki affirms with an approving smile. I made Molly's shirt different from mine, but Nikki is right—it's totally badass and I almost wish I had kept it for myself.

While I work on Nikki's shirt—yet another totally new and custom design—I learn the girls both met Van two years ago and that they usually follow Cutting the Line to most of their US shows. They get free tickets, backstage passes, and invites to all the parties. They don't seem to get much respect, I noticed, but they seem happy to be doing what they're doing. I guess Van's attention and the envy of other girls is what matters most to them, and I shudder when I realize that there was a time when I wasn't so different.

The girls ask me where I'm from, how I met Joel, if I'm in school. When I tell them I am, they ask what I'm majoring in, and I assure them I haven't the slightest clue.

They grumble about homework and wasted youth, and Nikki summarizes our collective sentiment. "That sounds miserable."

"It is," I agree, tying pieces of her shirt into knots.

"Do you know what you should go to school for?" Molly squeals, hopping off the counter and spinning around in the center of the kitchen. "You should go for fashion design!"

I chuckle. "I'm pretty sure 'T-shirt cutter' isn't an actual job."

I put the finishing touches on Nikki's shirt and hand it to her, and she marvels at the alterations. "Maybe it should be," she says, pulling the shirt over her head.

"Oh, wait!" Molly squeaks, yanking her own shirt back off. She roots through the junk drawer and thrusts a Sharpie at me. "You have to sign my tag! When you're a big famous fashion designer, I want people to be able to tell that my shirt is an authentic Dee creation."

I laugh and sign her tag, surprised when Nikki hands me her shirt and asks me to do the same.

Outside, we're nearly back at Van's circle when Nikki's hand clamps around my arm and jerks me to a stop. She nods her head toward the fire and says, "You want to find out if you're a groupie or a girlfriend?"

I follow her gaze to a trio of girls with Joel in their sights. He's sitting across the circle from Van, a beer hanging between his knees and an easy smile on his face as he talks to Mike sitting next to him.

Molly squeals and claps her hands, and Nikki pulls us farther into the shadows. I know what's going to happen—I could walk over and sit myself on his lap to stop it—but I *do* want to see it for myself, so I stand in silence between Nikki and Molly and watch as one of the girls by the fire separates herself from the herd to make her move on Joel.

When she steps in close, he gazes up at her. She says something to him, he says something back. They talk for what feels like forever, and then the girl nods her head toward what I don't doubt is a dark corner fit for blow jobs and quickies.

"She's going in for the kill," Molly whispers with far too much excitement. I resist the urge to smack her.

Joel says something back, and she reaches for his hand. My breath catches.

And then he pulls his hand away and shakes his head. He immediately follows by turning back toward Mike and brushing her off by talking to him instead. Molly skips wildly around me, chirping, "Girlfriend, girlfriend, girlfriend!"

If only they knew he told me just last night that I was *not* his girlfriend and that he was *not* asking me out . . .

Still, seeing that girl walk away from him gives me a little sort of thrill, and when I walk up to him and he tugs me into his lap, my heart skips just as gleefully as Molly had. The girls shoot me secret smiles, and they make a spectacle of showing off their shirts.

"What do you think, Van?" Nikki asks, spinning in front of him and practically trampling Ashley or Veronica or whatever the hell the blonde's name is.

Van traces his fingers intimately down her exposed back. "I like it."

Nikki's face lights up, and Van rewards her with a smile, but the moment is lost when the girl at his feet asks, "Can I have one?"

"Nope!" Molly chirps, tossing herself on Van's lap and draping her legs over the arm of his chair. "Dee has to keep production low to keep demand high. These are Dee originals. Besides, you don't even *know* her and you're just going to ask for a favor like that?"

I see Rowan give me a look, no doubt wondering when *these* girls got to know me, but the only answer I have is a noncommittal shrug.

"Can I pay you for one?" the blonde offers, standing up when Molly swings her legs around and nearly kicks her in the face.

I'm about to tell the girl no, since I really don't feel like missing any more of the party, but Shawn pipes in before I have the chance. "How much would you pay?"

"What do you charge?" she asks me.

T-shirts at the festival today were selling for twenty bucks. Curious to see if she'd pay it, I throw out twice that amount. "Forty bucks a shirt."

Nikki scoffs. "No way. At least fifty."

Molly nods in agreement, and before I can answer, Shawn says, "Keep an eye on our website."

Shawn is like the unofficial manager of the band. He's the one who books the shows, who keeps everyone in line, who networks with the right people. By the glint in his eye and the smile he gives me, I have an odd feeling I just became one of those people.

"Shit, that's a good idea," Van says, and my world stops spinning. "I'll talk to merch and have them get in touch with you."

I'm too stunned to reply, so instead I just sit there like an idiot until someone sparks up a new conversation. I'm mostly talking to myself when I finally say, "They can't be serious."

"Why can't they?" Joel asks, reminding me that I'm on his lap.

With my arm around his shoulder, I gaze down at him. "All I do is cut up shirts."

"All I do is play guitar," he counters.

I turn back around, settling against the ridges of his body, thinking they're *so* not the same thing.

His arms tighten around me and he says, "If you're good at something, you like doing it, and you can make money at it, you should go for it."

"So I should be a prostitute?" I argue, and he chuckles against my back.

"Don't sell yourself short. You could be a high-end escort."

I'm glad I'm facing away from him so he can't see my amused smile. "You'd never be able to afford me."

"You'd make me pay?"

"I'd charge you double."

"Why?"

"Hazard pay. I think I sprained my pinky when I jammed it in the toaster."

Joel laughs so hard that I have to laugh too. Everyone's attention turns on us, and when they ask what's so funny, he starts to say, "Dee and I were on the bus earlier and—"

I spin around and clamp my hand over his mouth, and his muffled laughter sounds into my palm. I turn back toward the group to make up a lie to finish the end of his sentence, but then his fingers are digging into my sides. He tickles me without mercy while I laugh hysterically and try to throw myself off his lap.

"TOASTER!" he yells when I free his mouth to pry his hands from my sides, and everyone looks at us like we're crazy as we laugh and wrestle until we're both falling out of the chair.

For the rest of the night, Joel acts like learning that I'm ticklish is better than Christmas coming early. He makes it his mission to discover all the places I'm sensitive, and I'm contemplating biting his fingers off, when someone brings up the flyers I've posted all around the festival about the auditions we're holding next weekend.

"I was actually wondering about that," Van says, his eyes glassy from one too many beers. Rowan and Adam have already gone back to the bus, but the rest of us are still hanging out under a sea of twinkling stars.

Van takes another sip of his beer and adds, "What happened to the little guy?"

"Wasn't his name Cody?" someone else says, and the name sends a cold shiver crawling up my spine.

"Yeah!" Van says. "I never liked him."

Joel's fingers stop exploring my sides to tighten around me reassuringly, but it's a pointless effort. This weekend has been make-believe. I should've always known I'd have to wake up sometime.

"Creative differences," Shawn offers dismissively. He's sitting on the edge of a cooler with a guitar on his lap and a fan club at his toes. His thick black hair is wild from the humidity, and his cargo shorts are a tattered mess. He doesn't even glance at me, his expression schooled and impassive.

"I heard it was a girl," a random guy says, ignoring Shawn's explanation. I feel Joel tense behind me.

"Who told you that?" he asks.

"Cody," the guy answers. "He said some psycho groupie was all over him but she started saying he was trying to rape her or something and you guys bought it."

All eyes turn to me and Joel, and it takes everything in me to make sure the heartbreak in my chest doesn't appear on my face.

"Cody is a fucking liar," Joel snaps, giving voice to the fight no longer left in me.

Cody is a liar about some things, but not all of them.

"He just doesn't want to admit he's a shit guitarist," Shawn says.

"My dead grandmother could play better than he could," Mike adds, and Shawn nods his agreement.

"He's lucky we kept him as long as we did."

I love the guys for lying for me. I hate myself for putting them in a position to have to.

"Did you seriously beat him up?" the same someone-from-before asks Joel, and I can't listen anymore. Each question is a memory unburied. This weekend at the festival, it's been easy to pretend that what happened with Cody was a lifetime ago, that it happened in a distant place to a different girl.

But I'm not a different girl. I'm the same *psycho groupie* who lured a guitarist to a bus and made sure to seduce him where his band mate would find us. I'm that same jealous, selfish, stupid girl. The same girl who started a fight she couldn't finish. Who played a game and lost.

"I'm heading to bed," I interrupt, standing up and giving the group a weak smile. I know they've all probably guessed that I'm the girl in question—it's written in my empty eyes, my forced smile, my broken voice. There's nothing I can do about it except hide until tomorrow and hope I never see them again.

I don't get far into the dark before Joel's fingers clasp with mine, firm and supportive.

I don't pull away, but I want to.

On the bus, I climb into the darkness of the upstairs level and kick my shoes and shorts off next to my bunk. Then I climb under the covers and try to disappear.

"Move over," Joel says. He starts sliding in next to me, leaving me no choice. I scoot toward the wall, too numb to argue.

He said some psycho groupie was all over him but she started saying he was trying to rape her.

"Those guys didn't know what they were talking about," Joel says, his hand coming to rest in the curve of my waist. We're facing each other with worlds of distance between us, and still it feels too close.

"I saw you turn that girl away tonight," I say. It sounds like an accusation, and it is. When I saw him turn her down, I had felt the glow of pride in my chest. Now, it's shadowed by something else. Something heavy.

"I didn't know you were watching."

"Why'd you do it?"

"I'm here with you."

He says it so simply. But the Joel from a week ago wasn't the type of guy to give girls thoughtful gifts, or to go away with them for the weekend. And he definitely wasn't the kind of guy to turn down a pretty girl regardless of where he was or who he was with. None of this is simple.

"Joel, last Saturday with Cody . . . I was trying to make you jealous."

"I know that."

If he really knew, he wouldn't be denying that I'm a "psycho groupie" just like Cody said. He wouldn't be lying in bed with me right now. He wouldn't be trying to make me feel better.

"I asked him to come to the bus with me," I continue, "because I knew you'd be there soon. He wanted to take me upstairs, but I insisted on staying downstairs. Do you know why?"

Silence.

"Because I knew you'd catch us there. I knew you'd see us making out, and I was hoping it would make you so jealous that you'd realize you wanted me more than anyone else." As the words leave my mouth, a horrible realization dawns on me, and I let out a humorless chuckle. "And you know what? It worked. You brought me to this festival, and you've given me all your attention, and you turned down another girl when you didn't even know I was watching. This is exactly what I wanted, Joel. Don't you get that? That's how fucking crazy I am. Cody got that part right."

Joel's hand remains motionless and heavy on my side. When he finally pulls it away, I brace myself for the emptiness I'll feel when the rest of him is gone.

"Do you know which part of that is the craziest?" he says in a soft voice, and I steel myself for his answer. He tucks my hair behind my ear and says, "That it took all of that for me to realize I always *did* want you more than anyone else."

His words sink deep beneath my skin, and I pray that in the dark, he can't see the tears welling in my eyes. I want to accept what he said, without reservation or argument, but clearly I haven't said enough. If I had, he wouldn't still be beside me.

"Do you know why I *wanted* you to like me?" I continue. "Because everything between us was just a game I wanted to win."

Sleeping with Aiden. Leaving Joel at the grocery store. Making out with Cody. Every outfit I bought, every fingernail I painted, every perfume I wore. All of it was a game, a stupid game played by a stupid girl who was way out of her league.

"I didn't actually want you to keep you," I confess. "I wanted you just to throw you away."

Joel's voice is quiet when he says, "Is it still a game?"

His thumb traces the curve of my jaw, and I manage not to shy away. "No."

"Good," he says softly, "because I'm done playing." He rolls onto his back, tucking his arm under me and pulling me against his side. And maybe I am different from the girl I was last week, because instead of resisting him, I rest my cheek against his chest and let him hold me.

We lie like that for long, stretching minutes, until his voice breaks the silence. "My mom is a drunk."

I keep still, my breathing steady. I don't know why he's telling me, but I know there's a reason, and the girl I'm becoming wants to hear it.

"She always has been. My grandma helped raise me, but she had a stroke when I was in high school and has been in a nursing home ever since." He trails off, and then shakes himself free of unvoiced thoughts. "Anyway, after that, my mom and I moved, and I started going to school with the guys. I heard they had a band, so I made them listen to me play guitar. One of the guys my mom dated had played, and when he split, he left his guitar behind and I taught myself to play." Another pause, more silent memories. "Most days, my mom was trashed and belligerent, so I stayed at Adam's house. Even when he wasn't home, most nights I slept on his floor just because I never wanted to be at my own house. I drew a lot back then. I got better at playing guitar. And you know what? I was happy. Those were the first years of my life when I felt seriously happy."

I never wondered about how Joel had grown up, about how he met the guys. I never wondered about him at all. Now, he's all I can think about, and I want to know everything. I want to know the answers to questions I haven't even thought of yet.

"Maybe that's why I don't have a car or an apartment or anything," he continues. "I like sleeping on Adam's couch because that's what I was doing the first time I ever really felt like I had a family. The guys were my brothers, and their moms bought me clothes and cooked me dinners . . . When I was little, one of my mom's boyfriends bought me birthday presents one year—he even bought me this awesome Hot Wheels Dragon racetrack I really wanted—but my mom turned around the next week and sold them all for booze money." Joel sighs, his chest rising and falling beneath me. I rub my hand over his downy-soft T-shirt, and he says, "I guess I just got used to not having anything."

After a long, long while, I say, "Joel . . . why'd you tell me all that?"

When he doesn't answer, I think he must be asleep, but then his quiet voice says, "Because I want you to know." His arms hug me closer, and he adds, "And I'm starting to think that maybe having nothing isn't such a good thing to get used to."

Chapter Fourteen

Without all the people in it, Mayhem looks strangely smaller. The ceiling seems a little higher but the walls appear a whole lot closer, like they've recovered from stretching to fit the flood of bodies that pours between them each and every weekend. We're here on a Saturday, but it's early afternoon—the line outside won't start forming for at least a few hours, when this husk of a building is brought back to life with the magic of too-bright lights and too-loud music.

The screech of a floor-cleaner echoes from somewhere behind me.

"Next!" I shout, and Leti leaves the cavernous room to bring in the next auditioner. So far, most of them have been airheaded groupies here for pictures or autographs. I may or may not have lost my temper on one of them and threatened to shove her Sharpie somewhere no one would find it.

There are six of us sitting at a long foldout table facing

the stage. Joel is on the left, next to me, Shawn, Adam, Rowan, and Mike. Before the festival, I wouldn't have felt like I belonged at this table. Now, I can almost believe that I do.

Last Sunday morning, after spending the night wrapped in Joel's arms, I woke up early, hopped into my shorts, and went downstairs to make a pot of coffee. Shawn was already standing in the kitchen with mussed hair and a steaming mug in his hands.

"You're up early," he noted as I poured myself a cup and shoveled into the sugar.

"Couldn't sleep." It was a total lie—I could have slept all day. A big part of me wanted to, as long as Joel stayed with me in bed. When he holds me, he doesn't snore, and I sleep better than I do alone.

"Looked like you were sleeping just fine to me," Shawn said with a smirk I deftly ignored.

I leaned back against the kitchen counter and blew tendrils of steam away from the lip of my mug. "So how did that conversation about the 'psycho groupie' go last night?" I asked. I said it like it didn't bother me, like *nothing* could bother me, but Shawn's grin slipped away.

"Honestly?" he asked, and the steam stopped wafting away from my cup. I held my breath, and Shawn said, "Mike and I told everyone about the time Cody slept with his cousin."

My jaw nearly dropped. "He *did that*?"

"No, but if he wants to spread bullshit lies, so can we." Shawn's grin came back ten times cockier, and when I laughed, he laughed too.

With his chin now resting heavily on the heel of his palm beside me, he says, "This is a disaster."

I can't argue. We all got our hopes up when the last person Leti brought in actually had a guitar with him, but those hopes were soon dashed when the guy revealed he had no idea how to play it and only wanted it signed.

"I'm screening everyone beforehand from now on," I say, casting a glance over my shoulder at the unmanned bar. The guys made an arrangement with the owner of Mayhem so we could hold auditions here—I wonder how mad he'd be if I deemed this an emergency situation and raided his liquor supply.

"*Driver?*" Rowan says, stealing my focus from the bottles behind the bar. At the right end of the table, she's been buried in a textbook and homework, but now all of her attention is on the lanky guy Leti just brought in. His hair is a curly burnt-orange mess; he has something-I-don't-think-is-a-cigarette tucked behind his ear; and . . . is that a freaking *banjo*?

"Is that a freaking banjo?" Rowan asks, and Mike groans and lets his forehead thump against the table. Adam and Joel both break into guy giggles, and Shawn lets out a heavy sigh.

"We're not looking for a banjo player, Driver," he says, and Joel leans in to tell me that Driver is one of their roadies and that he drives the bus when the band goes on tour.

"Hear me out, man," Driver says to Shawn. "This shit is gonna help your sound."

"What's wrong with our sound?"

Driver cocks his head to the side like he's thoroughly confused. "It doesn't have a banjo . . ."

Adam giggles harder, and Joel buries his face in the back of my shoulder to muffle his own laughter.

Shawn keeps a straight face for a moment before he can't help releasing a little laugh too. He waves his hand toward the stage. "Whatever, man. Do your thing."

The frayed bottoms of Driver's jeans drag over the dance floor as he walks toward the stage. He hops up to sit on the edge and removes the definitely-not-a-cigarette from behind his ear, fishing a lighter from his pocket and lighting up. He takes a long drag, holds it, and releases it in a thick cloud of smoke. He smiles at us, then takes another long drag.

"Driver?" Shawn asks.

"Yeah?"

"You wanna play?"

"Oh, shit," Driver says with the joint between his lips. He positions the banjo on his lap and says, "Yeah. You ready?"

Another bout of tiny giggles sound against my shoulder and echo from Adam's direction. Rowan smacks him on the arm and says to Driver, "Come on, Driver. We're hungry."

"Shit, me too. I'm *starving*," he says, and Adam howls with laughter. Joel rests his arm on my shoulder and buries his eyes in his forearm, his entire body shaking with giggles. I bite my lip to keep from joining him.

Driver laughs too, not minding how badly the boys are behaving.

"Hurry up so we can go eat," Shawn says with a smile on his face.

With the joint dangling between his lips and his feet hanging above the floor, Driver begins plucking at his banjo. And for a banjo player, he's pretty damn good. Joel whoops and slaps his knee before yanking me off my feet to do-si-do me around the room. Adam joins in, hooking his arm in mine when Joel passes me along, and Rowan drags Mike and Shawn on the floor to join us. By the time Driver finishes playing, all six of us have square-danced our asses off and are laughing hysterically. I lie down on the floor, laughing too hard to catch my breath, and Joel collapses beside me, grabbing my hand and holding on.

This week, he's spent most nights at my apartment, and on the nights he hasn't, Rowan has told me that he's attached himself to Adam's couch grumbling about how he wished he was at my place. We haven't talked about him not wanting me with other guys, and we *definitely* haven't talked about me not wanting him with other girls, but as far as I know, neither of us has been with anyone else.

Leti, who made sure to stay out of grabbing-range during our hoedown, moves to stand over me, giving me a smug smile. "Well aren't you two just totes adorbs."

I kick his ankle, and his smile widens.

"So do I get to be in the band?" Driver asks, and I lift my head off the floor to see Adam wrap his arm around Driver's shoulder.

"No fucking way, man. But we'll buy you dinner."

Driver seems to consider this for a moment, answering with a shrug. "Sweet."

At a Chinese buffet, I eat at a table with six hungry men and a bottomless pit of a best friend.

"Are you going to be able to eat all that?" Mike asks Rowan with a skeptical gaze directed at her plate.

I can't help laughing. Rowan and I are the same size, but I swear she can eat double our weight in food. Eating ice cream out of the carton with her is like competing for digging space with a backhoe. "She's just getting started."

She gives me a closed-lipped grin, her mouth already full of lo mein.

"So how are the shirts coming?" Shawn asks me, and I pick at my Chinese donut. My appetite is starting to come back, little by little.

"Almost done. I'm taking pictures this weekend, so you should be able to put them on the website next week."

"And you're seriously cool with doing this?"

"Are you kidding?" Joel asks. "You should see her apartment. There are shirts everywhere. All she talks about is knots and slits and bows and shit."

I chuckle and toss a piece of my donut at him, and he picks it off the table and pops it in his mouth, grinning at me.

Making the shirts has been a lot of work, but none of it has actually *felt* like work. Since talking to my dad, I've been more diligent about completing my overdue homework and studying for tests, since I promised him I would, but I keep catching my mind wondering to clothing designs. My college-bound notebooks are just as filled with shirt designs as they are with notes for class.

"You should see them," Rowan says, finally having swallowed down her food. "They're really good."

"Like *really* good," Leti adds.

"They're alright," I say. What I'm really proud of are

my other sketches—the ones of skirts and dresses and sexy little tops. But those are just for fun.

"You know what I've always wanted?" Driver asks. He's sitting at the end of the table, but I can smell the smoke on him from three seats away. He nods to himself and says, "A cape."

"A *cape*?" Adam asks, and Driver nods harder.

"Yeah. With hidden pockets and shit. That way if I get stopped by the cops, they won't be able to find anything on me."

"Couldn't you just get hidden pockets put in your coat or something?"

Driver's brows pull together with confusion. "You don't think that'd be too obvious?"

Adam chuckles, and Shawn closes his eyes and shakes his head. "You think a *cape* would be more subtle?" he asks.

"No, I think a cape would be more *cool*," Driver says, emphasizing the last word like Shawn's having trouble understanding.

Shawn releases a heavy sigh, and I find myself laughing quietly with Joel.

"If he gets a cape," Adam says, "I want one too."

"Can mine be sherbet orange with vanilla trim?" Leti asks. "Oh! Wait, no! Orange with fuschia sequins."

"That sounds hideous," I gripe, and Leti scoffs at me.

"Your *mom* sounds hideous," he counters.

I shrug. "My mom *is* hideous."

My mom was only beautiful in ways that won't matter once her skin starts to sag. On the inside, she's disgusting, and I pray the last seven years have taken their toll on her.

The rest of the group continues imagining their capes and arguing over whose sounds the coolest, and I find Joel watching me. He does this sometimes now—stares at me like I'm a puzzle to solve or a maze to navigate. A few times, I've asked what he was thinking, but since I never like the answer—because it *always* involves him asking me something personal—I've learned not to ask.

"You should make Joel a cape with mohawk spikes running down the back for his birthday next week," Adam says, and my eyes dart to him before settling back on Joel.

"Your birthday is next week?"

Joel looks back to his plate and scoops the peas out of his stir-fried rice. "Yeah. It's not a big deal."

My heart pulses painfully in my chest when I remember the story he told me about his mom selling his birthday presents to pay for booze. My childhood was filled with princess-themed birthday parties and more gifts than I knew what to do with. I doubt Joel has ever had a themed birthday party in his life.

"Are you guys having a party?" I ask.

"We usually take him out and get him wasted," Adam says with a laugh. "Does that count?"

Joel gives Adam a genuine smile, but I cut in with an uncompromising, "No." The guys stare at me, and I rush to resume my usual self-serving attitude. "It's been too long since we've had a party. I want to throw one."

"You don't have to do that," Joel stammers.

I brush him off with a flick of my wrist. "I love throwing parties. Ask Rowan about my Sweet Sixteen. It was amazing."

Rowan nods, keeping her eyes trained on me. She knows something is up. "It was epic," she says without missing a beat. "She had a DJ and everything. And she had three dates, and none of them were allowed to wear shirts."

I snicker at the memory, but Joel still looks skeptical.

"Just trust me," I tell him. "It'll be awesome."

Chapter Fifteen

THE FIRST TWO days after learning about Joel's birthday are spent gathering intel. The next three, collecting materials. The following two, running around like a chicken with my head cut off while cursing Joel's name for not telling me about his stupid twenty-fourth birthday a few months sooner.

"MOTHERFUCKER," I shout, raising my needle-pricked finger to my mouth to suck the hurt away.

Rowan ignores me and finishes hanging streamers from one of the card tables lining the walls of our living room. She stands up, brushes off her knees, and smiles wide. "Joel is going to flip."

Leti spins a mini Ferris wheel on top of one of the tables. Mini liquor bottles occupy each car as party favors. "You should be a party planner," he says, and I huff out a breath.

"Party planner. Shirt designer. Cape maker to the stars."

I lift a neon-green cape with black spikes running down the back of it off of my lap, silently praying Joel likes it.

Leti turns on music while Rowan finishes setting out snacks and I stand in the middle of the room with my hands on my hips making sure everything is ready to go. When someone knocks on the door, I take a deep breath before answering it.

"Holy shit," Shawn says as he walks inside, the expressions on the rest of the guys' faces echoing his sentiment.

"Do you think he'll like it?" I ask, but Shawn doesn't have a chance to answer before Adam squeals, "Are those *capes*?!"

He practically dives into the pile and pulls out one that looks just like the one he described last Saturday—it's red with a golden A stitched into it, just like Alvin the Chipmunk's shirt, and he beams like a little boy in a candy shop. Rowan helped me remember the capes all the guys described when they were joking at the buffet, and I did my best to create them. Adam's looks like Alvin's shirt, Shawn's is black with the Batman symbol stitched onto the back, and Mike's is camouflage with pockets stitched to the inside. He laughs when he finds the toy guns I stashed in the pockets, and I don't try to stop the smile that blooms across my face.

"Leti, yours is in my bedroom," I say, and Leti disappears down the hallway in an excited blur. He pouted when he saw I was making capes for the other guys but not for him, but really I just wanted to keep his hideous sherbet-and-magenta-sequined cape a surprise. He runs back out with it secured around his neck and strikes a flawless Superman pose. The rest of the guys are fastening their capes around their necks too when a knock sounds at the door.

"Close your eyes," I demand with my hand on the knob.

"Do I have to?" Joel whines from the other side.

"YES!" the guys all yell, and I chuckle.

"Are they closed?" I ask.

When he tells me they are, I open the door and lead him inside, plopping a plastic crown on his head and telling him to open his eyes. He opens them to find three grown rock stars and a very giddy-looking Leti wearing homemade capes and little-boy smiles.

"Oh my God," Joel says with a laugh that tells me he loves it. I hand him his cape, and he holds it up, laughing even harder. "This is fucking awesome."

His gaze travels around the room, skimming over the Ferris wheel carrying liquor bottles, the one-person beer-pong table with stuffed prizes hanging on the wall behind it, the painted cardboard cutout of two rock stars with holes for people to put their faces in. There's a table covered with red-and-white-striped bags of popcorn and mason jars full of candy. The star attraction is a cotton-candy maker, and the entire room is flooded with rainbow streamers and balloons.

When I was covertly prying intel out of Joel earlier this week in my attempt to get ideas for his birthday theme, I asked what his favorite childhood memory was and he told me about the time his grandma took him to the circus. I ran with it, throwing together an apartment-sized circus in a matter of days and never doubting it would be worth it.

His expression is utterly unreadable as he takes it all in, and I nibble at my bottom lip, worried that he doesn't like it. But then he finally looks at me, and his soft smile melts away all my apprehension. "This is too much."

I shake my head. It's not too much. It feels like it isn't enough—not after everything he's been through, not after everything *we've* been through—but I'm guessing no amount of streamers in the world is going to fix that.

Joel scoops me into a big hug and whispers in my ear, "Thank you."

"Happy birthday," I say, burying my face in his neck and squeezing him back. I've barely seen him over the past two days since I've been too busy setting up and wanted to keep the details a surprise, and I've missed him too much to try to hide it.

Another knock at the door interrupts our moment, and the rest of the guests begin trickling in—Driver, some other roadies, a bartender from Mayhem, a few guys from other bands, and a couple of Joel's friends from high school. I got all the names and numbers from Adam, Shawn, and Mike, and lucky for me, they were all names of guys. Girls show up too, but on the arms of dates, and pretty soon, my apartment is packed with people. Most of the guests don extra capes I made—I reserved a special one for Driver, complete with a giant pot leaf on the back and hidden pockets on the inside—and the guests who think they're too cool for capes seem content to guzzle down beer and shots and munch on pizza and mozzarella sticks. The cotton-candy machine is a huge hit, and so are the candy table and the rock-star cutouts. Guys play the beer pong game and win stuffed animals for their dates, and Joel nuzzles his chin into the crook of my shoulder as we watch.

He's laughing on my couch surrounded by a bunch of friends when I sneak to the kitchen to put the candles on his cake—vanilla ice cream with confetti sprinkles. I stick two tall candles at the sides and drape a mini carnival-style banner between them that says, "Happy Birthday Joel."

"He's so happy," Rowan comments, and I stare out to the living room, watching him pick at his blue cotton candy as he laughs at something Adam said. "So are you," Rowan adds, and I catch myself smiling. I wipe it from my face quickly, ignoring the knowing grin she gives me while I light the candles.

"Flick the switch," I order, and she gives Leti the signal to cut the lights. The room plunges into darkness, lit only by the brightness of the candles as I walk the cake toward Joel and start singing "Happy Birthday." Everyone joins in, some singing far more drunkenly than others, and I set the cake on the coffee table in front of him. "Make a wish."

With the light of the flames flickering between us, Joel's blue eyes find mine. They linger, neither one of us looking away, and a soft smile touches the corner of his mouth. He blows out the candles with one swift breath, and everyone cheers in the dark.

When the lights come back on, his eyes have already locked on me again, his smile making my cheeks blush. I escape back to the kitchen to grab plastic plates and a serving knife, and Rowan watches me with that annoying smirk on her face.

"Shut up," I say as I pass her.

"I didn't say anything."

"You thought something," I argue.

"Yeah . . . I tend to do that. I'm pretty sure normal people think things."

She chuckles, and I ignore her. "Grab the napkins."

"Okay, Miss Bossy."

As I leave the kitchen, I flick her off with the hand I'm using to hold the cake server, and she calls after me, "I'm thinking thingsss!"

"You're stupiddd," I sing back, and her giggle follows me to the living room.

I cut Joel a whopping slice of ice-cream cake before cutting tiny slivers for everyone else who wants one. By the time I'm done cutting, there's no cake left and I realize I haven't left any for myself, but then Joel is abruptly tugging me onto his lap and offering me some of his.

After cake, most of the party follows Adam outside for a smoke break, and I decide to make myself a margarita. I'm pouring ingredients into a mixing cup when Jenny, a girl who showed up with one of the guys Joel went to high school with, joins me in the kitchen to dump her plate and fork in the trash. She stands next to me, staring over the breakfast bar at Rowan and Mike playing on the hand-me-down Xbox Mike gave us as a housewarming present. They're surrounded by a group of guys drooling over their kill counts.

"I never thought I'd see the day when Adam Everest *and* Joel Gibbon got serious girlfriends," Jenny muses, and even though I'm not Joel's girlfriend, I don't correct her.

"Did you go to high school with them too?" I ask, putting the cap on my mixing cup. I begin shaking the margarita, and she nods.

"Yeah. I went to that school my whole life."

"What were they like?" I pour a glass for Jenny after pouring one for myself.

"Adam was a heartbreaker even in elementary school." She takes the glass I offer and laughs to herself. "We had class together in third grade, and I remember that his Valentine box was crammed full of cards on Valentine's Day. He picked the girl who gave him the most candy with her card, and she became his little girlfriend for the week. I think that was the only girlfriend he ever had until she came along." She nods toward Rowan, and a little smile sneaks onto my face.

"Shawn and Adam were almost always together, but they were so different. Adam spent most of his lunches in detention for skipping class or fooling around under the bleachers, but Shawn was always at the top of our class."

"Really?" I say, curious even though I don't find it hard to believe.

"Yeah. He was like this weird mix between a good boy and a bad boy. He always looked the part of a bad boy, but the teachers always loved him because he always pulled straight As." She chuckles and says, "I had a friend back then who had such a crush on him. I mean, a *lot* of girls had crushes on him, but she reeeally liked him. I think she's in a band now too."

She trails off, thinking about her friend, and I say, "What about Mike?"

"I don't remember Mike before middle school, but even then, he just kind of kept to himself. I played clarinet, and I remember he joined band for like . . . a month. Then he just walked out one practice and never came back."

"It was too easy!" Mike shouts from the couch, surprising us with his superhuman hearing.

Jenny laughs. "I think he started the band with Adam and Shawn shortly after that. He dated a girl for most of high school," she lowers her voice to a whisper, "but she was a total bitch."

"What about Joel?" I ask.

"I think he moved to town halfway through our freshman year. Back then he didn't have the mohawk. He just had a head full of messy blond hair, and the girls loved it. He had like this grunge bad-boy look."

I wonder if she knows about Joel's mom, that he probably didn't look grungy by choice, but I don't ask.

"He always spent classes doodling in a notebook instead of paying attention. A few teachers really got on his case because they said he was wasting his potential, but I think he always knew what he wanted to do with his life, you know? All those study halls he spent in the music room ended up being worth it."

Last Tuesday night, Joel came over with an acoustic guitar since he said he was working on a song but wanted to see me. We spent the evening sitting together in my living room, him strumming his guitar and working out the notes, and me working on a paper for English class while trying not to jump his bones. There was just something about seeing him play that guitar, so deep in concentration, that made me squirm in my seat. When he finally put it down, I was on his lap in a matter of seconds, tugging his shirt over his head and kissing him senseless.

I'm lost in the memory when Joel walks back inside, and I take a big gulp of my margarita to try to get my head straight.

"You two are really cute together," Jenny says. She pats my arm and walks away.

"What were you girls talking about?" Joel asks when he takes her spot.

"You," I taunt.

A tipsy smile consumes his face, and he says, "About how hot I am?"

I laugh and say, "Nope. About what a nerd you were in high school."

He follows me out to the living room, protesting the whole way. "I was *not* a nerd. If anything, *Shawn* was the nerd."

"Hey!" Shawn says, and a bunch of us laugh. "I was *not* a nerd."

"You were kind of a nerd," Mike says, and Shawn glares at him.

"Didn't you used to let Adam copy all of your assignments?" Jenny's boyfriend asks, and Shawn scoffs.

"What else was I supposed to do? Let him fail?"

Patting Shawn on the back, Adam says, "You're a good friend."

Shawn scoffs and knocks Adam's hand away. "Whatever. You still owe me thirty bucks for doing that history paper for you for Mr. Veit's class."

"Joel still owes *me* thirty bucks for when I took the fall for him denting my mom's car with that skateboard," Adam counters.

The boys start squabbling over who owes who what, and I break it up by bringing Joel one of his presents from the gift table. "This one is from Blake and Jenny."

He opens gift after gift, getting T-shirts and albums and gift cards and expensive liquor. Rowan got him personalized guitar picks, Leti got him a kickass pair of shades, and the guys all chipped in to get him a special kind of Fender guitar that everyone oohs and aahs over. I give him my gifts last, trying not to fidget as he opens them.

When he pulls back shiny green wrapping paper to reveal a graphite pencil set, he smiles down at the box.

"I didn't want you to be able to back out of our deal," I say, only half joking.

"What deal?" Rowan asks.

"He's going to draw me something for my birthday."

"You draw?" she asks Joel, and he finally turns his smile up to me.

"Used to."

"He was really good," Adam offers, and I hand Joel my next present before anyone can ask any more questions he might not want to answer.

"Another one?" he asks, setting his pencil set carefully aside before taking the box I hand him and shaking it next to his ear.

"Just open it."

Joel peels the wrapping paper away from the front of

the box in one clean swipe, revealing the Hot Wheels Dragon race track that he got for his birthday when he was a kid—before his mom sold it to fund her alcohol addiction.

Adam and Shawn start gushing about the track, reminiscing in their own childhoods, but it's all just white noise surrounding Joel's blank expression. My heart plummets as he stares down at the set, unmoving and unsmiling.

I open my mouth to say something. To apologize. But then he looks up at me, and his eyes are bright and glassy. I barely have time to register the tears in his eyes before he sets the gift aside and walks right toward me, lifting me off the floor without breaking stride. He carries me all the way down the hall to my room, closing the door behind us, and then we're just standing there, me with my feet off the floor and him with his face buried in my neck.

"Joel," I say, prepared to apologize, but his body begins trembling with little sobs and I no longer know what to say. I wrap my arms tighter around him and press my cheek against his temple. "Hey," I whisper, rubbing my hand over the buzzed hair next to his mohawk. I plant a kiss against his head and let him hold me.

Joel shakes his head, and I ask him what's wrong. He just shakes it again, and then he takes me to the bed and sits down with his arms still around me. I stand in front of him, and he holds me close. His cheek presses against my stomach and his body shakes with barely audible sobs that have tears spilling over my cheeks and dripping onto his back.

"Hey," I say again, rubbing my hand over his broad

shoulders. "Come on, stop that. You're going to mess up my makeup."

Joel chuckles against my stomach, and I smile and lift a hand to wipe my eyes.

He takes a deep, shuddering breath and stands up to take my face in his hands. He holds my teary-eyed gaze for a moment before giving me a soft kiss. "Thank you," he whispers.

I want to tell him it's just a toy, that there's nothing to thank me for. But I know it meant more to him than that, so instead of saying anything, I dry his tears. And when his thumbs wipe over my cheeks, I let him dry mine too.

Chapter Sixteen

"Don't answer it," Joel groans the morning after his birthday party, but I wiggle away from the warmth of his body to grab my ringing phone off the nightstand.

"Hello?"

My dad chuckles into the line. "Morning, sleepyhead."

I collapse back against my mattress and groan. "What time is it?"

"Almost noon. Late night clubbing?"

An amused chuckle answers him. "Dad, what do you know about clubbing?"

"What do you think I've been doing with all my time since you moved out?"

I laugh hard, waking Joel back up. He turns his face toward me and mumbles, "Who is it?"

"Is that a boy?" my dad asks.

"My gay friend, *Dad*," I quickly answer, emphasizing

the last word for Joel's benefit. "We had a sleepover last night after a birthday party."

"Gay friend?" my dad asks.

"Gay friend?" Joel mouths.

"Leti, remember?"

"Oh, yeah. Whose birthday was it?"

"My friend Joel's," I answer, and Joel's eyebrow lifts.

"A boy friend?"

"Yeah, a boy, space, friend," I say, rolling away from Joel so that I'm facing the edge of the bed. He brushes my hair away from my neck, and then his warm breath is on my neck and I'm struggling to listen to my dad.

"—just wanted to see when you're coming home for Easter," he says, and Joel's satin tongue curls behind the tender lobe of my ear. My eyes flutter closed, and I bite my lip between my teeth. "Dee?" my dad says, and I roll out of bed, padding out of Joel's reach.

"Yeah. I'm coming home the Wednesday before Easter," I say, watching Joel stretch out on my bed. His arms lift over his head, pulling his stomach muscles tight. When he catches me staring, he winks at me, and I spin toward the wall.

"I was thinking chicken cacciatore over garganelli pasta this year. Think we can figure out how to make it?"

The first Easter after my mom left, my dad attempted to cook Easter dinner, but the ham was burnt, the mashed potatoes were runny, and the green-bean casserole was charred to a crisp. We were both sitting at the table staring at our food, thinking of my mom, when he abruptly stood up and dragged me to the kitchen.

"Alright, we're going to make a linguini ala pomodoro caprese," he said, and at eleven years old, I had no idea he was just making shit up. We ended up boiling a bunch of miscellaneous pasta, cutting up fresh tomatoes and peppers, and mixing everything with a store-bought tomato sauce. My dad and I ate every last bit, swearing it was the best meal we had ever eaten, and in truth, it was. It was also the best Easter I'd ever had.

Every year since, we've attempted to make something especially complicated, and even on the years we've failed miserably, we've laughed our asses off and have eaten the scraps.

I smile at my lavender wall. "Yeah, I think we can manage. That sounds amazing."

I wrap up the conversation with my dad and turn back toward Joel, glaring at him. I point a finger at his smirking face and say, "*You* are evil."

"And gay apparently," he says, and I can't help laughing. "Are you really leaving next Wednesday?" he asks, suddenly more serious.

"Yeah. Heading home for Easter." I walk back to the edge of the bed and smirk at him. "Why, are you going to miss me?"

"Nope," he teases, tugging me back onto the covers, "I plan on being tired of you by then."

For the next few days, he makes it his mission to spend so much time with me that we're sick of each other by the time I have to leave. He sleeps at my apartment, he cooks me breakfast, we spend evenings on the couch watching movies. I watch him play guitar, he complains while I struggle over homework, and we spend more time in my bed than anywhere else in my apartment. Even the shower is no longer a safe zone, which is why we're late to auditions on Saturday. By the time we get to Mayhem, the first guitarist is about to start without us and Rowan scolds me with her eyes but encourages me with her smile.

"If I can't stay in bed," Adam gripes, tripping Joel as Joel walks to his seat, "neither can you."

"We weren't in the bed," Joel says with a smug voice and an even smugger smile. I muss his precious mohawk before taking the seat beside him. He glares at me, I blow him a kiss, and Shawn clears his throat.

"Can we get started now?"

We all quiet down, and after being patient with four guitarists who looked much better on paper than they sounded in person, Adam goes outside for a smoke break. The rest of the guys follow, and I slide into a seat next to Rowan.

"Listen to this," I say, playing her a song on my phone.

Her head nods to the beat. "I like it. Who's it by?"

"The next auditioner." My grin is downright giddy, and Rowan catches my good mood, her blue eyes lighting up. "His name is Kit. I have a good feeling about this one."

I got the email from Kit on Wednesday while I was walking back to my car from class. By the time I got home, I was overflowing with excitement and practically tackled Joel to get him to listen. He agreed that the song was awesome, and I immediately sent an email to Kit to give him an audition time.

"I think Shawn's head might explode pretty soon if

we don't find somebody," Rowan says, and I laugh. The last guy couldn't even figure out how to plug in his guitar. Shawn plugged him in, patted his back, and then immediately sent him on his way, shaking his head when the guy tried to talk his way back onto the stage.

"If this next guy doesn't work out, I'm just going to learn to play the guitar myself."

Rowan chuckles, and then she grins at me and says, "Sooo, you and Joel . . ."

When a knock sounds at the door, I seize the opportunity to bound out of my seat, not bothering to respond to my meddling best friend. Rowan thinks Joel and I are more than what we are, and no amount of arguing is going to convince her otherwise. My heels echo off the floor as I escape to the front door, and I swing it open wide to find Queen of the freaking Groupies.

Long black hair highlighted with dark blue highlights cascades down to a loose black tank top—low cut and showing copious amounts of lacy black bra. The girl's black jeans—which are more ripped up than any pair I've ever seen Adam, Shawn, or Joel wear—are practically painted to her legs. She's built like a freaking runway model with boobs. Complete with stacked bracelets, a tiny diamond nose ring, and combat boots, she's the definition of rocker chic.

I resist the urge to slam the door in her face.

"The band isn't here to sign shit or take pictures," I say, wondering how the hell she heard they would be here today.

"Okay?" she asks, a perfectly shaped eyebrow lifting to

emphasize her confusion. "I'm not here for autographs or pictures . . ."

"Great." I begin closing the door, but she slaps her hand against it.

"Are you Dee?" When I just stand there staring daggers at her, she wedges her combat boot against the door and holds out her hand. "I'm Kit. We spoke over email?"

"*You're* Kit?" Rowan asks from behind me as I dazedly shake Kit's hand.

Kit's eyes light with realization, and she laughs. "Oh, sorry. Yeah. I have four older brothers who thought Katrina was too girly of a name."

"And you're here to audition?" Rowan asks.

Kit pulls a guitar case from where she'd propped it outside against the wall. She shoots us a smile and says, "I hope so. It *is* okay that I'm a girl, right?"

"Yeah," Rowan rushes to say, but I'm skeptical. The song I listened to sounded amazing, but it's hard for me to reconcile the expectation I had in my head with the girl standing before me.

"That depends," I answer. "Are you a girl that can play the guitar?"

"I think so," Kit says with a perfectly straight face. "I mean, it's difficult since my vagina is constantly getting in the way, but I've learned to manage it just like any other handicap." Her brows pull down in a frown, and she says, "Sadly, I don't get special parking."

A long moment of silence passes between us, but then I can't help laughing. Kit's lips turn up at the corners and I lead her inside.

It isn't until we enter Mayhem that the first glimpses of her nervousness begin to show. With her guitar propped against the stage, she rubs her hands over her back pockets and stares around the room. "So it's just going to be us?"

"No—"

I begin to tell her that the guys should be back in at any moment, but then the back door opens and they all step inside.

"Guys," I say as they close the distance between us, "this is Kit. She's up next."

They're all staring at her, and I gauge Joel's reaction, suddenly very aware that we are auditioning a *girl*, with all girl parts. Long legs, perky boobs, and as she so kindly pointed out, a vagina. If this works out, the guys could soon be practicing, performing, and *touring* with a girl.

Joel steps beside me and wraps his arm around my shoulders. "We thought you were a dude."

Kit smiles. "Yeah, I gathered that when your girlfriend tried to close the door in my face."

Since Joel doesn't correct her, neither do I. I'm perfectly content letting her think Joel is taken.

"Have we met before?" Shawn asks, staring at her with a slight squint to his deep green eyes.

Kit stares back at him for a moment before a little smirk sneaks onto her face. "We went to the same school."

"What year were you?"

"Three under you."

"Didn't you used to come to our shows?" Mike asks, and Kit stares at Shawn for a moment longer, like she's waiting for something. When he only continues staring at her like she's a face he can't place, she turns to Mike.

"Sometimes."

The rest of the guys—with the exception of Shawn, who falls uncharacteristically quiet—continue asking her questions, and Kit finishes the introduction, telling them that she was in a band in college but that they broke up after graduation because some of them wanted to get nine-to-five jobs. Once everyone is all out of questions, she grabs her guitar and takes the stage. The rest of us seat ourselves at the table while she hooks her guitar up and does a quick sound check.

"Do you guys remember her?" I ask the guys when we sit down. The question is for all of them, but I'm staring right at Shawn.

"A little," Mike says.

"She looks *really* different," Shawn says, almost to himself. He's staring up at the stage, and I allow my gaze to travel there too. Kit is getting set up in record time, like she's done this a thousand times before.

"Did she used to wear glasses?" Joel asks, his head tilted to the side as he tries to place her face.

"Yeah," Shawn answers. "And she didn't have the nose ring, or . . ." he trails off when he notices we're all looking at him. "Her brother Bryce was in our grade, remember?"

The guys start reminiscing over some senior prank Bryce played, and Kit eventually leans into her microphone and asks, "What do you want me to play?"

"Your favorite song," Adam shouts to the stage, and

Kit thinks about it for a moment before smiling down at her guitar and stepping back. With her hair, her outfit, and the guitar strapped around her neck like it's just another accessory, she looks like she belongs there.

When she starts playing "Seven Nation Army" by the White Stripes—a song we've heard more times than we can count by now—we all begin to groan, but she quickly starts laughing and steps up to the microphone. "Just kidding!" she says, and then she starts playing a song I've never heard before but that the guys all seem to approve of. They sit straighter in their seats, watching her play it, until Adam lifts his hand for her to stop.

"Do you write your own stuff?" he asks, and when she nods, he tells her to play us something.

When she passes that test, the guys join her onstage. They all glance her way periodically as they play—all of them but Shawn, anyway, who seems dead set on not looking in her general direction. Afterward, he thanks her for coming and her face falls.

"She's perfect, right?" I ask when she's gone, wishing we could have told her she was in the band before she left. She walked out the door seeming so unsure of herself even though she knocked the audition out of the park.

"What do you guys think?" Shawn asks, and Adam speaks my mind.

"I'm wondering why we're even talking about it."

"Can we cancel the other auditions?" Mike asks, his stomach rumbling right on cue. "Please? If we don't, I'm going to scream like a little girl."

Rowan laughs, and Shawn says, "She was off on the third song."

"What planet were you on?" Joel asks. "She was perfect the whole time."

"Seriously Shawn," I complain, "what's your problem?"

He stiffens and scratches the back of his neck. "Nothing. I just want to make sure we don't make a mistake."

"You're going to have to pick someone sometime," I tell him.

"So we vote," Adam says. "All in favor of what's-her-name, raise your hand."

Everyone but Shawn raises their hand, and then he sighs and raises his too.

Later that night, I'm sitting with Joel on my couch when I ask him, "What was Shawn's problem today?"

I called Kit right after six hands went up in the air in Mayhem, and she sounded super excited on the phone, but I can't get Shawn's complete lack of enthusiasm out of my head. We've spent *weeks* looking for a guitarist, and he acted like finally finding her was the worst thing to ever happen.

"What is Shawn's problem ever?" Joel asks, flipping through one of my notebooks. We're at opposite ends of the couch, separated by a mountain of homework, since, under the arrangement I made with my professors in order to extend my Easter vacation, I need to finish all of my assignments and turn them in before I leave to go home. Like I haven't been struggling enough with this crap as it is.

"He was being weird," I argue.

"He's always weird."

I turn my attention back to the over-warm laptop resting on my crisscrossed legs, giving up on the Shawn conversation. "Do you think Kit is pretty?"

Joel's gaze swings up from my notebook, and when I glance at him out of the corner of my eye, he gives me a one-sided grin. "Not prettier than you."

I roll my eyes at him, trying to control the smile threatening to bloom across my face. "So you think she's pretty," I challenge, giving my attention back to my laptop.

"I prefer heels over combat boots."

"So you noticed what she was wearing."

Joel laughs and leans forward to close my laptop. "I think if you want to have make-up sex, you should just say so instead of picking a fight."

"You're an ass," I say.

"You're a—"

I flick a threatening finger into the air, and he grins.

"What, are we not fighting anymore?"

I glare at him, and he chuckles, settling back against the opposite arm of the couch as I open my laptop back up.

"I was going to say 'a goddess among men.' "

With my attention back on my screen, I snort out a laugh. "By all means, continue then."

"A rose in a garden full of weeds."

"What else?"

"A . . . plum . . . on a tree full of . . . bananas . . ."

I chuckle at my laptop. "Maybe leave the songwriting to Adam."

"Made you smile," he teases, and I quickly whitewash

my expression. "Still smiling," he says again, and I shoot him a look, rolling my eyes at the way he's grinning at me, but he's right—there's no disguising the smile on my face and it's pointless for me to keep trying.

Joel and I fall into a comfortable silence while I type my paper and he divides his attention between his phone, the TV, the cookies on his lap, and my notebook. Eventually, my paper-writing is interrupted by him asking, "Did you draw this?" He holds my notebook out for me to see, and I pale when I realize he's stumbled onto one of the high-fashion designs I sketched during class. I never intended for *anyone* to see those—him least of all.

"Yeah," I answer, all of my energy concentrated on *not* freaking out.

"Dee, this is really good." He continues flipping through the pages, and my fingers itch to yank the notebook out of his hands. It's like he's reading my freaking diary right in front of my face, but I know doing anything about it will just make it an even bigger deal than it already is. "Damn . . . this one is hot."

Too curious to resist, I peek over at him and say, "Which one?"

Joel turns the notebook toward me again, and this time it's open to a sketch I did of a dress. It's basically just a slightly longer and more fitted version of the shirts I've been making, but it would require some measuring and sewing, neither of which I've ever really done before with the exception of those last-minute birthday capes and a sixth-grade home sciences project that can't even count because Rowan did most of my work.

"You should make this," Joel says.

"I can't."

His brow scrunches. "Why not?"

"I've never made a dress before."

"That's a shitty reason to not try something."

When I don't respond—because how can I?—he goes back to flipping through pages, and my stomach coils into another knot with each and every sketch he looks at.

"Aren't you still trying to pick a major?" he asks with his focus still glued to my notebook.

Guessing where he's going with his question, I answer, "Fashion isn't a major at my school."

"Then maybe you're at the wrong school." When he glances my way, I'm nibbling on the inside of my lip, wondering if he's right and trying not to wonder about it. "I think there's a fashion school here in town, actually. You should apply . . ."

"Know what I think?" I ask, and he flashes me a smile since he knows I'm going to say something smart. "I think you think too much."

Joel gives a little chuckle and says, "I've also been thinking about what to draw you for your birthday. Am I allowed to think about that?"

"It's over a month away . . . but yes." If all he ever thought about was buying me presents, we'd be a match made in heaven.

"What do you want me to draw?"

"I don't know . . . something special."

"Anything in particular?"

"Make it a surprise."

"I think I can do that," he says with a soft smile. I go back to typing, and he adds, "You're going to miss me so much while you're gone."

I am, but that's for me to know. "You're going to miss me more."

Chapter Seventeen

THE ACHING IN my chest starts about an hour into the six-hour drive back home. The feeling is foreign and uncomfortable, and if I could physically claw it out of my heart, I would. The entire ride, my ears are half tuned in to Rowan and half tuned in to my phone, listening for text messages that never come. I drop her off at her house and finish the drive to my dad's, parking in the driveway and double-checking to make sure my phone isn't on silent. When I verify that it isn't, I huff out a disgruntled breath and climb out of the car.

My dad opens our front door even before I step up to the porch, and I set my overstuffed suitcase down to give him a big hug.

He's a few inches taller than I am, with a lean build and soft smile. He and my mom were both twenty years old when she had me, but he looks even younger than his thirty-eight years, with smoky blond hair and dark brown eyes. When I was in middle school, I banned him from chaperoning school events because all of my classmates developed creepy crushes on him, and even though he hasn't dated since my mom left, he could have started his own phone-book company with all the numbers women have tried to give him.

With his hands on my shoulders, he pulls away to smile at me. "Alright, let me look at you." He turns my chin from side to side. "No facial piercings." He lifts my arms up one by one, and I giggle while he inspects me. "No tribal tattoos. Turn around."

"What? Why?"

He spins me around and lifts the back of my shirt. "No tramp stamp. Oh thank God." I roll my eyes, and he laughs and kisses the top of my head.

"Are you done?" I ask.

"Worrying about you? Never."

"Being weird," I correct as he picks up my suitcase and opens the door.

"Also never."

He laughs at his own joke, and I try not to laugh too. I've missed my dad even more than I thought I would— probably because these last few weeks have been some of the messiest of my life.

"Your room is where ya left it," he tells me. "Your closet missed you."

This time, I do laugh. "I missed my closet too."

I start down the hallway, and he says, "Help me in the kitchen when you're done having a sobby reunion, will ya?"

"Be there in a minute."

My dad disappears into the kitchen, and I start toward my room, huffing out a slow, irritated breath when I pass through our hallway of misfit pictures. Ever since I was a teenager, my dad and I have waged a passive-aggressive war where I've taken down all the ones of my mom and hidden them, and my dad has always found them and put them right back up. He insists that they contain memories I shouldn't block out, and a certain person I shouldn't try to forget. I insist that some things are better off forgotten and some people are monster bitches who don't deserve to be displayed in our house when they couldn't even bother to stay faithful to their husbands or raise their daughters.

I ignore the pictures and walk straight to my room, dropping my suitcase next to my old bed and flopping face first onto my royal-purple comforter. My phone beeps in my back pocket, and I nearly pull a muscle throwing my arm behind my back to yank it out. I deflate when it's just a text from Rowan.

My parents both work tomorrow. Come over when you wake up?

I text her back to let her know I'll be there, and then I pick myself off the bed to prevent my mind from lingering on thoughts of Joel. I wonder what he's doing right now. Watching TV? Playing guitar? Sleeping with all the girls he's been abstaining from for the past month while I've been hoarding all of his time?

"Dee?" my dad asks from across the dining room table

at dinner, and I catch myself staring at my phone again, willing it to ring.

I look away quickly and busy myself with carving into my burnt pork chop. "Sorry."

"So the guys in this band," my dad says, reminding me that we'd been talking about the music festival, which got me to talking about the T-shirts that have been selling like hot cakes on the band's website, which got me to talking about the capes I made, which got me to thinking about Joel, "they're all just friends?"

"Yeah," I say, avoiding glancing at my phone. "They're all really cool."

"Even this Joel guy?"

I made it a point to talk about Joel no more or less than any of the other guys. And still, my dad picked him out of a damn invisible lineup. "Dad," I groan, "are we seriously going to talk about *boys*?"

"I'm just talking about the reason you keep staring at your phone," he says with a shrug, stabbing his pork chop and lifting the entire burnt thing to his mouth to take a bite out of it.

I turn my phone on silent and tuck it back into my pocket, making a serious effort to spend the rest of dinner giving my dad my undivided attention. We talk about everything—work, school, friends. Soccer, lasagna, neighbors. After hours of watching TV together and nodding off on the couch, I change into my pajamas and he insists on tucking me into bed. He kisses me on the head and disappears, closing the door behind him, and I immediately grab my phone off my nightstand.

Nothing. Eleven o'clock at night and *nothing*. Not a single word.

"You're an asshole," I tell my phone. Still, it says nothing back.

Are you awake? I text Rowan.

Sorta. What's up?

Really, I just wanted to make sure my phone was working. I growl under my breath and text back, *Nothing. See you in the morning.*

I want to call her and rant about how big of an ass Joel is for not calling or texting me after we've spent almost every day for the past few weeks together. But she already thinks I'm in love with him or something, so instead, I set my phone back on the nightstand and stare at it lying there for a few hours before I finally fall asleep.

The next morning, when I don't wake to any missed calls or missed texts or even apology roses delivered to my front door, I'm too frustrated to hold it in. On Rowan's couch, I dig my hand into a bag of potato chips and say, "I can't BELIEVE that asshole hasn't even called me."

"Maybe he's waiting for you to call him," she suggests while flipping through TV channels.

"Not going to happen."

"Why not?"

"Because he's the man."

Her head slowly turns in my direction, her eyebrow reaching for her hairline. "Should he also take away your right to vote and own property?"

I toss a chip at her, and she laughs and throws it back at me. We both turn back toward the TV, wasting the morning watching everything and nothing until she says, "I almost let it slip that I've been living with Adam."

I turn my head to see her gnawing on her thumbnail, and she glances my way before shifting to face me.

"I told mom and dad about Joel's birthday party, and I accidentally said we had it at your place. And my dad was all, 'Don't you mean *your* place?' And you know how bad I am at lying . . . It was cringe-worthy."

"Did they buy it?"

She nods her head with her brows turned in and her thumbnail locked between her teeth. "I think so."

"What do you think they'd do if they found out?"

She shrugs. "Probably throw a fit. Talk to me about how it's too soon."

"They'd want to meet him," I say, trying not to laugh when I imagine Rowan's burly, football-loving father meeting Adam, with his long hair and painted fingernails.

"The thing is, I *want* them to meet him," Rowan says, sighing and curling her knees up on the couch. "I mean, they know we're dating. I want them to know he's the one . . . I'm just a little worried they won't like him."

"Would it matter?" I ask, and to my surprise, she smiles. "Nope."

"Then stop worrying about it." I tap her thumb away from her mouth and add, "If they meet him and don't like him, whatever. But if it helps, I think they'll love him." I stand up and start walking toward her bedroom. Her nails are a jagged mess I can't stand to look at anymore. Filing and polishing them will be a better waste of my time than sitting around stressing about Joel.

"You think so?" she asks.

"Yep."

"How do you know?"

I walk backward, giving her a smile. "Because your parents love you. And so does Adam."

My afternoon is spent doing her nails and trying not to hate her when she gets constant text messages from Adam. I attempt to distract myself by talking to her about Kit and how weird Shawn acted around her—which Rowan observed too—but it doesn't stop me from noticing that my phone remains painfully silent while Rowan's beeps and dings and rings like a winning lotto machine. By the time I crawl into my bed later that night, I'm convinced that what I had with Joel was a fluke and that he's forgotten all about me.

I don't hear from him until three o'clock the next afternoon.

My dad and I are outside at my favorite year-round ice-cream parlor eating sundaes at a picnic table, and I'm teasing him about the way the ice-cream girls batted their eyelashes at him, when my phone beeps and Joel's panty-melting smile flashes onto my screen. My heart does parkour off the walls of my chest, and I snatch my phone off the table.

I miss you.

Three little words from him lift an impossible weight off my chest, and my mouth curls into the smile to end all smiles.

"Who is it?" my dad asks, and I quickly slam my phone face down on the table.

"No one."

When he doesn't look convinced, I ask if he's going to eat the cherry on top of his sundae, and then I steal it without waiting for an answer.

As soon as I get home, I speed-walk into the privacy of my bedroom and whip my phone out of my pocket.

Why haven't you called? I type, and Joel's response is immediate.

Why haven't *you* called?

I debate saying something snarky, something clever and insincere. Instead, I type back, *I miss you too.*

I hit SEND before I can change my mind, and then I listen to the clock on my wall tick seconds into minutes. Hours later, long after dinner and late-night TV with my dad, I'm still waiting for Joel's reply. I turn my ringer all the way up so that I'll wake if he texts, and then I crawl under my covers, wondering what he's doing and who he's doing it with. Maybe he found someone to help him stop missing me—God knows his phone is full of plenty of numbers of girls who would jump at the chance.

I'm not sure how long it takes me to fall asleep, but when I wake up later, it's still dark. Even though the sound that wakes me is familiar, it takes me a moment to place—because I haven't heard anyone tap on my bedroom window since I moved away from home.

Chapter Eighteen

"WHAT ARE YOU doing here?" I whisper-yell through the glass.

Joel smiles at me and points to the lock, and I quickly push it over and throw the window open.

"What are you doing here?" I whisper again. Cold night air gets sucked inside the warmth of my room, and I wrap my arms around myself to ward off the chill. I'm wearing nothing but a cami top with nothing under it and a pair of oversized pajama shorts.

"Can you lift the screen?"

I do, and Joel climbs into my bedroom, forcing me to take a step back. My brain barely has time to form another question before his arms wrap around me and his lips steal my words. Two days without him and I'd forgotten how intoxicating those kisses can be.

"I missed you," he says against my mouth, his feet already walking me backward toward the bed, his hands already removing my clothes. My cami gets pulled over my head, his jeans fall to the floor, and we sink into the mattress. He nestles between my legs, and when I tug his shirt off, his bare chest molds against mine. With only thin layers of cotton between us where it counts, I moan against his mouth. It's been eight hours since he texted me to tell me he missed me, and he's making it clear he meant every single word.

Joel's chilled lips drop to my neck, and I muster the sense to ask, "How did you get here?"

"I bought a car," he says as he trails kisses down my stomach and pulls my pajama shorts down.

"You bought a—" my breath catches in my throat when his warm tongue envelopes me. His ice-cold lips follow, sucking my tiny bud into his molten mouth and squeezing it tight. "Joel!" I gasp, my toes curling against the mattress. He tenderly slides his lips away, and my fingernails claw at loose sheets.

"Shhh," he whispers against me, his breath sending shivers up and down my skin, making my nipples perk and my heart race.

"My dad is home," I warn without any conviction.

"We'll be quiet." His tongue strokes through my folds again, and my back arches away from the mattress. Joel rolls his tongue over me, and I moan against the lip I'm biting.

He chuckles and presses a soft, wet kiss against my thigh. He knows he's torturing me, and he's loving it.

"You're a jerk," I say, and he looks up at me from under thick black lashes. He's on his stomach at the foot of my bed, and he shifts so that his lips are hovering above the most sensitive part of me.

"I'm a what?" Each word sends a fresh warm breath drifting over me, another wave of tingles.

"A jerk," I maintain in a quiet, timid voice, and Joel gives me a dark smile before planting an impossibly light kiss against my tense little bud.

Another light kiss. A light nibble, a light lick, a light suck.

"Joel," I whine.

"Is this not nice?"

"No," I growl, but I've barely said the word when his eager mouth devours me and I moan far louder than I mean to.

Joel crawls over top of me a second later, shimmying out of his boxers, bracing his elbows along my sides, and then—

"Oh," I gasp as he sinks deep inside me.

"Fuck," he breathes with his forehead pressed against mine. His body shudders under my fingertips, and my thighs tremble around his hips. "I really, *really* missed you."

I tilt my chin up and suck his bottom lip between my teeth as he sets a steady pace. I kiss him and control my breathing to keep from crying out. My fingers sink into the tight skin of his back, and my headboard knocks against the wall.

"Shit," I hiss, breaking my lips from Joel's so that he'll stop moving and the wooden headboard will stop threatening to wake up my dad. It's not the first time I've had a boy in my room—far from it—but that still doesn't mean I want my dad to hear his little girl having sex under his roof while she's home for Easter vacation.

In the moonlight filtering in through my still open window, Joel reaches one arm up to grab the top of my headboard, pulling it away from the wall. Cold air wraps itself around us, and he holds the headboard steady as he rocks back into me. The sight of him like that, with one hand braced on the mattress beside me and the other supporting his taut body above me, makes it hard to breathe, and I can't help myself—I lift away from the warmth of my sheets to suck his cold nipple ring into my mouth, flicking my tongue inside the metal hoop and scratching my fingernails up his sides.

"Dee," Joel pleads. His voice cracks, and I know he's close.

I lower my head back to my pillow, and he never takes his eyes off me as he resumes his movement in slow, long thrusts. They grow slower and slower until they stop altogether.

"I wish you could see yourself right now," he says. "You have no idea how beautiful you look."

Maybe it's the cold, maybe it's something else, but I suddenly need him in my arms, and I need to feel myself in his.

"Come here," I say, and he releases my headboard to settle over top of me, lowering his lips to mine and kissing me slowly, leisurely. "Just go slow," I whisper.

Joel's hips move slowly, his fingers brushing my cheek, my hair, my neck. We move together until early morning, when I whimper against his mouth and he pulses inside me. Afterward, with him still buried all the way inside me, I wrap my arms around him and hold him like I've never held any man ever.

After a while, he kisses the side of my jaw and gets up to close the window, but then he crawls back into bed with me and wraps me in his arms. I play the role of the little spoon, content to let him hold me.

We fall asleep together, we wake together, and the next morning, I'm lying on my stomach watching him get dressed. His back muscles ripple as he bends over to pick his worn-soft jeans off the floor, and my blood heats when I remember the way those muscles flexed under my finger-tips just a few hours ago.

"I'm not going to call you," he says as he buttons his jeans, and my brow furrows.

"Why not?"

He lifts his gaze, and I can see he's serious. "It's your turn. I did it first the last time." He leans down and kisses me, softly. A fragile breath escapes me. "If you miss me," he instructs, "then pick up the phone."

When he pulls away, I collect myself and tease, "I think I'm set for a while."

Joel tickles my side until I take the tease back so that I don't end up screaming and waking my dad, and then he stands and motions for me to give him his shirt. I pull it over my head and hand it back, doing my best not to pout when he covers all of that gorgeously toned skin. He licks his fingers and tries to salvage some semblance of the spiked mohawk he arrived with last night, and then he wipes his hands on the front of his jeans while I find my own shirt bunched under the covers and pull it over my head.

"Where are you parked?" I ask.

Last night, before we fell asleep, I asked about his new car and he told me he bought a clunker from a friend. He got the name of my hometown from Adam, looked my dad up in the white pages, and crossed his fingers while guessing which window was mine. I still can't believe he finally bought a car, or that he did it just to see me, but it makes me want to forgive him for not talking to me these past three days.

"Down the street," he answers, his eyes traveling around my room. "You like Stephen King?" He picks a book off of a shelf on my wall, turning it over in his hand.

"No, I just like books about teenage girls who go crazy and kill everyone," I say with a sweet smile.

Joel laughs and sets it back on the shelf, picking up a DVD in its place. "*Dirty Dancing*? Seriously?"

"Oh," I croon, "Johnny Castle could wipe the floor with you."

Joel scoffs and sets it back down; then he moves to my desk and picks up a picture frame, his mouth pulling into a wide smile. "Paintball?"

He turns the frame toward me, and I smile at the picture of Rowan and I at an eighth-grade graduation party. We're covered in paint, each with an arm draped around the other and a paint gun propped on our hip, looking entirely badass.

"The boys had no idea what they were in for," I say,

and Joel laughs. He continues perusing my room, scanning pictures and books and knickknacks. "Don't you have somewhere to be?" I ask, climbing out of bed and propping myself against my windowsill.

Joel sighs and opens my window. He slides one leg into the early morning cold and says, "I wish I could stay."

When I say nothing back, he finishes sliding the rest of the way out, dropping between the bushes and turning to face me. I bend low, kiss him slowly, and confess, "I do too."

Something sparks in his deep blue eyes, and his hand threads into my hair and practically pulls me out the window. He crushes my lips against his, and I grip the windowsill to keep from falling out. When he pulls away, he flashes me a white smile, and then he spins around and walks toward the street.

I pull back into my room in a boneless heap, sitting on the floor and touching my lips. A tiny giggle escapes me, followed by a whole fit of them that have me flopping onto my back and smiling up at the pale green stars on my ceiling. I'm still swooning when my doorbell rings and the stars explode into apocalyptic fireworks.

I rush to the doorway of my room, in full view of the front door, and helplessly watch as my dad beats me to it.

"Hi," I hear Joel's voice say from the doorstep, "is Dee home?"

My dad, already dressed in khaki pants and a checkered button-down, stares out the door for a second before letting out a little chuckle. "Dee!" he shouts. "The guy who snuck in your room last night is here!"

My dad turns to me and smirks at the way my jaw is

hanging on the floor. Then he walks into the kitchen and I rush to the front door.

Joel looks just as stunned as I do. He's standing on my doorstep—with his bad boy mohawk, his wrinkled day-old shirt, and his tattered jeans—and we're just staring at each other with wide eyes and no words until my dad shouts, "Are you going to invite him in or are you just going to make him stand out there in the cold?"

I seriously contemplate closing the door and making him stand out in the cold, but instead I grab his hand and yank him inside. My dad appears around the corner a moment later, smirking around a cup of coffee. He takes a sip and asks me, "Are you going to introduce us?"

I cross my arms over my chest, realizing I'm severely underdressed. "Dad, this is Joel," I say, flicking my fingers in Joel's direction. My dad's eyes light up with recognition that makes my stomach fall, and I continue, "Joel, this is my dad."

"Keith," my dad says, extending his hand to Joel.

They shake, and afterward, my dad scrunches his nose at his palm.

"Hair gel," Joel rushes to explain, and I could just die and dissolve into the floor.

My dad chuckles and stares up at Joel's mohawk. "Right . . . You kids want some breakfast?"

Together? No! Not now, not ever!

"Sure," Joel says, and he follows my dad into hell's kitchen.

They eat breakfast together. And lunch. Laughing and sharing stories and becoming best freaking buds. At noon,

I'm sitting between them at the dining-room table furiously texting Rowan on my phone.

It's like they're BFFs.

Isn't that good?

ARE YOU BEING SERIOUS RIGHT NOW?

Yes?

NO!!!

. . . I think I'm confused.

I huff and lay my phone on the table, but my dad and Joel barely seem to notice.

"I got it when I was eighteen," my dad says, pulling his arm out of his shirt and showing Joel his Celtic armband tattoo.

"Badass," Joel says, and my dad grins.

Joel stands and lifts up his shirt, showing my dad the script stretching up his side. It says "I am the hero of this story" in delicate, curling letters, and I never put much thought into what it means. Now, I want to know when he got it, why he got it, where he got it. I want to trace my fingertips over the letters and feel his marked skin. "I got this when I was twenty-one," Joel says, letting my dad read the words before lowering his shirt.

"Nice," my dad says, and I roll my eyes. "When did you get the guitar one?" he asks.

Joel studies the tattoo on his inner forearm. It's sepia-toned, of the neck of a guitar hidden beneath torn skin. "I got that one when I was nineteen."

"So that was your first one?"

"Nah," Joel answers, showing my dad the tiny music note hidden where his middle finger usually rests against his index finger. "I got this one when I was fifteen. Did it myself."

"How?" my dad asks.

"Razor and pen."

My dad chuckles. "I bet your mom was thrilled."

Something flashes across Joel's expression, something I'm guessing was too quick for anyone but me to catch, but then he smiles.

I bet his mom couldn't have cared less.

"Are you going to your parents' for Easter tomorrow?" my dad asks, and I find myself wondering the same thing. Where does Joel go for Easter? Where does he go for Thanksgiving and Christmas? I pick at a cold breadstick left over from the pizza lunch we ordered, waiting for his answer.

He shakes his head. "We're not close. I'll probably go to my friend Adam's. Last year I just ordered Chinese and played video games. It was pretty awesome."

My dad frowns, mirroring my expression. "Would you want to stay here and have dinner with us?" he asks, not bothering to ask for my approval.

Joel turns toward me like he's hoping I'll have the answer, and my dad adds, "It's usually just Dee and me, but we'd love to have you if you want to stay."

"Yeah," I say after it feels like I've been silent for too long, "you should stay."

Joel studies me for a moment, but if he's trying to figure out how I feel about him spending Easter with us, I'm pretty sure he'll have to wait until I figure that out first. Ever since my mom left, it's always been just my dad and me. My insides twist, and I'm not sure if it's because of the possibility of Joel spending the holiday alone or because of the possibility of him spending it with me and my dad.

"I'll think about it," he says, and then he thanks my dad for the offer.

Later, after lunch, my dad leaves for the grocery store to get ingredients for tomorrow, and Joel finds his way into our hallway of misfit pictures. This morning, my dad told him all sorts of personal stories about me as a baby, me as a toddler, me as a mouthy child, me as a mouthy teenager. Now Joel gazes up at a picture on the wall and asks, "Is that your mom?"

He's staring at a picture that was taken when I was around three. I have little chocolate curls everywhere, and my mom is holding me on her lap. My dad is standing behind her with his hand on her shoulder, smiling and looking as handsome as ever. But my mom is the one shining bright at the center of the photo, wearing my olive skin, my high cheekbones, and my smooth lips.

"Yeah," I answer, because what else can I say?

"You look just like her," he says, and I inwardly cringe.

"I know."

"Are you ever going to tell me about her?" Joel asks, turning on me.

"Do I have to?" I ask. It's a smartass question, but he answers anyway.

"I'd like you to . . ."

When I walk out to the living room, he follows me. I flop down on the couch, and he sits beside me.

"I told you about *my* mom," he says, and I know, I know he did. I know I should open up to him like he did to me. And it's not that I can't. It's just that I don't want to. I didn't plan for him to show up at my house, or for him to become best friends with my dad, or for him to get invited to Easter dinner. I didn't plan or want or ask for him to be here.

"Mine isn't worth talking about," I say.

"So she's alive . . ."

"Unfortunately." Guilt hits me the minute I say it. I don't actually wish she was dead, but I've gotten used to ignoring the shame I feel every time I wish it on her. It's always been easier than missing her.

When Joel starts to speak again, I cut him off. "Joel, look. You've seen my house. You've slept in my bed. You've met my dad. Can't that be enough for now?"

I know he wants to get to know me. I'm aware that what's going on between us is more than just sex now. But I didn't ask him to come here, and it's not fair for him to expect that I'm going to bare my soul to him just because he showed up at my bedroom window in the middle of the night.

He searches my face for a long moment, and then he sighs and sits back against the couch, tugging me against his side. "I like your dad," he says after a while, and I could kiss him for changing the subject.

"I can tell."

"He loves you."

"I know."

"We have a lot in common."

I tilt my chin up to search his face, to see if he just implied what I think he did, but he kisses my forehead and turns on the TV and it's like he never said anything at all.

Chapter Nineteen

WAKING UP IN my old room is always kind of strange. Like waking up in a past life. It's easy to imagine that moving away for college was a series of dreams. That the people I've met are all just characters my subconscious invented to teach me life lessons.

Leti, to teach me to be more open. Adam, to teach me that anything is possible. Cody, to teach me to always go for the eyes.

And Joel, who seems to be teaching me a lot of things.

Last night, he agreed to stay for Easter dinner, and my dad set him up in the spare room. When it got late, we all went our separate ways, and I lay in bed for what seemed like forever wondering if Joel was actually going to stay in his own room all night. I waited for him until my eyelids got too heavy to hold open, and then I drifted off.

I was sleeping when my door creaked open and he

slipped into my room. He closed it silently behind him, and the mattress behind me sunk low.

"I thought you weren't going to come," I whispered into the dark as his arm wrapped around me and pulled me tight.

"I wasn't going to," he whispered back, nuzzling my hair away from my neck and kissing my sensitive skin.

If I wasn't still half asleep, that kiss would have been enough to have me turning over in his arms to feel his lips in a million other places. Instead, I stayed facing away from him, my eyes closed and my body languid. I expected him to keep kissing me, to wake my body up so that the rest of me would follow. Instead, he simply snuggled tighter against me and held me until I fell back asleep.

In my dreams, I asked him why he came to my room if he wasn't planning to, why he drove more than three hundred miles just to see me. But I woke myself up before he answered, certain that I didn't want to know.

I was alone in my bed, and for a moment, I wondered if it had *all* been a dream. But then I remembered the way his arms had felt around me—warm, safe, real.

When our eyes locked in the kitchen before breakfast, I had the strangest urge to go to him. To wrap myself around him and mold my cheek against his chest. I wanted to feel his arms around me, and I pushed the feeling as far away as I could.

Every moment I spend with him now feels like holding my hand in the fire and liking it. The longer I stay in the flames, the more it will hurt later, but for now, we're burning. And I like it too much to step away.

We have a breakfast of coffee and marshmallow Peeps and Cadbury eggs, and then we play board games with my dad until lunch. Then more chatter, more burning, until it's time to start Easter dinner. My dad is in charge of boiling water while Joel and I stand side by side at the counter chopping vegetables.

It's unsettlingly perfect.

Joel steals kisses when my dad isn't looking, and it's strange how a simple brush of his lips or graze of his fingertips feels infinitely more intimate, more dangerous, than having sex under my dad's roof. And not just because my dad is nearby, but because of that flicker—that something between us that I'm becoming more and more aware of.

It's like swimming with sharks. Like running with wolves.

It's like falling. Like *leaping*.

"It's usually just Dee and me at Christmastime, too," my dad tells Joel after dinner. We're all still sitting at the table, with our bellies full and mine tangled in knots. "You should come this year. We'd love to have you."

Falling. Leaping. Vertigo.

I abruptly stand up, and my dad and Joel stare up at me.

"I feel like going for a walk," I say, backing away from the ledge.

"Now?" Joel asks.

I need to get him away from this table. Away from my dad. Away from conversations about a future that will probably never happen. "Yeah. You coming?"

He follows me without further hesitation, and after he helps me into a jacket and borrows an oversized hoodie from my dad, we finally escape the house. As soon as I'm outside in the chilled night air, I feel like I can breathe again.

"What was that about?" Joel asks, falling in step beside me as I follow a trail of streetlamps leading away from my house.

"What was what about?"

He stops walking, and I stare back at him. In three-day-old jeans and a black hoodie, he's wearing an uncompromising expression.

I know he wants me to explain, but what the hell am I supposed to say? That my brain is full of chemicals making me want to melt against his skin? That the feeling fucking terrifies me?

I reach out to him, unwilling to say a word, and Joel studies my extended hand before clasping his fingers with mine. We walk in silence all the way to a place I didn't even know I was taking us.

"Where are we?" he asks as I punch a key code into the security system of the clubhouse where one of my exes works. We used to sneak in after-hours to skinny-dip in the pools or just hook up, and I still know the code by heart.

"A pool," I answer. The club sports three pools of varying sizes, all of which are empty now—concrete husks drained of water until Memorial Day. Even though I still mess around with my ex from time to time, and I've brought other boys here during the season, I prefer to come alone. This place is different without the water—magical, private. Bringing Joel here is like sharing a secret, one I've never shared with anyone, not even Rowan.

"How do you know the security code?" Joel asks, and I turn around to walk backward, smirking while drawing him inside.

"One of the perks of dating a lifeguard."

I lead him through the girls' shower room, and we grab armfuls of towels before emerging out back in the fenced-in pool area. Most of the security lights around the chain-link fencing dimmed out ages ago and haven't been replaced. The white moon and pale stars light what the rare orange bulb doesn't, and Joel and I walk through the shallow pool to get to the lap pool, walking deeper and deeper inside concrete walls until we get to the middle of the twelve-foot-deep circular pool.

We lay the towels down and stretch out on our backs, our shoulders brushing under a blanket of pinprick stars that glow against the walls of the pool and make the dark feel a little less dark.

"I feel like we need to have some cliché conversation about the stars," Joel says as we lie there staring up at them, and my light laughter echoes off the walls.

"Do we need to?"

"What if someone is watching a movie of our lives? We'd be a huge disappointment." He smiles over at me, and when he looks back toward the sky, his fingers thread with mine.

We lie there like that, silently breathing in the cold and bearing the weight of the universe, until he says, "I always thought this shit was cheesy. Like when it happened in movies. But it's kind of nice . . . being here with you."

Falling. Leaping. His hand should be a lifeline, but it's pushing me over the edge. His words, batting at my heart.

"Have you brought many other guys here?" he asks after a while, his voice unreadable.

"Not when the pools are empty like this."

"What about the lifeguard?" he prompts.

I stare up at the sky, knowing I should lie but not having the heart to. "No. Just you."

I don't know what we're doing here. Joel and I aren't the kind of people to lie under the stars—not holding hands, not having conversations that will haunt me fifty years from now when we barely remember each other's faces because too many others have come in between.

"I feel like I'm keeping a secret," he says, and I feel like I'm keeping a secret too. A lot of them. So many. Like how badly I want to pull my hand away and then cry in his arms for doing it.

I know he's keeping secrets too. I've been trying not to guess what they are.

"Some secrets are better off kept," I say, pleading with him to keep it.

"I love you."

I close my eyes, my heart silently breaking. Part of me knew this would happen, but I was too selfish to stop it. "No, you don't."

The words have been said to me before. From some guys, that's all they were—words. From others, they were a misguided belief that left them brokenhearted. This time, I'm the one who breaks.

Joel sits up, still clinging to my hand. "Dee, I nearly killed a man for hurting you. I changed my whole life to be with you. I bought a car to drive three hundred miles just because I was going crazy not seeing you. You don't have to say it back, but don't tell me how I feel."

I don't say it back. I can't.

"Say something," he begs after a while. My eyes are still closed. If I don't have to see his face, maybe this won't hurt as much.

"What am I supposed to say?"

"Anything."

"I'm sorry." I open my eyes, and the broken way he looks at me grips at my heart. I sit up, wanting to hug him close, wanting to apologize for apologizing, but I'm doing this for both of us. Because neither one of us is the type of person anyone should give their heart to. Not if they want it kept in one piece.

I take my hand from his.

"I think you should go home."

"What?"

Years of practice help keep my face blank. "You should go home." I begin gathering the towels, but Joel grasps my hand again, like he's the one falling and he needs me to hold on to.

"Why? Why are you doing this?" I pull my hand away, and he says, "Is it because of your mom?"

Ice shoots through my veins, freezing me in place. "What do you know about my mom?"

"Your dad told me about her this morning—"

"He *told* you?"

"I didn't ask. He just brought it up. I know that her leaving must have messed with your head but—"

"You know *nothing*," I spit, standing up in a rush of frustration.

"Dee . . ." Joel says, standing up to face me. His voice remains soft in spite of the way I'm glaring at him. "I want to be with you. I don't give a shit about your mom. You're right, I don't know anything. I only know that I'm in love with you. Like *seriously* fucking in love with you."

I gather the blankets while he just stands there. "I'm sorry you think you fell in love, Joel. The good news is you'll get over it."

"I won't."

"You'll have to."

His expression hardens, and I'm glad. If he hates me, this will be so much easier.

"Are you fucking kidding me right now? You made me fall in love with you just to throw me out like the fucking trash?"

There it is. I *made* him fall in love with me. Just like all the others. I'm no better than my mother. The only difference is, I care enough about him to walk away before it's too late—before this spark between us grows and grows and fucking grows until there's nothing left but ashes when it finally runs out of fuel.

"Is this what you wanted all along?" Joel snaps. "Was this your fucking plan? To fucking *crush* me?"

"Go home, Joel."

With the towels in my arms, I walk away from him.

I don't look back. I can't.

Chapter Twenty

I ARRIVE BACK at the house before Joel, walk right into the dining room, and pull a bottle of tequila from the liquor cabinet.

"Dee?" my dad asks when he enters the room behind me. "Joel just pulled out of the driveway. Did something . . ." He trails off when I finish pouring myself a glass and turn around. "What the hell are you doing?"

"What, it's okay for me to date rock stars with tattoos and piercings but I can't have a freaking drink?"

My dad's brows turn in as he studies me. "What happened?"

"Oh, you know," I say, swirling the liquid in my glass. "Classic case of girl meets boy, boy saves girl, girl hangs out with boy, boy tells girl he loves her, girl tells boy to get lost."

When my dad just stares at me like I'm a creature that possessed his daughter, I say, "Why'd you tell him about

Mom?" His face pales, and I challenge, "It wasn't enough for you to ask him to stay for Easter and invite him to Christmas, you had to go and tell him about Mom too?"

"She just came up," my dad stammers.

"Of course she came up!" I slam my untouched drink on the table, and it splashes onto my hand. "It's been seven years and you still can't stop fucking talking about her!"

"Deandra," my dad says, but I'm too far gone to heed the warning in his voice.

I wipe the back of my hand on my jacket and say, "No, Dad, tell me. It wasn't enough to have her pictures all over the walls, you had to rub her in my face by telling Joel about her too?"

"That isn't fair—"

"You know what's not fair?!" I shout, startling him. "You not letting me forget her! It's not fair I had to teach myself how to put on makeup or how to shave my legs. It's not fair that Rowan's mom had to tell me how to use a goddamn tampon!" Tears burn my eyes, but I ignore them and shout at the top of my lungs, "She doesn't deserve to have her pictures on our walls, Dad!"

He reaches out to touch me, hesitant like he's afraid I'm going to burst into pieces. "Dee . . . calm down and just tell me what happened."

"No," I say, shaking my head. The tears are coming. They're acid in my eyes, sulfur in my nose. I walk past him and grab my keys off the breakfast bar.

"Where are you going?" he asks as he follows after me.

"AWAY!" I shout, and I slam the front door behind me.

In my car on the way to Rowan's, I can barely see the road through the tears that have sprung free from somewhere deep inside me. They're clouding my vision, and the sob that tears from my throat racks my whole body. In her driveway, I'm crying too badly to move, so when my car door opens, I don't bother lifting my head from the steering wheel to see who it is. Slender arms wrap around me, and I shift to let them hold me.

"Shh," Rowan whispers, hugging me tight. "I've got you. You're okay."

"I can't fucking do this, Ro," I cry, hating myself for being this person. This person who can't take care of herself. I can't believe I snapped on my dad, or that I was so cold to Joel, or that I cried about my mom after seven years of managing not to.

"What happened?" Rowan asks me, rubbing my back.

So much has happened, I don't even know where to start. I just shake my head against her shoulder, and she holds me until I calm down enough to breathe.

"Let's go inside," she tells me, but since I'm not sure I'm done crying and I don't want to wake her parents, I shake my head again. "Then let me take you to the hideout," she says, and I let her help me out of the car.

We enter her garage and climb up into its attic, a tiny space we set up in seventh grade. It's filled with oversized pillows, beanbag chairs, and old lamps we collected from yard sales. I turn on my favorite one and it flickers purple and green light all over the eggshell walls before I sit down in my zebra-print beanbag and drop my head to my hands.

Rowan sits on her blue beanbag across from me, rubbing my shoulders and my knees until I take a deep breath and say, "He told me he loves me."

"Joel?" she asks, and I huff out a single humorless laugh. Even Rowan can't believe he'd say it. He was supposed to be different.

"Yeah. Joel."

"Then what?"

His broken face flashes into my mind, his words echoing in the fissures of my heart. *Was this your fucking plan? To fucking crush me?*

I sit up, wiping my eyes with the heels of my palms. "I told him to go home."

Rowan frowns at me, and I stare down at the floor.

"Why?" she asks.

"I don't want anyone to get hurt."

"Dee," she says, rubbing my shoulder, "you're hurting right now."

"I'll be fine."

"What about him?"

Another wave of tears stings my eyes, and I hurriedly wipe them away. "He'll be fine too. This is for the best, Ro. We're no good for each other. You said so yourself."

"I said that *months* ago, Dee . . ."

"Nothing's changed."

"Are you sure?" she asks. I know she has a point, but it's one I don't want to think about.

"I yelled at my dad," I say to avoid her question. More silent tears. I lift the bottom of my shirt to wipe them away. "He told Joel about my mom, and Joel used it to try to psychoanalyze me when we were fighting and . . . I don't even know, Ro. I just . . . I was just so . . ." A sob bubbles out of my chest, and I bury my face in my arms.

Rowan drops to her knees beside me to drape her arm over my back, trying to rub my pain away.

"I threw it all in my dad's face. I took it all out on him. He didn't deserve that." The sobs start coming hard and heavy, my entire body aching with the force of them, and I say, "He's been through enough. He's always been such a good dad."

"I'm sure he'll understand," Rowan says, and I know she's right, but that doesn't make me feel any better. If anything, it makes me feel worse.

"I just don't know what to do." My words are muffled and stuffy. My eyes are swollen and I'm too congested to breathe.

"Just tell him you're sorry—"

"No, I mean about *everything*." I sit up and wipe my nose with the back of my wrist and my eyes with the tips of my fingers. "He's never going to talk to me again."

"Your dad . . . ? Or—"

"Joel," I answer. "We can't be friends. Not anymore."

"Do you love him?" she asks, and I shake my head, tears falling between my knees.

She waits for a long moment, holding my gaze, and then says, "Are you sure?"

I shake my head again, and she sighs and brushes her thumb over the apple of my wet cheek. "When you told Joel to go home, what happened?"

"He went."

"Did he say anything?"

He told me he wouldn't get over me. He practically pleaded with me not to push him away. He told me I was crushing him.

I shake my head. "He just left."

"Maybe you should call him . . ."

"And say what?"

She frowns, because we both know there's nothing to say.

"I need a fucking drink," I say, already feeling the sting of new tears and desperately trying to hold them at bay. I need a buffer, something to help me forget. Something to help me sleep until being awake doesn't hurt so much.

Rowan stares at me for a moment, and then she nods. "I'll be right back."

A few minutes later, she returns with a bottle of Jack Daniels I'm guessing she stole from her parents' liquor cabinet. She unscrews the cap and hands me the bottle, and I take a big swig before holding it back out to her. "Let's just get drunk."

"Are you sure that's a good idea?" she asks, not taking the bottle.

"Yes," I insist, never so sure of anything in my entire freaking life. I push the bottle into her hand, and Rowan takes a little swig before handing the bottle back to me. I take a big swig, then another, before sending it back her way, and we keep going like that until my tears stop falling—until most of the whiskey is gone and so is the aching in my heart.

"Dee," Rowan says later that night, waking me with

a light touch to my shoulder that makes my head throb. "Dee, your dad's here."

I try to sit up, and the whole room spins. I feel big hands steady me as the world slowly comes into focus, and then there's my dad's face.

"What . . ." I mumble, not sure where I am or why I'm being woken up.

"Come on, kiddo," he says, and then he helps me to my feet. The night seeps back into my consciousness in bits and pieces. Joel, crying, Rowan, Jack Daniels.

"I'm sorry, Dad," I slur, my eyes thick with burning tears as we walk down the stairs into Rowan's garage. He shushes me, but I turn under his arm and wrap my arms around him. "I didn't mean it."

"I know," he says, holding me upright and rubbing my back. I hear him whisper something to Rowan, and she whispers back, but I'm too busy sobbing in my daddy's arms to care. "Let's get to the car, okay, sweetheart?"

I nod but don't stop hugging him, and eventually he picks me off my feet and carries me the rest of the way.

I fall asleep sometime during the car ride home and don't wake up again until four o'clock in the morning. The alarm clock on my nightstand glows an angry, fuzzy red, and I realize I'm still in my clothes, but my shoes and jacket are off and I'm snug under my covers. My eyeballs feel too big for their sockets—and my brain, too big for its skull. I press my fingers against my temples until I'm sure my head isn't going to explode, and then I reach for my lamp and flinch away from the light when it smacks me in the face.

I lie in bed with my eyes squeezed closed for another few minutes before summoning the strength to roll out of bed. Then I lumber down the hall and rummage through the bathroom medicine cabinet until I find the aspirin. With three of them in my hand, I turn on the faucet and dip my mouth under the water; then I swallow the tablets down and brace my hands on the sink, lost in deep blue eyes and a voice I'll never forget, words I'll always remember.

I only know that I'm in love with you. Like seriously *fucking in love with you.*

I pat the back pocket of my jeans, closing my clammy fingers around my phone and pulling it out. I have missed calls from my dad and missed texts from Rowan and Leti.

Nothing from Joel.

Go home, Joel.

My heart twists, and I bite the inside of my lip to keep from crying again.

I did what needed to be done. I extinguished the fire before it consumed us both. Now I need to let it go.

After shutting off the water, I find myself walking away from my room instead of toward it. I slip into the guest room at the other side of the house and stare down at the unmade bed Joel was sleeping in less than twenty-four hours ago.

I feel like I'm keeping a secret.

Some secrets are better off kept.

I take off my jeans and crawl under his covers, wanting to be close to him even though I can't be and won't ever be again. My knee brushes against something soft, and I pull a T-shirt out from under the covers. Yesterday morning, he borrowed a clean one from my dad, and last night, he didn't come inside to get his old one before leaving.

I love you.

You don't have to say it back, but don't tell me how I feel.

I lift the shirt to my nose—breathing him in, missing him, wanting to go back in time even if nothing could have changed—and then I tuck the shirt under my cheek and fall asleep alone.

Chapter Twenty-One

"Do you want to stop at IHOP?" Rowan asks from the driver's seat of my car. This afternoon, she drove my Civic from her place to my place and picked me up to head back to school. I didn't bother offering to drive, and she didn't bother asking if I wanted to.

"I look like crap," I mutter with my forehead resting on the cool glass of my passenger-side window, every single hair follicle reminding me of how much I had to drink last night.

"You're wearing alien-sized sunglasses," Rowan counters. "No one can even see you."

I turn my head to give her a look, but it's lost behind sunglasses that are just as big as she said they are.

"Are you glaring at me right now?" she asks.

"Something like that." I lay my head back against the glass with delicate precision, careful not to wake the troll hammering at my brain.

This morning, after dry-heaving in a hot shower and finishing washing up in a cold one, I got dressed and faced my dad in the kitchen. He slid a coffee and a stack of home-made pancakes in my direction as I took a seat at the breakfast bar.

"How are you feeling?" he asked.

The truth was, I felt too shitty to even *look* at his pancakes. I slid them to the side and glued my cheek to the cold granite countertop. "Bad."

"Do you want to talk about what happened with Joel?" my dad asked, and my heart pinched at the mention of his name.

"Not really."

My dad rested his big hands on the counter and said, "Okay . . . but you know you can, right? I'm here to listen if you need me to . . ."

I closed my eyes for a long moment before I began to sit up. My head protested, but I managed to get my elbows on the bar and the rest of me into an upright position. "Dad, about yesterday . . . . I'm really sorry. I didn't mean anything I said."

He frowned at me. "Sweetheart . . . we both know that's not true, and I think it's time we talk about it."

I didn't want to talk about it, but my dad lured me into a conversation, and every confession I made felt like a weight lifted from my soul. I told him about how much I hated my mom, about how much I *needed* a mom because, even though he had been the best dad a girl could ask for, there are some roles a dad just can't fill. I told him about the night I heard him crying after she left, and his eyes filled with fresh tears as he apologized for me having over-heard. I told him that I hated her for what she did to him, that I hated that he never moved on or dated anyone else.

And my dad told me things too, things I didn't want to know but that he said I should understand.

"Your mom got pregnant with you when we were nine-teen, Dee," he said as I finally began picking at my pan-cakes. It was easier than looking him in the eye. "We hadn't even been dating that long." He sighed and raked his hand through his dusty blond hair, like he was trying to work up the courage to tell me something he didn't want to admit even to himself. "She never loved me," he said, quietly, "not really . . . I thought I could love her enough for both of us, but . . ." He shook his head at some unseen memory he was reliving. "Anyway, when I found out she was pregnant, I immediately got all these ideas in my head about a marriage and a house and a family. And your mom went along with it because—even though you don't think she did—she loved you. She did her best . . . it just wasn't enough."

I sat in my chair, my headache forgotten while I lis-tened intently to every word my dad was sharing. I clung to each new piece of information, saying nothing because I didn't want to risk him shutting down and leaving me in the dark.

"Sometimes, I would come home from work and your diaper would be filthy, and it was just because your mom was too overwhelmed to even change it. Looking back now, I realize she needed help, like professional help, but at the time, I thought I could do it all. I tried to be every-thing for you both, and I'm sorry."

"Dad—" I began to say, hating that he was blaming himself for being a loving father and a devoted husband, but he just put his hand up.

"Just let me get all this out, okay? I'm not trying to excuse your mom, and I know you'll still hate her when I'm done talking, but . . . she really did love you, Dee. She just didn't know *how* to love you. She tried and tried to be who she thought she should be, but over the years I think she just . . . she just lost herself."

"There's no excuse for walking out on your eleven-year-old child, Dad," I said, stern in my convictions in spite of everything he said.

"No, there's not," he agreed. "And I guess that's why I can't hate her. I feel *sorry* for her, Dee." His almond eyes became glassy, and he stared across the counter at me. "Because look at the beautiful woman you've become, and she missed it."

When we met each other at the side of the bar and hugged, I wasn't sure who was being strong for who. Maybe we were being strong for each other. Like we've always been.

"You alive over there?" Rowan asks, pulling me from the memory.

"Yeah."

"Sure you don't want IHOP?"

"Yeah . . . I just want to go home."

Over the entire week, I spend my days wanting to ask her a single question that dare not be spoken: *Is this how you felt when you broke up with Brady?*

I can't sleep. I can't eat. I make T-shirts for the band's

website, but I don't enjoy it. I'm a robot—I go to classes, I suffer through homework, and all of it *hurts*.

I don't hear from Joel, but neither does anyone else. He's a ghost, haunting me with his absence through a phone that never rings. On Friday, after he skips out on the the band's first practice with Kit, Rowan threatens to file a Missing Persons Report and he finally texts her back. But all he says is that he's fine, and he refuses to say where he is. I spend my nights imagining the girls he's with, the ways they might look, the ways he might touch them. I wonder how long it will take him to forget me, but then on Saturday afternoon, my phone rings and Rowan is on the other end. "They think he might be at his mom's."

"His *mom's*?" I ask, the memory of my own voice echoing in my ears.

Go home, Joel.

"Yeah. The guys are leaving to go check."

"Stall them," I say, already grabbing my keys and heading for the front door of my apartment.

"Why?"

"Because I'm coming."

It's my fault that Joel is there, and it's my responsibility to bring him back. I pull my car into the parking lot of Adam's apartment complex just as he and the rest of the guys are walking out of the building. I park next to his topless Camaro and hurry out of my car. "I'm coming with you."

Shawn, who doesn't look at all surprised to see me, just shakes his head. "I don't think that's a good idea."

"It might be . . ." Adam offers. He puts his cigarette out

under the toe of his shoe and climbs into the driver's seat, waiting for Shawn and me to figure out what we're doing.

I climb into the back with Mike, challenging Shawn to try to remove me.

"Dee," he sighs, "you don't know Joel's mom."

"I know enough." I give him a meaningful look, and something passes between us. I'm trying to tell him I *know* about Joel's mom. Even if I don't know *her*, I know all I need to know. I know we need to bring him home.

Shawn hesitates, hearing my unspoken words, and then climbs into the passenger seat beside Adam.

An hour later, we turn onto the derelict road of Sunny Meadows trailer park.

If I were in my own car, I'd roll up my windows and lock my doors. But Adam rolls onto Dandelion Drive with his roof down and his radio blasting. People on porches turn their heads to follow us as we drive by, and I flip my shades down, sinking lower in my seat.

We park next to Joel's brown clunker in the stony drive-way of a rusted brown trailer with wind chimes hanging on the porch. Tulips hide in a neglected garden, choked out by overgrown grass and weeds.

"How is that dog not dead yet?" Adam asks of a one-eared mutt barking at us from the next yard. He picks a stick off the ground and throws it over the chain-link fence, frowning when the dog doesn't chase it. I slide out of the car on Mike's side to stay as far away from the dog as possible.

"Maybe you should wait in the car," Shawn tells me, and I give him a look that asks if he seriously wants me to get murdered.

"Yeah, I don't think so," I say, and he rubs his eyebrow like a serious pain has taken root there. Then, without another word, he climbs the stairs to the trailer's porch and knocks on the broken screen door. It clangs against the frame as I climb up behind him, each stair creaking under my weight.

He knocks again, and when no one answers, Adam huffs out a breath and opens the door. He disappears inside, and I file in between Shawn and Mike.

"Hey Darlene," Adam says to the woman on the couch who has just stirred awake. A white cat jumps down from the cushion beside her and rubs against my leg, but my attention is fastened on the woman I can tell is Joel's mom. She has a certain something about her—a certain beautiful something that I can tell Joel inherited from her—but she doesn't have his blond hair or blue eyes. Her hair is a washed-out brown with choppy layers and split ends, and her eyes are a murky brown. She has her legs stretched out on the built-in recliner of the sofa and an ashtray sitting on her lap, and she's pretty like a ruby coated in years of neglect. This is the same woman who sold her son's birthday presents, the same woman Joel can't bear to talk about unless it's quietly in the dark.

"Who are you?" she slurs at me, and I catch myself glaring at her.

"This is a friend of ours," Adam offers simply, nodding in my direction while I push my sunglasses on top of my head. "Where's Joel?"

Darlene's gaze swings back to Adam like she forgot he was standing there. "His bedroom."

Adam immediately heads down the hallway while

Shawn, Mike, and I stand awkwardly on the ragged brown carpet. The entire house smells like vanilla air freshener, and I dread to think of what it would smell like without it. Every available surface seems littered with something— liquor bottles, beer cans, full ashtrays, empty cigarette packs, magazines, old paper plates, old chip bags.

Darlene's bushy brows pull together as she watches Adam head down the hall, and then she turns her attention on the boys at my sides. "Who let you in?" She has a smoker's voice and a drunk person's patience, irritation lacing the confusion in her voice.

"Door was open," Mike lies, and Darlene lets out a disgruntled breath. She tries to put the footrest down but eventually gives up. I doubt she could walk a straight line even if I held a gun to her head, which I kind of want to.

I pry my eyes away from her to stare at the pictures on the walls—angels, Jesus, a wooden cross. Beside them hang pictures of Joel, with his dark blue eyes and innocent little smile. I stand in front of one of him with a head full of spiky blond hair, smiling in a bright orange T-shirt in front of a laser-filled blue background, and then I move to the next, and the next, taking them all in and realizing that he isn't older than eight or nine in any of them. Maybe they were framed by his grandma before she had a stroke, or maybe by one of the ex-boyfriends Joel told me about. Maybe even the one who bothered to buy him a Hot Wheels track and leave behind a guitar.

My gaze travels back to Darlene to find her tracking me with cold, narrowed eyes. I don't know why she doesn't like me, but I *know* why I don't like her.

"What'd you say your name was again?" she asks, her words all running together.

When Joel emerges from his bedroom, I don't bother answering her. He freezes in the hall, shirtless and barefoot with his mohawk soft and messy like he just woke up. His skin has lost some color, and his eyes are hangover-red. "You've got to be fucking kidding me."

"He says he's not coming," Adam tells Shawn from behind Joel, but Joel never breaks eye contact with me.

"Why the fuck are you here?" he asks, his voice holding not one ounce of the boy who told me he loved me less than a week ago.

"To make sure you come home," I answer sadly, but Joel just laughs and rakes both hands over his scalp.

"So let me get this straight," he says, "you tell me to go home, but when I go home, I'm not allowed to fucking stay there? Where the fuck am I supposed to go, Dee?"

"This is *her*?" his mom growls from the couch. She finally manages to get the leg rest down, and she sits forward, pointing an unsteady finger at me. "You've got some nerve coming to my house."

"I'm not leaving without Joel," I state calmly, realizing I mean it. He doesn't belong here, with this selfish woman who stole his childhood. He belongs with his friends, with people who love him.

His mom's finger jams farther forward. "You'll do what I tell you, you stupid little bitch!"

"Mom!" Joel barks, silencing us. Claws scratch into the carpet as the cat glued to my legs darts down the hallway and into Joel's room.

Joel's mom glares at him and then me. "You break my son's heart and think you can just come in my house and take him away from me?"

I want to tell her that someone should have done that a long fucking time ago, when he was young enough for it to matter, but that's between Joel and his mom, and it isn't my place to say. I fist my hands at my sides and bite the inside of my cheek until I'm sure the words aren't going to burst free the second I open my mouth. Then, with pleading eyes, I look at Joel and say, "Joel, please."

He's staring at me like he's debating coming with me when his mom says, "She ain't even that fuckin' pretty."

"Mom," Joel warns, but Darlene isn't done.

She locks eyes with me and snarls, "I used to be prettier 'n you."

"And look at you now," I counter, and a molten red flush erupts across her cheeks. She begins trying to stand, and if she were sober, I don't doubt she'd be in the midst of yanking my hair out. Instead, the couch cushion gives under her palm and she struggles to find her footing.

"YOU THINK YOU'RE BETTER THAN ME?" she hollers while teetering dangerously to the side. "YOU AIN'T NOTHIN' BUT A DUMB FUCKIN—"

"SIT THE FUCK DOWN!" Joel bellows, and his mom literally falls back into her seat. She gapes at him for a second before resuming that ugly mask of anger again. Shawn and Mike, who were moving closer to the couch to intervene on my behalf, just stand there frozen in time like they're not sure what to do with themselves. Adam puts his hand on Joel's shoulder, but Joel barely seems to notice.

"You're going to take that slut's side over mine?" Joel's mom asks him.

"She's not a slut," he snaps back.

"She doesn't care about you!"

Joel laughs, quietly at first and then louder. "There's some money in my room," he says. "Keep it. Pretend I'm still here for a while. We both know that's the only fucking reason you've ever wanted me around."

"How dare you talk to me like that in my own goddamn house!" his mom shouts.

"I PAID FOR THIS FUCKING HOUSE," he thunders, "so yeah, I'm going to do whatever the fuck I damn well please!"

Joel and his mom stare each other down, and then she starts to cry and he rolls his eyes.

"I'm out of here," he says, snatching a set of keys off the counter and practically steamrolling me out the door. The rest of the guys follow. I hear Joel's mom yelling behind them, apologizing and begging him to stay, but he ignores her. With his hand on my back, he ushers me down the porch stairs, and then he pulls away like I'm carrying something contagious. He walks to his car, opens the door—

He hesitates.

When he turns around, the world stops turning and I'm caught in one of those moments—the kind that have the power to change everything or nothing. A crossroad. A turn in the tide. A moment you can never come back from. "Why did you come here?"

I give him the simplest answer there is, the one that

says just enough and not too much. "Because I wanted to make sure you went home with Adam."

"Why?"

If there's a right answer, I know the one I'm about to give isn't it, and yet I give it anyway, because it feels like the safest. "You would've done the same for me. I owed you."

"You owed me?"

When my response is to say nothing, his gaze lowers to the ground beneath his bare feet and he turns away from me. He climbs into his car, waits for Mike to climb into the passenger seat, and then they're gone.

On shaking legs—still rushing with adrenaline from my near fight with Joel's mom, and weakened from watching him drive away—I manage to get myself into Adam's backseat, and he takes his sweet time lighting a cigarette before starting his black Camaro and heading toward home.

"Well," he says with the cigarette between his lips, "*that* went well."

"I told you we shouldn't have brought her," Shawn says, frowning at me in the rearview mirror. "No offense, Dee."

"She," Adam says, pointing a thumb in my direction, "is the only reason he's coming home."

I flip my shades back down and pretend to stare at the trees to avoid meeting their eyes. "No. He's coming back for you guys."

I'm the reason he left.

Chapter Twenty-Two

———————————————

WHEN ROWAN ENTERS our apartment a few minutes after I get home, I'm sitting on our couch with my head in my hands. I look up at her through tear-filled eyes, and she frowns at me.

I didn't break down during the ride home from Joel's mom's house. I didn't break down when I saw his beat-up car sitting empty in Adam's parking lot. I didn't break down during the drive back to my own place. And even at home, in the privacy of my own living room, I haven't broken down.

I don't deserve to cry. Even though I do it—almost every day—I don't have any right to.

"They told me what happened," Rowan says, taking a seat on the coffee table across from me. "Dee, this has got to stop."

My expression hardens, and I blink away unshed tears before they have a chance to fall. "What are you talking about?"

"Joel looks miserable. He *is* miserable. And you're sitting here crying . . ." She puts her hand on my knee, her voice soft but insistent. "You need to tell him how you feel."

"And how do I feel, Rowan?"

"You love him."

A tear escapes the corner of my eye, and I shake my head.

"Really?" she challenges. "Then why are you crying?"

Another tear, and another. I'm crying because he drove off with no shirt and no shoes, because he never should have been there in the first place, because when he asked me why I came to get him, I should have told him how horrible this week has been without him, how I miss his smile, his laugh, the way he used to kiss me goodnight. How I still sleep in his T-shirt because I miss his arms around me, how I can't even bring myself to wash it.

"Just drop it, Rowan."

"No," she argues. "This is ridiculous. I'm your *best* friend, and I know you've never been in love before but—"

"Stop," I warn, feeling all the hurt inside me burn into anger, which feels more familiar, more safe. I cling to it.

Rowan sighs. "He loves you back, Dee. No one's breaking your heart here but *you*."

"You don't know what the hell you're talking about," I snap. I get up and walk down the hallway toward my room, but she follows me.

"Oh really? Why did you go to his mom's tonight? And don't give me the same bullshit reason you gave Joel."

I close the door between us, but Rowan throws it open.

"Why the fuck do you care?" I shout at her. "Your life

is perfect! You have a perfect guy and a perfect family and everything's so goddamn fucking easy!"

"Oh, excuse me while I cry you a river, Dee," she snaps back. "Joel is a GREAT fucking guy. And he ADORES you. So let's all cry about it! Because that makes ANY sense."

I head into my bathroom, but Rowan jams her foot against the door before I can close it. I turn around and glare at her, my cheeks hot with tears.

"I'm trying to help you," she says, everything about her stony and uncompromising.

"You can help me by minding your own fucking business."

"Excuse me?"

"You heard me. Leave. Me. The fuck. Alone!"

She bites the inside of her cheek to keep from lashing out at me, and I already know I shouldn't have said what I said. But I don't take it back, not any of it, and she finally says, "Fine. You want me to leave? I'm leaving. Call me when you're ready to stop lying."

"Lying to who?" I yell at the back of her head when she gets to the front door.

"Yourself!" she shouts back, and then the door slams behind her.

That night, when I cry in the shower, it's not just because I miss Joel. It's because I miss my best friend. Because I miss my old self. Because I miss a time that never really existed—a time when I was happy.

I change into pajamas and wrap my hair in a towel, not bothering to dry it before I crawl into bed with Joel's T-shirt, breathing in his scent and wishing he were here with me to hold me close and tell me I'm not broken.

The closest I ever got to happiness was when I was on the receiving end of his smiles, his kisses, his secrets. When we held hands and made each other laugh. When he loved me.

Tears soak into my pillow when I remember him standing barefoot in his mom's gravel driveway asking me why I came to get him. Rowan asked me the same question. I didn't give Rowan an answer, and I gave Joel a lie.

Because I wanted to make sure you went home with Adam, I said.

But what I should have said was, *Because I love you.*

A heavy sob breaks free from some locked-away place inside me, and I hug Joel's T-shirt tighter, letting myself say the words, even if they're only in my head while I sob into my pillow.

I tell him I love him on Easter at the pool. I tell him I love him while we're cooking dinner with my dad. I tell him I love him when he crawls in my bedroom window.

I say it while he cries in my arms on his birthday. I say it while I lie on his chest on the bus.

I cry myself to sleep, knowing it's too late but saying it over and over and over again.

I love you, I love you, I love you.

I'm sorry, I'm sorry, I'm sorry.

Chapter Twenty-Three

I WAIT SEVEN days to text Rowan. Seven days to sort through my feelings and figure out what I'm going to say. On Saturday morning, we meet at IHOP. I'm sitting in a booth when she slides into the seat across from me. Her long blonde hair is up in a messy bun, her blue eyes shining with worry she's doing her best to hide.

"I missed you," I say, and she abruptly stands back up and slides in beside me, capturing me in a bone-crushing hug.

"I missed you too," she says against my hair. "I'm sorry I was such a bitch."

I shake my head against her cheek, holding her just as tightly as she's holding me. "No, you were right."

She loosens her hold around my neck, like she's just realized she's hugging a stranger, and when she pulls away, she looks at me like one.

I take a deep breath, intending to tell her that I've realized I love Joel, but the words get caught in my throat.

"Right about what?" she asks.

"About . . ." I rub the spot between my eyes. "God, this was so much easier when I practiced it in my head."

Rowan studies me for a moment before realization lights her eyes and the corners of her mouth begin to tip up. I'm dreading her giddy reaction when I'm saved by the server who pops by to take our orders. Rowan slides back into her own seat, never taking her eyes off me or losing her full-faced smile. I order for both of us, hand back the menus, wait for the server to walk out of earshot, and scold my best friend. "Stop smiling at me like that."

"I can't help it," she says, her smile growing even bigger. "Just say it."

"You already know."

"Pretend I don't."

God, she's so excited, I really want to smack her. "Why are you doing this?" I groan, but her smile is indestructible.

"Because I love you." She says it easily, like it's the easiest thing in the world. And maybe it should be.

"I love you too," I say, and she props her hand on her fist, still wearing that goofy grin.

"And who else?"

I inhale and exhale a deep breath. "And Joel."

"All together now."

"God I hate you."

She starts laughing, and I close my eyes and just say it. "I love Joel."

When I peel my eyelids open, she looks like she wants to launch herself across the table to wrap me in another hug.

"Happy?" I ask, and her eyes start to well. The backs

of mine begin to sting, and I say, "What the hell are you crying for?"

"You," she says, running a knuckle over the corner of her eye.

"Stop," I complain, turning my gaze to the ceiling. I blink rapidly to hold the tears at bay. "Seriously, is it so much to ask for just one day without ruining my mascara? Why the hell are we crying?"

"Because we're girls," she laughs. "This is what we do when we fall in love."

"We get stupid?" She laughs even harder, and I find myself laughing too. "God, this is a mess."

"When are you going to tell him?" she asks, and I finally turn my chin back down, losing myself in another kind of feeling.

The shadow of our server falls over the table, and she pours us both a cup of coffee. "Your pancakes will be right out," she says with a smile.

"Thanks." I force a smile back at her, and when I look back to Rowan, hers has fallen away.

"You *are* going to tell him, right?"

Scratching my pointer finger over a scuff on the table, I say, "Do you think I should?"

"Is that even a question?"

I let out a slow breath. "How's he doing?"

When I turn my attention back to her, she's frowning. "I haven't seen him much. He promised not to go back to his mom's, but he hasn't been sticking around the apartment. I think he might be sleeping in his car."

"Or in other girls' beds," I counter, and when she doesn't deny it, I sigh. "Maybe it's better he not know."

"How is it better?"

"What happens if I tell him?" I stop scratching the table to tuck my hair behind my ear. "I know he told me he loved me, but I doubt he really thought it out. What happens after you tell someone you love them?" She waits for me to continue, but I just shake my head. "Joel and I don't know how to be in a relationship, Ro. We're not that kind of people."

"You've had boyfriends," she argues.

"Yeah, and look at what I did to them." Guys have told me they've loved me before, but I never believed them. They've given me flowers and gifts and declarations I didn't want, and all it did was make me run away even faster. I've made grown men cry, and all it ever did was make me lift an eyebrow and wonder why I dated them in the first place.

"But you *love* Joel."

"And look at what I've already put him through."

Rowan frowns at me for a moment before reaching across the table and taking my hands in hers. "Listen to me, okay?" I nod, and she says, "I know this is all really new, and I know it's scary, but you're going to keep loving Joel whether you tell him or not, and if you don't tell him and see where it goes, it's going to be a mistake that haunts you for the rest of your life."

Our hands separate when the server drops our pancakes off. This time, Rowan thanks her since I'm still lost in the darkness of her words. "What if we end up breaking each others' hearts?" I ask once we're alone again.

"You're already doing that," she answers, her voice matching her solemn expression. "What do you have to lose?"

THAT EVENING, AFTER I finish zipping up a pair of sparkly stiletto ankle boots, I consider all the answers to Rowan's question: my pride, my heart, my independence. But when I gave her those answers at breakfast, she asked me one more simple question: Are they more important than Joel?

I stand up, command my knees to stop shaking, and take one final look in my bedroom mirror. My purple wrap dress squeezes me in all the right places, flaunting my curves and complementing my dark chocolate curls. My makeup is flawless, my body is killer, and I feel like a fucking wreck.

Rowan told me that Joel is definitely going to be at Mayhem tonight. One of his favorite bands is playing, and all of the guys are going to go see them. The plan is just to go, be as hot as humanly possible, and say the words I should have said a long time ago.

"I love you," I practice in the mirror, rolling my eyes at myself. I take a deep breath and stare at it again. "I love you. I love you, Joel."

When someone knocks on my door, I nearly jump out of my skin.

After collecting myself, I let out a little chuckle and swing open the door to find Leti dressed in a dark purple button-down and dark-wash jeans. I smile when I realize we matched without even planning to. When he's not wearing ridiculous T-shirts and bleach-stained jeans, the boy definitely knows how to dress.

"Happy to see me?" he asks.

"Took you long enough."

"You do realize *you're* the one with the car, right?"

Ignoring him, I do a twirl and say, "How do I look?"

"Like a hot little succubus," he says with a grin. "What's the occasion?"

I grab a light leather jacket from the coat closet and toss Leti my keys, leading him into the hall outside my front door. "Joel is going to be there."

Leti locks up for me, pausing long enough to show that he's weighing his words. "I thought you two were done?"

"Turns out, I love him." When his jaw drops, I shrug and say, "Go figure."

He bursts out laughing and throws his arm over my shoulder as we navigate the hallways of my apartment building. "So you're going to tell him at Mayhem tonight?"

"I'm going to try."

"Say it to me," he prompts when we get to my car, opening the passenger-side door for me.

I put my hand on his shoulder and flutter my eyelashes up at him, saying in a 1960s-romance vixen voice, "Oh, Leti, you hot chunk of man, I love you." His laugh makes me smile.

"I think I just went straight for a minute."

"It was only a matter of time." I wink at him and get in the car, rubbing my hands over my thighs when I realize I'm really, seriously about to do this.

"Don't be nervous," he says when he slides into the driver's seat.

"I'm not," I lie.

"Don't be."

"I'm not," I say again, and he pats my knee.

"Good."

By the time we get to Mayhem, the club is pulsing with music and swimming in a thick cocktail of perfume, cologne, and sweat. Layers of people are packed in front of the bar, but since that's where I know Rowan will be, I grab Leti's hand and start weaving. I'm the small end of our human wedge, tugging him through the open space people make for me and hearing him make apologies for his wide shoulders the whole way.

"Hey," I say to Rowan when we finally get to her and Adam. I release Leti's hand and we both wipe handcooties onto our clothes.

Rowan hands me her full drink, and I gladly suck it down. "That dress is killer," she says.

I glance down at myself, getting an eyeful of cleavage. "I may or may not have caused a few heart attacks on my walk over here."

"That tends to happen when you torpedo through a crowd towing a big purple chunk of man behind you," Leti quips, and I crack a smile.

"Chunk of man?" Rowan asks with a lifted eyebrow.

"Her words, not mine," he says with a thumb in my direction. I smile and shrug while I finish off Rowan's drink and covertly scan the bar for Joel.

"Alright, who's dancing with me?" I ask, and Adam

takes that as his cue to go outside for a smoke break. Rowan and Leti both follow me toward the dance floor, and I get swallowed by the crowd with my two best friends.

"He's not here yet," Rowan says as soon as we're far enough away from Adam.

"Are we sure he's coming?" Leti asks. He's at my back, and Rowan is at my front. I rest my hands on her shoulders and try to pretend my heart isn't balanced on a tightrope waiting for her answer.

"Yeah. Adam texted him to make sure."

"*Adam* knows?" I ask, my cheeks flushing.

"Of course not," Rowan scoffs before I send myself into a tailspin. "What kind of a best friend do you think I am? I just told him I was worried about Joel and thought he could use a fun night out and to make sure he was coming."

"And he bought it?"

Rowan nods. "It was true, so yeah."

With Leti at my back, I mouth to Rowan, *I'm nervous.*

She smiles and shouts over my shoulder to Leti. "Leti, do you know what I love best about Dee?"

"Her wardrobe?" he shouts back.

"Her heart!"

"Not her butt?"

Rowan and I both laugh, and she says, "Her attitude!"

"Her boobs!"

I completely lose it, laughing so hard I have to stop dancing and grip Rowan's shoulders to stay upright. By the time I collect myself, I have an unshakeable smile on my face, mirrored by Rowan's bright blue eyes and rosy pink cheeks.

I dance until my thighs are burning and my hair is sticking to the back of my neck. "Drinks?" I ask during a lapse between songs, and we make our way back to the bar.

My heart teeters precariously on the wire while I scan the bar for Joel, and it nearly falls when I realize he's still not here. Before, I couldn't bear the thought of telling him how I feel. Now, every second that he doesn't know feels like a second we're drifting further apart.

I miss him. I miss him so much that I can't even think about it without tears threatening to form. It's been a full week since I've seen him, two weeks since he could stand to look at me.

"I need to go to the bathroom," I tell Rowan and Leti before we get to where Adam, Mike, and Shawn are sitting at the bar.

"Want me to come with?" Rowan asks, but I shake my head. I need a minute to myself to pull my game face back on.

"Nah, I'll be right back."

I turn on my heel before she can argue, weaving through clusters of people to get back toward the front of the building where the cleanest bathrooms are. When I get there, the women's bathroom is taped off with a sign that deems it "Out of Order," but I push open the door anyway and duck under the yellow tape. The other bathrooms are at the other side of the building, and I need the alone time too much to wait. In front of the wall-width mirror above the sinks, I take a deep breath and begin freshening my makeup, mentally rehearsing what I'm going to say to Joel.

I love you. I'm sorry I didn't tell you sooner. I want to be with you.

In my head, he furrows his brow at me. *You broke my heart, and now I'm supposed to take you back?*

I brace my hands on the sink and close my eyes, telling myself over and over again that it's only been two weeks. You can't stop loving someone in two weeks—not if you ever really loved them at all.

When I leave the bathroom, I'm telling myself not to worry, that everything will be fine, that he'll want me and we'll have each other. But when I get close to the bar, I see him, and my heart slips off the wire.

He's walking toward where Rowan and the guys are gathered, his arm around a girl with long blonde hair and a dress even shorter than mine. He's smiling, he's laughing. His blue-eyed gaze is traveling around the room, and my heart is breaking.

When his eyes land on me, his smile falls away. Tears flood my vision, and I turn on my heel to race back toward the bathroom, turning this way and that to melt through the crowd. I push through the press of bodies and duck under the yellow tape, slamming into the bathroom door and stumbling inside.

He was happy. It's only been two weeks, and he's happy without me. Two weeks, and he's happy with someone else.

Ugly tears are dripping onto the floor when the bathroom door pushes open and Joel ducks under the tape. He stops and looks at me, and all I do is stare back at him while letting the tears fall. There's no use trying to hide them.

"No," he says, his long stride eating the distance between us. He takes my face between his hands and stares down at me. "No. You don't get to do this."

A tiny sob sounds from inside me. Even though my heart is breaking, it feels so right having his hands on me. I want to press them tighter against my cheeks. I want him to hold me.

"You don't get to do this, Dee," he says again, his voice cracking. He brushes his thumbs over my wet cheeks and presses his forehead against mine. "Stop crying," he says in a voice so soft and sad, it breaks my already crushed heart. "You don't get to cry."

I want to tell him I love him. But what would be the point? I thought he would be better without me—now I know I was right.

Joel's lips brush over mine, his blue eyes closing. "You don't get to do this anymore." He kisses me again, and my fists bunch in his shirt as I kiss him back. Tears are pouring down my cheeks when he says, "You don't want me." He says it between kisses growing increasingly more insistent, and when he backs me up against the wall, he kisses me so deeply that the sound that comes from my lips is more moan than sob. In the next instant, he's lifting me into the air and I'm pushing my hands under his shirt, needing to feel his skin on my skin and his lips on my lips.

A spark flares between us, and we're lost. Our kisses are bruising and frantic. My dress is being pushed up, his pants are being unzipped, and my panties are being yanked to the side.

When he sinks inside me, my fingernails dig into his back and a low moan crashes between us. His. Mine. Tears are still dripping down my cheeks, and when I open my eyes, his eyes are glassy too. I hold his face between my hands and kiss him desperately as he thrusts inside me over and over again. We breathe each other as he takes me, kissing and pulling and never getting close enough. I want to tell him I love him, but when I remember the girl waiting for him back inside the club, the way he laughed with her, I can't. Instead, I kiss his mouth, his jaw, his neck, his ears.

Joel shudders against me, his fingers gripping tighter around my thighs and his hard body pinning me to the wall. I kiss away the sounds coming from his parted lips while he empties inside me, and afterward, his head drops to my shoulder and he slowly sets my heels back to the tile. My arms are still around him, and I don't want to let him go, but then he lifts his head and stares into me with bloodshot eyes and tear-stained cheeks. His voice is raw with an emotion I feel in my own bones. "I can't do this anymore."

When his blurred form turns away from me, I don't stop him.

When he walks out the door, he doesn't look back.

Chapter Twenty-Four

AFTER JOEL WALKED away from me, I wanted to fall to my knees. I wanted to collapse and cry until I had no tears left to shed.

Instead, I ran after him.

It took a few seconds for my feet to move, but eventually, something clicked in my brain. A desperate voice said, *this is your last chance*, and I took it. I swung open the door, I pushed through the crowd, I searched for him. And I froze.

He was leaving—with her. My gaze lowered to their joined hands, and I stared at them until they were burned into my brain. Then, the hands disappeared, and I knew with crushing certainty that my chance with Joel was gone. The chance had passed two weeks earlier in an empty pool, and now it was too late.

I left Mayhem as soon as I was sure Joel wouldn't still be in the parking lot. In my car, I texted Rowan to tell her I had changed my mind about telling him how I felt. I asked her to give Leti a ride home, and I also asked, very politely, for her to please give me my space.

She showed up at my apartment half an hour later, but by then, I was already numb. It was easy to tell her that I had simply decided I didn't want to be tied down, that I was sure Joel wouldn't want to be tied down either. She argued with me and repeatedly asked me if something had happened, but I had no intention of ever telling her about what happened in the bathroom.

Gradually, days turned into weeks and she let it go.

I thought of Joel every day, every night, but I eventually stopped crying about him. He never texted, never called, and neither did I. I avoided Mayhem, and even though I still got asked out on dates almost anytime I bothered brushing my hair and going out in public, I turned them all down. Instead, I focused all my energy on finishing my classes and making T-shirts for The Last Ones to Know.

THE WEEK BEFORE finals, Rowan drags me to IHOP and I let her because I've come to a decision she needs to know about sooner rather than later. We sit in a booth, we place our orders, and we're both carving into high stacks of strawberry pancakes when she says, "How do you think you're going to do on your finals next week?"

"Honestly?" She waits expectantly, and I give it to her straight. "I'm not even going to bother taking two of them because there's no way I can pass the classes even if I ace the finals." Her lips part like she's going to say something, but I don't leave her time to interrupt. "Two others are papers, and I've already started working on them, but I'll be lucky if I pass the classes with Cs. The other one is the marketing class, and I better get an A on that one or I'm seriously going to burn the entire school to the ground."

Rowan's worry lines are deep when she says, "You really can't pass two of them even if you ace the finals?"

"Don't look at me like that," I say. "I tried, Ro. I really did. I mean, you saw me, I—"

"I know you did," she assures me. "You've been working really hard . . ."

I take a deep, heavy breath. "I promised my dad I'd get my grades up . . . but the damage was already done before midterms. I couldn't get caught up, and then . . . stuff happened." I don't need to say what stuff. I stopped saying Joel's name a few weeks ago. "It just wasn't going to happen."

"There's always next semester," she suggests after a while, forcing a smile at me even though her eyes are still sad.

I take another weighted breath, knowing I have to tell her and hoping I don't cry. "Ro . . . I'm not coming back next semester."

She stops cutting into her pancakes to stare at me. "What do you mean?"

"I'm going home. I'm not coming back. I—"

"You're *not coming back*?"

My eyes start to sting, so I close them. "I just can't be here anymore. This isn't working out for me."

When she slides into my side of the booth, I open my

eyes and look at her. She takes my hand. "Dee, I know you miss Joel, but—"

"This isn't just about Joel," I say, and it's the truth. The past few weeks have been some of the most miserable of my life, but while part of my brain insists that it's all because of a certain boy I can't forget, the other part knows that's not entirely true. It's also because I've honestly been giving college my all, and the more seriously I take it, the more *wrong* it feels, like I'm not doing what I'm supposed to be doing or in the place where I should be. Over the past year, I've tried to quiet the voice, convincing myself that it's just because I'm lazy or disinterested—because everyone with half a brain goes to college, right?—but it's gotten to the point where I no longer care what the voice says because I just want to go home.

I want to go back to a place where subjects like math and biology don't matter. Back where homework doesn't exist and boys are predictable. Back where I can figure out who I am, because right now, the only thing I'm absolutely sure of is who I'm not. I'm not the same girl who accepted that college was her only option. I'm not the same girl who obsessed over Joel, or who let Aiden drool all over her, or who thought she could use Cody as a pawn to get what she wanted.

And I'm definitely not the same girl who blamed herself for what Cody did.

The girl I am now knows better. Even though there are days when I still think about that night, each time Cody's face enters my mind, I become more and more sure that I didn't deserve what happened. A kiss, even one that I enjoyed, does *not* equal consent. I was *not* to blame for what he tried to do to me.

It wasn't my fault.

It took me a while to believe it, and some days, it's still hard, but I know Rowan was right when she told me I did all I needed to do when I told him that one word: "STOP."

Before that night, I was broken, and after, I was destroyed. It was a broken girl who turned Joel away when he told me he loved me, and a broken girl who watched him leave Mayhem holding another girl's hand. I'm still trying to put myself together, but I need to be able to think to do that, and that's the last thing I can do when every single breath I take in this town pulls at the fissures of my completely broken heart. If my future doesn't involve college or the only guy I ever gave my heart to, I don't know where that leaves me, but I need to figure it out.

"It'll get better," Rowan says. "Next semester—"

"My mind's already made up, babe." The corners of her lips start slipping into a frown, but my voice stays sure. "I'm moving back home at the end of the month. I already talked to my dad."

Rowan shakes her head, her blue eyes welling with unshed tears. "What about me?"

I smile and smooth her hair over her shoulder. "You'll be fine. You'll stay here with Adam and finish school and be awesome, and we'll visit each other. And we'll talk all the time."

"Dee . . ."

I pull her in for a hug, and she squeezes me close.

When the server stops by to ask how we're doing, she takes one look at us and gives us another few minutes.

"What will *you* do?" Rowan asks when she pulls away. She wipes her eyes and sniffs in the rest of her tears.

"Call Jeremy, see what he's up to." She chuckles when I bring up the name of the lifeguard, and I force a smile even though I'm lying out of my teeth. I have no interest in seeing anyone, especially considering it's taking all of my energy just to crawl out of bed in the morning.

Last week, Rowan told me Joel got his own place, and I asked her to stop giving me updates. She told me she didn't think he was seeing anyone, and I told her I didn't care.

I'm happy that he finally has a place he can call home, but I don't believe for a second that he's been alone all this time, and I hate that some other girl is the one who got to sleep in his bed first. Or at all.

"I actually got an email from Van last night," I say, showing Rowan my phone to distract us both. This will make her happy, and hopefully that will help me block Joel from my mind for another five minutes. If I take life five minutes at a time, maybe I'll never need to think of him again.

"From *Van*?" she asks.

"He wanted to let me know he finally got in touch with his marketing people. I got an email from them half an hour later with a contract attached."

"Seriously?" she says, her face lighting up. "You're going to make T-shirts for Cutting the Line?"

I force another smile, hoping it looks as excited and genuine as hers. Last night, when I got the email, I should have danced, screamed, called my best friend and freaked the hell out. Instead, I burst into tears.

All I could think was, *This should make me happy. I should be happy. Why am I not happy?* But there I was, crying into a box of tissues.

"Yep," I answer. "Van actually came through."

"How are you not freaking out?!" she asks.

"I did, believe me."

"Did you sign the contract yet?"

"I wanted to sleep on it, but I'm going to."

Rowan slides back into her own seat as we talk about the terms. Van told me not to be afraid to negotiate any I didn't like, but the contract was more than generous. Based on the time it takes me to make the shirts, I'll be making nearly triple minimum wage. My "brand" will also be featured on the band's website and at their merchandise booth. They want me to send a picture and a bio and make it a whole big thing.

"I think I might also apply to fashion school," I add, and Rowan's eyes get big.

"Really?"

Nikki and Molly had been the first to suggest it, and Joel had been the last. "Yeah, maybe. I mean, it's just something I'm thinking of. I—"

"I think you should do it," Rowan says. "You'd be really good at it, Dee."

"You think so?"

"I know so." She presses the heels of her palms against

her eyes when she starts getting choked up again. "I still don't want you to go though."

"I know," I say, because we both know I'm going to anyway.

"I'll miss you."

I give her a weak smile. "Nah, you're going to hate me when you realize what this means."

She pulls her hands away from her eyes, and I manage a sincere smirk in her direction.

"You're going to have to tell your parents about you living with Adam."

Chapter Twenty-Five

OUR FINAL WEEK in the apartment, Rowan spends every night either in my bed or camped out with me in the living room. We build a massive fort out of pillows and blankets and leave it up until it's time to pack everything away.

"They want to meet him," she tells me as we fold a sheet together, and I laugh. I wish I could see her dad's face when he sees Adam's black nail polish.

"Of course they want to meet him."

We bring the edges of the four-hundred-thread-count sheet together and Rowan gives me a flat stare as she takes over the folding. "You don't have to sound so happy about it." When I just smile at her, she says, "He's going to drive the moving van for us on Sunday and stay the night at my house."

"They're going to make him sleep on the couch," I warn, and Rowan nods.

"I just hope he stays there."

I laugh and ask, "Are you going to make him dress up?" Adam could be considered "dressed up" if he just wore jeans without rips, took off some of his bracelets, and wore a shirt with buttons.

Rowan shakes her head. "No. I love him the way he is, so they should too."

I smile, pretending her words don't sting the open wound in my chest. I wonder if Joel loved me like that—just the way I am—and if he did, how he could stop doing it so quickly. He was the first boy I ever loved, the first boy I ever let inside me with nothing between us, the first boy I ever wanted to really *be* with, and it took him approximately two seconds after fucking me against a bathroom wall to haul some other girl out of Mayhem and probably fuck her the same way.

I broke his heart first, but he broke mine last.

"Do you know what *I* love?" I ask, ignoring memories of Joel, pretending to feel normal. Pretending to be myself. I flop onto the couch and watch Rowan fold. She tucks a long-edged seam under her chin and works her magic.

"What?" she asks once her chin is free.

"This new you. Adam has been really good for you. You don't take shit anymore."

"I took enough shit from Brady to last me a lifetime," she says, and I toast a half-empty margarita glass into the air. I'm sucking at its salted rim when Leti knocks on the front door. He pushes it open without invitation and strolls inside with Kit on his heels. I've seen her a few times since she joined the band, and if I were sticking around, I think we might've even become friends.

"Help has arrived!" Leti says with both arms thrown in the air.

Rowan, the genius that she is, insisted on throwing me a packing party disguised as a girls' day, and I figured it was a brilliant way to secure some cheap labor. Tomorrow, she's throwing me a birthday-slash-going-away party, for which everyone is required to bring a present *and* help us load the moving van. We're having the party in my empty apartment, and then I'm going to Rowan's to spend the night at her place. By then I will have said all my good-byes, and on Sunday morning, I'll leave this life behind.

"You're not packing up the fort, are you?" Leti asks with an exaggerated amount of alarm, keeping me in the present instead of a future that feels just as lonely.

"Yes?" Rowan says.

"But I brought my jammies!" He lifts a backpack in the air, and I manage a chuckle.

"I was promised a fort," Kit says, and Rowan shrugs before shaking the blanket back out.

With Kit's help, we pack up most of my things and build a fort even better than the one we had before. Mismatched bedsheets—some lavender, some pink polka-dot—are hung over couches and lamps and packed cardboard boxes, and the entire fort is full of comforters and pillows. Two tiny lamps illuminate the inside, and we camp out within the dryer-sheet-scented walls.

Kit credits her fort-building skills to her older brothers, who I suspect can also be credited with her willingness to cram herself into a tiny space with Rowan, Leti, and me. Even though we've only hung out a handful of times since her audition a couple months ago, I like her, and as long as she continues lacking any interest in Joel, I'll keep liking her. She's pretty and she knows it—but in a tough, impenetrable kind of way. She's not sweet like Rowan or girly like me, but she's got a sort of playfulness about her that is as feminine as it is tomboyish.

"I feel like I've been a horrible friend," I say to Leti while he finally lets me paint his fingernails. He said it would be his birthday present to me, and I was twisting off the cap of the sparkliest, purpliest nail polish I own before he even finished his sentence. "What ever happened with that Mark guy?"

"Who?" Leti asks, not looking at all comfortable to be on the receiving end of what I insist is the most fabulous manicure he'll ever get. He furrows his brows at the polish like it might make his fingers fall off, and he only half seems to hear what I'm saying.

"Mark. The fireman." Leti raises his eyebrow and I say, "You met him at Mayhem a few weeks ago . . . dated for a while . . . We joked about him being hot enough to be Mr. February in the firemen's calendar . . ."

"Oh!" Leti chuckles. "Mark, right. You know he wasn't an actual fireman, right?"

Now it's my turn to raise my eyebrow. Leti's smirk sinks even deeper.

"I just nicknamed him that."

"Why?" Rowan asks, and a mischievous spark glints in Leti's eye.

"Because he put out a fire in your pants?" I ask, and Leti grins while shaking his head.

"Because he had a really big hose."

"Oh my God," Rowan says, and she and I break into a fit of giggles.

We're still giggling when Kit, staring at a random polka dot on the wall of our fort, says, "I slept with Shawn."

All of the sound gets sucked out of the room. Three sets of eyes lock on her and three jaws drop open. She glances at each of us, as if just realizing that she said it out loud, and gives an embarrassed smile.

"You *slept* with *Shawn*?" Rowan asks, and the apples of Kit's cheeks redden.

"Not recently . . . It was a long time ago. When we were in high school."

Rowan shares a look with me. She's gone to a few of the band's practices with Kit, and she's told me how weird Shawn acts around her, but I know Rowan's loyalty is to Shawn over Kit, so she chooses her words carefully. "Has he brought it up?"

Kit shakes her head. "He doesn't remember."

"Are you sure about that?" I ask. The girl code in me wants to tell Kit I think she's wrong, based on what he said about her at her audition, but just like Rowan, I've been friends with Shawn for a lot longer.

"Why, has he said something?" she asks, and I can hear the dusting of hopefulness clinging to the edges of her voice.

I shake my head. "No, but . . ." I don't even know how to finish that sentence. I don't want to give her false hope, but I recognize something in her that I see in myself every time I look in the mirror anymore. A quiet longing for something lost. "But I think you'd be hard to forget."

She gives me a smile that seems bigger than it should be, like she's fighting to keep it on her face. "I didn't look the same in high school. I was way more of a tomboy—T-shirts and flannels, less makeup, no tattoos or piercings, glasses."

"Hot enough to sleep with," Leti offers, and Kit gives another forced smile.

"Why don't you say something to him?" I ask, watching as her smile grows both warmer and colder. It's a troublemaker smile, the smile of a girl who grew up with four older brothers and knows how to take care of herself.

"It's fun playing with him. I'll tell him eventually . . . maybe."

I chuckle, and Leti pouts. "Well, it's official. I'm the only one here who hasn't slept with someone in the band. Shawn, Adam, J . . ." He trails off on the 'J' sound, and we all know why. Shame colors his face, and his apologetic eyes swing to meet mine. "Shit."

"Consider yourself lucky," I say, taking one more purple swipe over his pinky before twisting the nail polish shut. "It looks like Rowan is the only one who got a happy ending out of it."

When I sit back, she frowns at me. "Are you sure you don't want me to invite him tomorrow?"

"In what world would that turn out okay?"

"What happened between you two?" Kit asks, and Leti subtly shakes his head, freezing when I catch him doing it.

"A lot," I answer, and when she continues waiting, I add, "Too much."

"Were you in love?"

The answer is that we were. The answer is that I still am. I love him, and I hate that, and if I could shut it off, I would. Part of me wants him to be happy, in his own place with his new life, but the other part of me hopes that he can't sleep, can't eat, and never gives his heart to anyone else. I hope that when the next girl tells him she loves him, he tells her to go home. "Who wants another margarita?"

That night, after I've drank enough to forget about Joel and everyone else has drank enough to stop bringing him up, Leti and Rowan both wrap me in a cocoon of arms. They do it as a joke, and we all giggle, but no one pulls their arms away, and eventually we fall asleep like that. In less than thirty-six hours, I'll be moving home, and next semester, Leti will be graduating. The cocoon is precious, a memory not yet a memory, and we hold on to the night for as long as we can.

In the morning, I wiggle out of my tight spot between them still feeling more like a caterpillar than a butterfly. I crawl over an unsteady mountain of pillows, slip through the exit of our fortress, and find Kit groaning in the kitchen.

"I can't believe we packed away your coffeemaker," she says, her layered black-and-blue hair wild and untamed. Her lashes are so thick and dark that they frame her eyes even without eyeliner or mascara, and I hate her just a little for it.

"Let's wake up Sleeping Beauty and Prince Charming so we can go to IHOP," I say.

I'm walking back toward the fort when Kit replies, "I *love* their pancakes." My mouth tips up at the corners, and I know with absolute certainty that we found the right girl for the band.

After pancakes, Adam, Shawn, and Mike show up at my apartment with the moving van and start loading my stuff into the back—my bed, my dressers, my boxes and boxes and boxes of shoes. Not all of this stuff is going to fit into my room at my dad's, and I wonder if maybe I should get my own apartment back home. Maybe a roommate. Hopefully not a weird one like I had at the dorms. If I can find the band a kickass guitarist, I should definitely be able to find myself a not-weird roommate, right?

Considering Rowan will still be here, over three hundred miles away, I can't imagine liking anyone I'd be living with. She could be the most amazing person in the world and she'd still feel counterfeit—I'd always hate her for not being Rowan.

"What's wrong?" Rowan asks as we watch Mike and Shawn carry my dresser into the van. Leti and Kit are taking a break on the grass, and Adam is sitting in a basket chair waiting to be loaded, smoking a cigarette and looking downright cozy.

"Nothing."

"Liar."

I sigh, and she turns her gaze back toward the boys. There's no point in telling her I'll miss her. I've told her a thousand times.

"Me too," she says, and she bumps her shoulder against mine.

I wish she was the only one I'll miss, but looking out at the boys, I can't help thinking that I'll miss them too. And I can't help knowing that one of them is missing.

Chapter Twenty-Six

PACKING AWAY MY glassware was our first mistake. Forgetting to buy Solo cups at the store was our second. Now, everyone is passing around a collection of liquor bottles and soda cans. We're all sitting on the empty hardwood floor of my apartment, boxes of pizza in the middle of our circle and a cake Rowan won't let me stick my finger into hiding in the fridge.

"To getting an A on that marketing final," Shawn says, toasting a bottle of tequila in the air.

"To fashion school," Leti adds, toasting a bottle of vodka.

"To drinking straight from the bottle," Adam quips, toasting a bottle of whiskey.

I chuckle, and Rowan toasts a hard lemonade in the air. "To Dee."

I smile and steal the tequila from Shawn, holding it out

toward Adam. "To Adam, for being the only not-corny person here."

He laughs and clinks his bottle to mine, and we both take big gulps.

"To everyone who bothered to work today," Mike adds, and Rowan laughs and toasts her lemonade bottle to his beer bottle. Adam laughs too because he knows Mike is referring to him. For the most part today, Adam did a miraculous job of looking like he was helping without actually doing anything.

"How many pairs of shoes do you think you own?" asks Kit. She somehow ended up sitting next to Shawn, but he's doing a remarkable job of not acknowledging the bombshell at his side, and Kit is doing a remarkable job of being extra bombshelly. I wonder what would happen if they accidentally rubbed elbows. Would they glare at each other and show their teeth, or would sparks fly and lead to a whole lot of clothing being ripped off right in the middle of this room?

"Easily a thousand," Leti answers, "judging by how much those boxes weighed."

"You should see my closet at home," I say, and then I laugh and add, "and the basement, and the guest bedroom."

Rowan nods. "It's true. When I lived at home, I almost never needed to buy shoes because we're the same size."

"What size are you?" Kit asks.

"Seven and a half," Rowan and I both answer.

"I'm a nine," Kit replies. "Your feet are tiny."

"Yours are just big because you're tall and built like a freaking supermodel," I point out, mostly for Shawn's benefit.

Kit smiles but shakes her head at the compliment. "Everyone in my family is tall. My older brothers are huge. They're all over six foot."

"So are we," Shawn says of himself and the rest of the guys.

"Yeah, but you," Kit says, pushing her finger into his bicep, "are scrawny. You don't look big at all."

Shawn stiffens, and I nearly burst out laughing. Kit just smiles that warm-cold smile of hers, making me wonder what happened after they slept together in high school. It must not have been pretty.

"Are you ready for cake?" Rowan asks to diffuse the tension.

"I'm ready for presents," I say, eyeing the stack piled in the corner of the room. It's always so easy to tell which were wrapped by boys—loose edges of wrapping paper and extra tape everywhere.

"You know the drill," Rowan says. When she pushes off the floor, I attempt to follow her to the kitchen, but she shoos me back out to the living room. "Don't look."

"I hope it's vanilla," Kit says, and I shake my head.

"It's going to be chocolate with chocolate icing."

The lights cut, and Rowan starts the birthday song. Everyone joins in, and in the dark, a lump forms in my throat. I'm going to miss them. Every single one of them. I try to clear my eyes before the candles illuminate my face.

"Dear Deeeeee," everyone sings, "Happy birthdaaay to yoooou."

"Make a wish." Rowan holds the cake in front of me, and I think about making one. I could wish to get accepted into fashion school. I could wish for the T-shirts to make me famous. I could wish for Joel to appear in my doorway. He'd tell me he still loves me and ask me not to go. When I realize that's what I want most of all, I blow out the candles without wishing anything at all. Rowan smiles, my friends cheer, and I pretend to be the kind of girl who still believes in wishes and who still bothers to make them.

"We *did* buy plastic plates and silverware, right?" Rowan asks, and everyone looks at each other.

"Not it," Adam calls, initiating a frenzy of not-it calling and nose touching. In the end, Mike and Shawn take a road trip to the grocery store. They return with plates and silverware, and when Rowan asks them why they didn't get cups too, since we still need those, they simply shrug and tell her because she only told them to get plates and silverware.

"Alright," I say, licking a fourth swipe of icing off my finger as she huffs at them, "someone give me a present."

Rowan cuts the cake and begins handing out slices as Leti slides the pile of gifts in front of me. I open them at random, getting a gift card from Kit, a scented candle from Shawn, a kickass perfume from Leti, and a second scented candle from Mike, who I suspect brainstormed gift ideas with Shawn. Rowan and Adam give me a ridiculously expensive sewing machine that almost makes me cry, and then she gives me a second present which is a set of the coolest-looking pairs of scissors I've ever seen—with sparkly purple handles and lots of differently shaped edges.

"Who's this one from?" I ask as I tear open the final gift. It doesn't have a tag or a card, but it's neatly wrapped in a plain dark purple paper, so I suspect it's from one of the girls. When I glance at them, they both look just as curious as I do. I finish unwrapping a long poster-tube and open it up, pulling out a sturdy piece of paper and unrolling it.

A penciled image of myself stares back at me. She's lying on her back with her hair lying in thick pools around her smooth face. The sky is dark and full of stars that the pale wall behind her tries to catch. She smiles at me, and the love in her eyes is so clear that my breath catches.

It's a memory preserved on paper. And even though I'm smiling at myself now, I wasn't smiling at myself when I was in that pool.

"Who drew this?" I ask, unable to tear my eyes from the sketch in front of me. When no one answers, I lift my gaze and demand to know, "Who brought this?"

"What is it?" Shawn asks, and I turn the sketch around for him to see. It steals everyone else's breath just as it stole mine.

We all know who drew it.

"I just grabbed all the presents that were on the table," Mike says.

"I thought it was one of yours," Adam adds.

"Shit," Shawn breathes.

I look back inside the tube—for a card or a note or *anything*—but there's nothing else inside.

"Why would he do this?" I say to myself, angering when no one answers me. "Why the fuck would he do this?" I ask Rowan.

It's been three weeks since he fucked me against a bathroom wall, four weeks since he yelled at me at his mom's, over a fucking month since he told me he loved me, and now he sends me this drawing? Why, just to remind me of a time when I was actually fucking happy?

"Where does he live?" I snap, rolling the sketch back up and stuffing it into the tube.

"Dee," Rowan says in that voice she sometimes uses to charm the viper inside me. "I think you should just—"

"Where. Does. He. Live?" I growl again, barely containing my calm. I'm saving my anger for Joel. Every fucking shred of it.

Again, no one answers me. They're all sitting around me in a shell-shocked circle, staring at me like I'm a grenade with its pin pulled. I'm glancing at Rowan, at Leti, expecting them to tell me, and when they don't, I look to Adam, Shawn, Mike. More looks, more silence. Betrayal courses through my veins like burning poison, and I'm about to tell every single one of them to go to hell, when Kit is the one who speaks.

"Adam and Shawn's complex," she says, and all eyes swing to her. "First floor . . . I can't remember which number."

I thank her and grab my keys off the counter with all intentions of busting down every single door on the first floor if that's what it takes to find him.

I'm almost out the front door when Rowan shouts, "C!" I glance over my shoulder at her, and she gives me a worried but apologetic nod. "C. He's in 1C."

I close the door behind me.

Chapter Twenty-Seven

OVER THE PAST few weeks, I've thought more than a few times about what I would say to Joel if I ran into him. I'd smile, I'd ask how he's been, I'd exaggerate all of my good news, and I'd walk away first.

"What the fuck is this?" I ask when I burst into his apartment. I hold up the poster tube as evidence, and from his position on the couch, he stares at me like I just broke his door down—which I would have if it had been locked.

There's a guitar on his lap and an amp at his feet. With no shoes, no shirt, and a single earbud dangling from his ear, he calls to my heart in a way that makes it want to open wide.

"Joel?" a girl asks, popping her head out of a room in the hallway.

And then the poster tube is flying right at his head.

"What the hell!" he barks, barely getting an arm up in time to prevent the tube from hitting him in the face.

It bounces off of his forearm and ricochets onto the hardwood floor.

"What's going on?" a second girl asks, poking her head out of the second room in the hall.

"Why the fuck would you send me that!" I shriek. I sound hysterical. I *am* hysterical. Two fucking girls? TWO?! "Is a slut going to pop out of the coat closet next? Should I not look in the fridge?!"

"Who are you calling a slut?" the first slut asks.

"YOU!" I shout down the hall. If I had more poster tubes, I'd be launching them like rapid-fire ammunition.

She takes a step toward me, I take a step toward her, and Joel steps between us. "What are you doing here?"

"Ruining your fucking orgy since you ruined my fucking birthday!"

He puts his hand on my arm, and I knock him away. Fully aware that we have an audience, I glare up at him—hating him for hurting me and hating myself for letting it happen—and then I turn on my heel to leave.

"What was I supposed to do?" he asks in a cold voice that snakes after me. "Be miserable forever so you could finally be fucking happy?"

My fists clench at my sides, and I whirl on him. "You think that's what I wanted?" When he just stares at me, a silent affirmation, I shout, "I went to Mayhem to tell you I wanted to be with you, Joel! And you fucked me in a bathroom and left with some stupid bitch two seconds later!"

The angry mask dissolves from his face, revealing a slack expression. Shock. Confusion.

I lean to the side to speak to the girls in the hall. "Congratulations, ladies, you've caught yourself a real winner!"

I turn away again, needing to get the hell out of Joel's apartment before I snatch the poster tube off the floor and literally impale someone with it. I make it to the door, I wrap my hand around the knob, and then my feet jerk off the ground.

"Get out," Joel orders with his arms tight around me.

He spins me away from the door, and I scream at him to put me the fuck down.

He begins carrying me toward the hall, and the girls there just stare at us like we're a train wreck bursting into flames. "Get out!" he barks again, and they both blanch as they realize he's talking to them.

"GET OFF ME!" I shout as I bat and kick at his arms and legs. He shoulders past the girl in the doorway of his bedroom to get me inside, and then he kicks the door shut behind us and pins his back against it to block me from leaving.

"Stop," he says, lifting a hand between us when I take a determined step toward him.

"You can't just lock me in your room," I growl, grabbing his extended palm and throwing it to the side.

"If you wanted to be with me, why the fuck didn't you say so? Why did you tell me to go home at your dad's, and shrug me off at my mom's? And not fucking say anything at Mayhem?"

"You were with . . . another . . . GIRL," I say, getting louder and louder with each word.

His feet carry him forward and his fingers wrap tight

around my shoulders. "Because you broke my fucking heart, Dee!"

I let out a humorless chuckle, and he stiffens. "That's funny, Joel, because it only took you *seconds* to move on, but I haven't been with anyone else in *months*."

"You think I've moved on?" he asks.

I shrug out of his hold and cross my arms over my chest. I'm sure the girls that may or may not still be in his apartment—including the ones hiding in the coat closet and refrigerator—would agree with me.

"You think I'm fucking happy?" he asks, and when I don't answer, he picks a crumpled piece of paper off the floor. Looking around, I realize the room is full of them. They litter the floor and overflow from a wire wastebasket in the corner of the room. "I drew you over and over and over again, and I could never fucking get you right," Joel says, uncrumpling paper after paper. He pushes them at me one by one, each sketch a slightly different version of the image he gave me for my birthday. "I was terrified I was forgetting your face, and then when I finally got it, all I wanted was to give it the fuck away so I'd never have to see it again."

"Then why bother drawing me?" I snap at him.

"Because I promised you I'd sketch you something special for your birthday."

"You also said you loved me," I scoff. "What's one more lie?"

"You're one to talk," he snarls, and fury flashes through me.

"What the fuck is THAT supposed to mean?"

He meets my raised voice with a gaze that burns through me, his voice threatening to bring down the walls. "WHY ARE YOU HERE, DEE?!"

Every cell in my body trembles, demanding I yell back at him.

"TELL ME THE FUCKING TRUTH!" he booms, and something inside me snaps.

"BECAUSE I LOVE YOU!" I scream at the top of my lungs, watching the words hit him and nearly send him stumbling back. "I fucking love you, okay?! Are you happy?!"

"YES!" Joel shouts, the corners of his lips already tipping up in spite of the anger in his voice.

I'm so livid and confused that I just want to cry, but Joel steps forward and cradles my face between his hands.

"Yes," he says again, softer. "Say it again."

"No."

"Say it again. I'm going to say it back, and then I'm going to kiss you."

I want that so badly, my heart pulses in my chest. Once, twice, three times. He's waiting. He's waiting on me, just like he has for the past few months. I need to trust that. I need to trust him.

"I love you," I confess in a quiet voice.

He doesn't smile at me, or say it back, or even wait for me to finish. One moment, I'm saying the last word, and the next, his lips are on mine. Kissing Joel feels like drowning in a memory, a secret place where I'm always happy, always home. His kiss is desperate but soft, and I part my lips to him, needing to feel his tongue, his lips, the heat between us. My fingernails scratch over the buzzed sides of his mohawk, and he lifts me off the ground, hugging me around my waist and kissing me until the past five weeks cease to exist. Our hearts thrum against each other, and eventually, I summon the willpower to hold his head in place and pull mine away. He smiles up at me, his blue eyes bright and his lips an irresistible, thoroughly kissed red.

"You didn't say it back," I say, and he sets me down, smiling at me in a way that gives flight to the butterflies in my stomach. Normal girls have butterflies that flutter, but Joel stirs mine into a full-blown riot.

"I fucking love you," he says, and he nips at my lips and kisses me again. He's still kissing me when he says, "Dee?"

"Hm?" I say, but it comes out sounding much more like a moan than I intended.

Joel chuckles and pulls away. "There's one more thing." I have no idea what he's talking about, so I wait, but not patiently. My hungry eyes are locked on those pretty red lips when he says, "I want to be with you. Just me and you."

My gaze lifts to his.

"Are you asking me to be your girlfriend?" I tease, but those butterflies are swarming into a frenzy. I've asked him this question before, and his answer has always been no.

This time, he gives me a soft smile and says, "Are you saying yes?"

"Do you always have to be so difficult?"

He laughs and kisses me playfully on the mouth. "Do you?"

"Yes," I say, and he furrows his brow at me.

"To the girlfriend part, or to the being difficult?"

"So you admit you're asking me to be your girlfriend," I say, and Joel laughs hard.

"Fine. Yes. Deandra Dawson, will you please for the love of God be my fucking girlfriend?"

I lace my fingers behind his neck and give him a smile only he can bring out of me. "I thought you'd never ask."

Chapter Twenty-Eight

IN A MOSTLY empty bedroom, I tap my finger against my chin and point to a corner. "There."

Shawn and Mike begin carrying my dresser to the spot I indicated, and I shake my head. "No, there." I point to the other wall, and they huff and change direction.

"Tell me again why I have to get you a housewarming present when I just got you a going-away present?" Shawn asks, quickly adding, "*And* I just got you a housewarming present for your last place a few months ago?"

"That was a birthday present," I scoff, ignoring the part about the housewarming present.

"Tell me again why *I* have to get you a housewarming present when I'm living here too?" Joel asks, and I smile and wrap my arms around his neck.

"Because you love me."

He lowers his mouth to mine in a single kiss that makes

my insides flutter, and then he pulls away and curses himself. "Damn it."

I give him my sweetest smirk, someone behind us gags, and we all get back to moving my things into Joel's bedroom.

Yesterday, after I burst into his place, threw a poster tube at his head, and agreed to be his girlfriend, I remembered that I was moving six hours away. Reality settled heavily in my stomach, and I told Joel it didn't matter if we wanted to be together because someone new was already set to move into my apartment and I was in the process of moving back home. I told him about how wrong college was for me, how I was thinking about going to fashion school, how popular the T-shirts were getting, and most importantly, how I had to move back home because I had no other options. Rowan had already told her parents about her living with Adam, so even if I could find another apartment in town, we couldn't keep lying about living together. I'd have to find a roommate, and I had no idea how long that would take.

"Move in with me," Joel had said, interrupting me mid-rant.

The only response I could muster was, "Huh?"

"Stay here," he answered.

"Joel—"

"If you think I'm letting you go again, you're even crazier than I give you credit for," he challenged, and I ignored the taunt since, for once, I didn't feel like fighting.

"You don't think it's too fast?" I asked, and his voice softened.

"I think that all we do is fast. When we try to slow it down, we mess shit up."

When we emerged from his apartment, after the hottest make-up quickie I've ever had, everyone from my birthday party was already gathered in the lobby anxiously waiting for me. Rowan, who was gnawing on a fingernail, lowered her gaze to our clasped hands, and her hand fell away from her mouth as a big smile lit her face.

"Shut up," I warned, but I couldn't stop smiling and she started laughing.

"Her stuff is already packed up?" Joel asked the guys.

"Yeah," Shawn cautiously answered. "Why?"

When Joel announced I was moving in with him, Adam burst out laughing, Rowan's jaw dropped, and Leti grinned like a goofball. From the expressions on everyone else's faces, they thought we were batshit crazy. And maybe we are, but it's either go crazy with him or go crazy without him, and that choice is finally easy for me to make.

This morning, I called my dad to let him know I was going to move in with Joel instead of moving back home.

"Are you there?" I asked in the long moment of silence that followed my announcement.

"Yeah . . . Give me a minute, I'm trying to figure out how to feel about this." I gave him what felt like the full minute, and he finally said, "Is Joel with you?"

I cast a worried look at Joel, who was sitting next to me on his couch. "Yeah . . ."

"Put him on."

"Why?"

"Because my little girl is moving in with him and we need to have a talk first."

I worried my bottom lip. "Dad?"

"Dee."

"There's something you should know first . . ."

Another long moment of silence passed while I tried to work up the nerve to tell my dad I'd fallen in love, and he interrupted it by stating matter-of-factly, "You're pregnant."

"No!" I shouted into the line, my outburst making Joel flinch. "No! Oh my God, no! NO."

An audible sigh of relief sounded from over three hundred miles away. "Thank God."

"Jesus, Dad. What the heck?!"

"I think I just aged thirty years."

"This is ME we're talking about!"

"YOU are acting strange lately," he argued. "Now what were you going to say?"

Joel leaned closer to try to hear more than one side of our conversation, and I rubbed a spot between my eyes as I confessed, "I love him. I just wanted you to know I love him."

"Sweetheart," my dad said, "I knew that at Easter."

"How?" I breathed.

My dad chuckled into the phone. "Because I'm your dad. I know things."

"So you're okay with me living with him?" I asked.

"I didn't say that. Now put him on the phone."

I reluctantly handed Joel the phone, and he and my dad had a long talk during which he told my dad that he loves me and that he'd never do anything to hurt me. By the time he handed my phone back, all I wanted to do was hang up on my dad so I could kiss Joel senseless for saying all of those perfect things.

"Okay," my dad said. "You have my seal of approval, but if he ever gets out of line, you tell him I have a gun."

"But you don't . . ."

"But he doesn't need to know that."

I laughed and told my dad I loved him, and when he finally let me off the phone, I beamed at Joel. Rowan and the guys showed up a short while later with the moving van, and I immediately got to work bossing people around, which I'm still doing when Shawn and Mike carry my dresser into the room.

Moving the furniture in is easy, but the little things are hard—like positioning my coffee mug next to Joel's, or spreading my comforter on his bed. When I drop my purple toothbrush into a plastic cup next to his green one, my heart lashes against the walls of my chest and I have to take deep breaths to calm it. The little things feel like bungee jumping, like skydiving.

Like falling.

And there are moments when I want to back away from the ledge again, but when I remember how lonely that felt—how *bad*—I let myself fall. I cling to Joel on the way down—holding his gaze, brushing his fingers, and planting soft kisses on his lips as we unpack—and he falls with me.

Later that night, after the little things are done and I haven't passed out even once, I change into a pair of teeny pajama shorts and one of Joel's T-shirts.

"So your dad is really okay with this?" he asks me for the second time that day as I watch him tug his shirt over his head. God, that will never get old.

"My dad loves you," I say, climbing into bed—under my crisp covers, on top of his firm mattress. *Our* bed. My heart pounds again, but this time it feels a little warmer, a little nicer.

Joel gives me a skeptical glance and climbs in next to me. "He didn't sound like he loved me on the phone . . ."

"What did he say?"

"He said he wasn't a fan of seeing his baby girl cry over a boy." Joel slides closer, his hand coming to rest on the curve of my waist. His voice is soft, careful, when he says, "Did you cry?"

I fight the urge to deny it, to downplay the misery I felt. Instead, I admit, "I fell apart."

"I thought you'd be relieved I was gone . . ."

I curl up against his chest so I don't have to look him in the eyes, and he wraps his arms tight around me. "When you left, I lashed out at my dad. Then I went over to Rowan's and cried my heart out. I got sloppy drunk and passed out, and my dad had to come get me."

His firm fingers rub my back, and he says, "I'm sorry."

I shake my head against his bare skin, closing my eyes and breathing his scent deep into my lungs. "I slept in the guest room that night and cried into the T-shirt you left behind. After I came back to school, I wore it to bed a few times just because I missed you so much."

"You did?"

"Yeah. I still have it."

Joel pulls away to lower his lips to mine, giving me a soft kiss that tells me he loves me more than words ever could.

"I love you," I say anyway, getting better at saying it. My heart beats strong and steady.

"I love you too," he says back, giving me another sweet kiss and asking, "Did you love me at Easter?"

"I loved you at the festival," I confess. I snuggle against him again, knowing it's true. "I just didn't know it."

"Same here," Joel says. "I didn't know it until you went home and didn't text me."

"I should have known it earlier. I just didn't want to admit it."

"Why?"

"I never wanted to fall in love. My mom . . ."

"You don't have to tell me," he offers when I trail off, and I take a steady breath. I've never talked about my mom to anyone but Rowan, and to some extent, to my dad. But I want Joel to know about her. I want him to know about me.

I need to stop hiding. I need to let him see me.

I pull away from him so I can lose myself in his blue eyes. "My mom had an affair," I say, strengthened by the steady way he looks at me. "I have no idea how long it had been going on, but she left when I was eleven, and when she did, my dad was broken. I never wanted anyone to have that power over me."

"You know I'd never do that to you, right?"

"How do you know?" I ask, and when he just stares at me like he's not sure what I'm asking, I say, "The band is getting huge, Joel. You have girls throwing themselves at you every time you perform."

"They aren't you," he says simply.

"What happens when you get tired of me?"

"Not going to happen."

"But how do you *know*?"

He studies his fingers as they gently tuck my hair behind my ear, and I study his face as he touches me. "You're the only girl I've ever wanted to draw," he says, his gaze coming to settle on mine. "You're the only girl I've ever wanted to date. To live with. You're the only one with a dad I wanted to meet. You're the only one I've wanted to fall asleep with and wake up next to. A lot of girls came before you, Dee . . . a *lot* of girls . . . but you're the only one. I know it'll always be you because it's only ever *been* you."

I close my eyes to prevent the tears from falling, and Joel leans forward to plant a tender kiss against my brow.

"I mean it when I say I love you," he says.

"I know."

"How I feel isn't going to change." I open my eyes, and he brushes his thumb across the wet apple of my cheek.

"Do you promise?"

"I'm promising it every time I say those three words," he says. A moment passes, and then he says them. "I love you, Dee."

A soft smile touches my lips, and still lost in those deep blue eyes—which hold the secrets of my own heart—I make a promise back. "I love you too."

Epilogue

Joel

ONSTAGE, THERE ARE different levels of multitasking. There's Adam, who belts out lyrics while working the crowd. There's Mike, who pounds at the drums with his hands and the pedals with his feet. There are Shawn and Kit, who pretend to be focused on the performance instead of each other—whatever *that's* about. And there's me, trying to keep the beat while Dee is standing offstage in a tiny black skirt that I swear to God is riding higher and higher every time I look her way.

Between songs, I reach behind my guitar to shift myself inside my jeans, knowing it's a lost cause. She gives me a little smirk, and my answering groan is lost to the screams of the crowd.

Mike's drumsticks start the next song, and I turn my attention back to the pit. Adam has it fired up tonight, and the waves are rolling in a storm that makes my skin hum. Under the searing blue and green lights, my T-shirt is clinging to the sheen of sweat on my skin and my blood is boiling hot. My bass pours through Mayhem's massive speakers, and my entire body bounces with the beat. The girls who aren't focused on Adam or Shawn scream lyrics at me, reaching with braceleted arms and desperate fingers. A pair of panties flies in my direction, but I take a step back to let them fall to the stage. I turn a smile on Dee, who, with her arms crossed and a grin on her face, shakes her head at me.

I turn back toward the crowd, knocked completely off my game. My fingers play on auto even though what I'm really thinking about is why the hell Dee just stood there shaking her head instead of tossing her panties at me. For the past couple weeks, we've played a little game: if I catch her panties when she throws them, I get a reward. If I don't, she gets one. Either way, I'm the luckiest fucking guy I know. Half the time, I've let them fall at my feet just so I have an excuse to taste her.

"Why didn't you throw your panties onstage?" I ask in her ear as soon as our first "last song" ends. The crowd is chanting for "one more song" over and over again, but the guys are busy chugging down water and taking a much needed break from the lights. Dee tugs on my damp sleeve so she can answer in my ear.

"I'm not wearing any," she says, and my hand instantly slides over the curve of her ass. No panty lines. *Christ.*

Unable to keep my lips off her any longer, I kiss the salt on the curve her neck and begin dipping my fingers under the waistband of her skirt to check for the strap of a thong or a g-string in case she's only teasing.

"Last song, man," Shawn says, smacking me on the shoulder before taking the stage.

I press my mouth back against Dee's ear, intending to warn her about all the things I'm going to do to her as soon as the set is over. But my brain is too fucking fried to even know *what* I'm going to do, so instead I curl my tongue behind her earlobe and nip at the soft skin. Her curled fingers tighten around my bicep, and a smirk touches my lips. I walk away from her and don't look back.

When the song is over, I'm the first one off the stage. I unstrap my guitar from my neck, prop it against the first surface I find, and grab Dee's hand. She makes a little noise and nearly trips behind me in those sexy stiletto heels she's wearing, but she catches her footing and manages to fall into a quick step beside me. Next month, I'll be leaving for a month-long tour to promote the album the band recorded this past week, but until then, I'm all hers.

"Where are we going?" she asks, but the fact that she's following me instead of bitching me out for nearly tugging her off her feet tells me she already knows.

"Anywhere." I push open the first door I find, relieved when it's an empty office. I tow Dee inside, lock the knob behind us, and pin her against the heavy wooden door. My lips cover hers, and my hand sneaks under her skirt to see if she was telling the truth about not wearing any panties.

My calloused fingers brush over silky smooth skin,

and when I find her bare little button and press, the gasp that tears from her lips makes me throb inside my jeans. Her hands are fumbling with my zipper a second later, and then I'm lifting her against the door and squeezing between her thighs. Her fingers scratch over the back of my T-shirt as I sink inside her, and I kiss the moan that sounds from her lips.

"I love you," I say between thrusts. There was a time when the words made her stiffen, made her pull away from me. Now, she turns into putty in my hands. "I fucking love you," I say again, and she melts against my skin.

She's moaning, her ankles crossed tight behind my legs when someone jiggles the doorknob.

Her eyes get wide, and I stop moving for only a second. "Just a minute."

"This is my fucking office!" the person outside yells.

I move Dee to another wall and go back to fucking the hell out of her. "Be. Right. Out!"

I can see the anxiety and desire warring in her eyes, but when I kiss her, the battle is easily won.

The person outside doesn't stop jiggling or knocking, and I thrust into Dee until her moans in my ear are all I hear. When I finish giving her all I've got, my forehead resting heavily on her shoulder, she taps her fingers against my hands and I lower her feet back to the ground. She cleans up with some tissues from the desk, tosses them in a wastebasket, and takes my hand. I give the owner of Mayhem an exhausted, apologetic smile as we leave his office, and he mutters something about me being an asshole as we pass.

"You're going to get in trouble one of these days," Dee warns.

"Worth it," I counter, and her giggle makes it that much more true.

On the bus, she and Peach talk about Dee starting fashion school next week, and even though Dee just blushes and tells me to shut up, I make sure to tell everyone how proud I am of her. She applied, she got in, and I know she's going to be amazing. The shirts are great, but her designs are what she's passionate about, and if she can learn to see in herself what everyone else sees in her, there will be nothing to hold her back.

At home, I give her a much more satisfying version of what happened in the office, and afterward, she lies snuggled against my side with her purple fingernail tracing invisible patterns on my chest. I watch her, breathing slow so I don't bring her back from wherever she is. She's so damn gorgeous, especially in moments when she's lost in thought and showing me she loves me without even realizing that's what she's doing.

Her almond eyes slowly lift to catch mine staring, and I kiss the top of her head. She lets out a contented sigh and snuggles closer against me. "Why do you love me?"

With her silky brown hair spilling through my fingers, I tease, "That'd be like me asking why you love ice cream."

"Because it tastes good," she argues, and I contain a chuckle.

"*You* taste good."

"Oh, you're such a—"

I cut her off by digging my fingers into her sides, and

she laughs hysterically while wiggling out of my reach. When she stops laughing and shoots a glare at me, I plant a surprise kiss on her lips and wrap her back up in my arms. She growls but lets me do it, and I smile because I can't help it.

"I love you because I can't *not* love you," I say, and her fingers curl around my ribs to hug me close.

The night I almost killed Cody was the night I realized just how much she meant to me—more than any girl ever has or ever will. I don't think I loved her yet, not like I do now, but it was the start of something, and I couldn't have stopped it even if I tried. I spent the next few weeks falling—fast and hard, just like she and I do everything. I fell at the festival, at my birthday, during quiet nights at her apartment. I fell every time she smiled at me, every time she let me hold her.

"Do you think we'll last?" she asks, her words a quiet whisper floating across my chest.

I keep her close, not answering because I don't know. Loving Dee is like loving fire. The night I first told her I loved her, when she told me to go home, it broke my heart in a way that it had never been broken before. I ended up drinking myself sick with my mom, toasting the girl who burned me and hating everyone who wasn't as miserable as I was. Then Dee showed up, giving me hope and taking it away again, and I drove back to town that day vowing to forget her.

"Do you?" I counter. I don't know if we'll last—I only know that I hope so. The more time passed after what happened between us in the roped-off bathroom at Mayhem, the more girls I used to try to forget her face, but every night, I found myself drawing her with the pencils she gave me for my birthday. There was no forgetting her, and it took her chucking a poster tube at my head and screaming that she loved me at the top of her lungs to make me realize I'd never want to. Things between us will probably never be easy, but the best things never are. What matters is that every day, I promise to love her forever, and every day, she promises it back.

"I hope so," she says, and I smile when she echoes my thoughts.

Brushing her silky hair through my fingers, I say, "Me too."

We lie like that until there's nothing between us but her heartbeat and my heartbeat and a future we both want—until I quietly say, "I wished for this." When Dee lifts her gaze to mine, I explain, "On my birthday. When you had me blow out the candles, this is what I wished for."

"You wished for me?" she asks, and I give her a smile.

That night, with her face illuminated behind soft flames, I wished for the only thing I'd ever really wanted. I wished to be happy.

"Yeah," I say, lifting her fingers to my lips and planting a soft kiss against her palm. "I wished for you."

The End

New to the series?
Don't forget to read Adam and Rowan's story in

Mayhem

Available now from Avon Impulse!

And don't miss Shawn and Kit's story . . .

Chaos

Coming July 21st from
Avon Impulse!

Read on for a sneak peek!

An Excerpt from Chaos

Nearly Six Years Earlier

"You're *sure* you want to do this?" my twin brother Kaleb asks with his arms crossed firmly over his lanky chest. His bottom lip twists into a knot that he sucks between his teeth, and I roll my eyes.

"How many times are you going to ask me that?" One of my legs is already dangling out my second-story bedroom window, my weighted combat boot stretching my leg toward the grass. I've snuck out of my house a million times—to play flashlight tag, to spy on my brothers, to steal some desperately needed alone time—but never have I felt as nervous as I do tonight.

Or as desperate.

"How many times do I need to before you realize this

is CRAZY?" Kaleb whispers brashly, casting a nervous glance over his shoulder. Our parents are sleeping, and for tonight to go as planned, I need to keep it that way. When he returns his gaze to me, he has the decency to look guilty for almost ratting me out.

"This is my last chance, Kale," my quiet voice pleads, but my twin remains unfazed.

"Your last chance to *what*, Kit? What are you going to do? Confess your eternal love just so he can break your heart just like every other girl those guys ever come into contact with?"

I sigh and throw a second scrawny leg over the window sill, staring out at the clouds rolling over the crescent face of the moon. "Just . . ." Another heavy sigh escapes me, and I say, "If Mom and Dad wake up, just cover for me, okay?"

When I look over my shoulder, Kale is shaking his head.

"Please?"

He walks to meet me. "No. If you're going, I'm coming with you."

"You don't—"

"I'm coming with you or you're not going." My brother's eyes mirror my own—dark and determined, a brown so dark they're almost black. I know the look he's wearing, and I know there's no point in arguing with it. "Your call, Kit."

"Party boy," I tease, and before he can push me out the window, I jump.

"So what's your plan?" he asks after hitting the ground after me and breaking into a sprint at my side.

"Bryce is going to take us."

When Kale starts laughing, I flash him a smug smile, and we both hop into our parents' SUV and begin our wait.

Adam Everest is throwing a party bigger than he's ever thrown tonight. He and the rest of his band all graduated this morning, and rumor is they're all moving away to Mayfield soon. My brother Bryce would have graduated too if he hadn't gotten suspended for vandalizing the principal's car as part of a senior prank. Our parents grounded him for life—or at least until he moves out—but if I know Bryce at all, that isn't going to stop him from making an appearance at the party of the year.

"You sure he's coming?" Kale asks, tapping nervous fingers on the passenger-side armrest, and I point my chin toward the front door. Our third-oldest brother steps onto the porch, sporting that midnight-black hair that all of us Larson kids are known for. He shuts the front door quietly behind him, shoots nervous glances both ways, and jogs toward our parents' car, slowing when I give him a little wave from the driver's seat.

"What the fuck, Kit?" he asks after swinging my door wide open, letting in the late spring air. He shoots an angry glance at Kale, but Kale just shrugs a bony shoulder.

"We're coming too," I say.

Bryce's head shakes sternly from side to side. He learned to give orders as star quarterback of our football team, but he's apparently been hit in the skull one too many times to remember I don't take them.

"No fucking way," he says, but when I rest my hand on

the horn, he tenses. I'm the baby of the family, but having grown up with Kale, Bryce, and two other older brothers, I know how to play dirty.

"Yes fucking way."

"Is she kidding?" Bryce asks Kale, and Kale lifts an eyebrow.

"Does she *look* like she's kidding?"

Bryce sneers at our brother before gluing his eyes back to my weaponized hand and asking me, "Why do you even want to come?"

"Because I do."

Impatient as always, he throws his attention back at Kale. "Why does she want to come?"

"Because she does," Kale echoes, and Bryce bristles when he realizes we're doing the twin thing. I could argue that the sky is pink right now, and Kale would have my back.

"You're seriously going to make me take you?" Bryce complains. "You're fucking *freshmen*. It's embarrassing."

Kale mutters something about us technically being sophomores now, but it's lost under the snark in my voice. "Like we'd want to hang out with you anyway."

In my frustration, I accidentally push too hard on the horn, and an impossibly short, impossibly loud beep silences the crickets around us. All three of us are frozen in place, with wide obsidian eyes, and hearts that are racing so fast, I'm surprised Bryce doesn't piss his pants. Silence stretches in the space between our getaway car and our five-bedroom house, and when no lights come on, we breathe a collective sigh of relief.

"Sorry," I offer, and Bryce laughs as he rakes his hand nervously over his short-cropped hair.

"You're a pain in my fucking ass, Kit." He offers me a hand and yanks me out of the car. "Get in the back. And don't blame me if Mom and Dad ground you 'til you're forty."

The ride to Adam's place takes forever and no time at all. When my brother parks in a long line of cars on the street, shuts the ignition off, and turns to me, I'm pretty damn sure this is the dumbest idea I've ever had. I've lost count of how many telephone poles and street lights have separated me from home.

"Okay, listen," Bryce orders with his eyes flitting between Kale and me, "if the cops break this thing up, I'll meet you at the big oak by the lake, okay?"

"Wait, what?" Kale says, like it just occurred to him that we'd be at a party with underage drinking and a record-breaking number of noise-ordinance violations.

"Okay," I agree for both of us, and Bryce studies my twin for a moment longer before letting out a resigned breath and climbing out of the car. I climb out too, wait for Kale to appear at my side, and follow Bryce toward the sound of music threatening to crack the asphalt under our feet. The party is already in full swing, with kids swarming all over the huge yard like ants harvesting red Solo cups. Bryce walks right into the mayhem inside the front door, and when he disappears, Kale and I share a glance before making our way in after him.

Inside Adam's foyer, my eyes travel up and up to a chandelier that casts harsh white light over what is most definitely a million freaking bodies crammed into the space. I maneuver my way through a sea of shoulders and elbows, through hallways and overstuffed rooms, to get to the back patio door, the music in my ears growing louder and louder with every single step I take. By the time Kale and I emerge outside, it's beating on my eardrums, pulsing in my veins. A massive pool flooded with half-naked high schoolers stands between me and where Adam Everest is belting lyrics into his microphone. Joel Gibbon plays the bass to Adam's left. The new guy, Cody something, plays rhythm guitar next to Joel. Mike Madden beats on the drums at the back.

But all of them are just blurred shapes in my peripheral vision.

Shawn Scarlett stands to Adam's right, his talented fingers shredding lead guitar, his messy black hair wild over deep green eyes locked on the vibrating strings. Heat dances up the back of my neck, and Kale mutters, "He's not even the hottest one."

I ignore him and command my feet to move, carrying me around the pool to where a huge crowd is gathered to watch the band. In my combat boots, torn-up jeans, and loose tank top, I'm severely overdressed standing behind bikini-clad cheerleaders who wouldn't know the difference between a Fender and a Gibson even if I smashed both over their bleach-stained skulls.

The song ends with me standing on my tippy-toes trying to see over bouncing heads, and I turn on Kale with a huff when the band thanks the crowd and starts packing up their stuff.

"Can we go home now?" Kale asks. I shake my head. "Why not? The show's over."

"That's not why I came."

Kale's gaze burrows under my skin, and he reads my mind. "You're seriously going to try to talk to him?"

I nod as we walk away from the crowd.

"And say what?"

"I haven't figured that out yet."

"Kit," Kale cautions, his navy-blue Chuck Taylors slowing to a stop, "what do you expect to happen?" He looks at me with sad dark eyes, and I wish we were standing closer to the pool so I could push him in and wipe that expression off his face.

"I don't expect anything."

"Then why bother?"

"Because I have to, Kale. I just have to talk to him, even if it's just to tell him how much he changed my life, okay?"

Kale sighs, and we both let the conversation go. He knows that Shawn is more than just a teenage crush to me. The first time I ever saw him play guitar was at a school talent show when we were both still in junior high. I was in fifth grade, he was in eighth, and he and Adam put on an acoustic performance that gave me goose bumps from my fingers to my toes. They both sat on stools with guitars on their laps, with Adam singing lead vocals and Shawn singing backup, but the way Shawn's fingers danced over the strings, and the way he lost himself in the music—he took me with him, and I got lost too. I convinced my parents to buy me a used guitar the next week, and I started taking lessons. Now, my favorite thing to do will forever be linked with the person who taught me to love it, the person I fell in love with that day in the junior-high gym.

Love, as much as I hate to admit it. The kind that makes me ache. The kind that would probably be better kept secret since I know it will only break my heart.

I know I'm fucked, and yet an undeniable part of me still needs him to know what he did for me, even if I don't tell him what he *is* to me.

With my body on auto-walk and my mind a million miles away, Kale and I find Solo cups in the kitchen and head toward the keg out back, my thoughts slowly coming back to the present. I've had beer with my brothers before, but I've never operated a keg, so I watch a few people fill their cups before me to make sure I don't make myself look like an idiot when it's my turn at the tap. I nervously pick it up, fill my cup and Kale's, and then wander Adam's property while my brother and I begin our underage drinking. Adam's yard is big enough to be a public park, surrounded by a wrought-iron fence that protects the pool, a few large oaks, and enough teenagers to fill the school gym. I spare a glance at my brother and follow his gaze to a group of guys laughing by the side of the pool.

"He's cute," I offer, nodding my head toward the one that Kale is now pretending not to have been staring at, a cute tan boy in Hawaiian board shorts and flip-flops.

"He is," Kale challenges with feigned indifference. "You should go talk to him."

I give my twin a look, he gives me one back, and I say, "Don't you ever want a boyfriend?"

"You do realize Bryce is still hanging around here somewhere, right?"

I scoff. "So?"

Kale gives me a look that says it all, and I try not to let him see how much his refusal bothers me. It's not that I don't love being the one who keeps his secrets—it's just that I hate that this is one he feels needs to be kept.

"So if Shawn isn't the hottest one," I say to change the subject, "who is?"

"Are you blind?" Kale asks while pushing his face close to mine to inspect my eyes. I use my free hand to push his forehead away.

"They're all pretty cute."

A girl nearby screams bloody murder as the boy in board shorts picks her up and jumps in the pool. Kale watches them and sighs.

"So which one?" I ask again to distract him.

"Mount Everest."

I chuckle. "You're only saying that because Adam is a man-whore. He's the only one you could probably get to switch teams."

"Maybe," Kale says with a tinge of sadness in his voice, and I frown before taking his cup to the keg to refill it. I'm squeezing the tap when he elbows me in the arm.

When I look up, Shawn and Adam are walking toward the keg. Toward *me*.

There are two ways this can go. I can pretend to be confident, offer to pour their beers for them, smile and start a normal conversation so I can say what I need to say, or—nope! I drop the tap, nearly twist my ankles in a supersonic twirl, and bite my lip all the way to a secluded spot that doesn't feel nearly secluded enough.

"What the hell was that?" Kale asks breathlessly from behind me.

"I think I'm having an allergic reaction," I say through a throat that feels too thick.

Kale laughs and pushes me. I stumble forward as he says, "I did *not* come all this way to watch you turn into some kind of girl."

With my lip still pinned between my teeth, I glance back toward the direction we came and see Shawn and Adam, beers in hand, slip inside the house through the patio door.

"What am I supposed to say?" I ask.

"Whatever you need to," Kale says, and then he circles behind me and nudges me toward the door again.

In a daze, I continue walking forward, my feet eating the long distance step by step by step. I don't even realize that Kale hasn't followed until I turn around and he's not there. My Solo cup is empty, but I cling to it like it's a security blanket, avoiding eye contact with everyone around me and pretending I know where I'm going. I navigate a narrow path through a few familiar faces from school, but not many seem to recognize me, and the ones that do just kind of raise an eyebrow before going back to ignoring me.

Everyone from school knows my older brothers. *Everyone.* Bryce was on the football team before he decided getting into trouble was more important than a scholarship. Mason, two years older than Bryce, is infamous for breaking the school's record for number of suspensions.

And Ryan, a year and a half older than Mason, was a record-shattering track star back in his day and remains a legend. All of them straddle this weird line between treating me like one of the guys and acting like I'm coated in porcelain.

I find myself looking for Bryce, desperately wanting to see a familiar face, when I spot Shawn instead. He's sitting in the middle of the couch in the living room, Joel Gibbon on one side and some chick I instantly hate on the other. I'm frozen in place when some idiot slams into me from behind.

"Hey!" I shout over the music, whirling around as the jerk leans on me to steady himself.

"Shit! I'm—" Bryce's eyes lock with mine, and he starts laughing, wrapping his hands around my shoulders to steady himself in earnest now. "Kit! I forgot you were here!" He beams like a happy lush, and I scowl at him. "Where's Kale?"

"By the keg out back," I say, crossing my arms over my chest instead of helping my drunk-ass older brother stay on his feet.

His brows turn in with confusion as he finally finds his balance. "What're you doing in here by yourself?"

"Needed to pee," I lie with practiced ease.

"Oh, want me to take you to the bathroom?"

I'm about to chew him out for treating me like a baby when one of his on-again, off-again girlfriends sidles up next to him and asks him to get her a beer.

"I think I can find my way to the bathroom, Bryce," I finally scoff, and he studies me through a glassed-over gaze before agreeing.

"Okay." He eyes me some more and then unties the over-sized flannel from around my waist and man-handles my arms into it. He pulls it closed over my chest and nods to himself like he's just safeguarded national security. "Okay, don't get into trouble, Kit."

I roll my eyes and take my flannel back off as soon as he walks away, but then I regret dismissing him so quickly when I find myself standing alone in a crowded room. I root myself to a spot by a massive gas fireplace and pretend to drink an empty beer while trying not to look awkward, which is probably useless considering I'm spying on Shawn from afar like a freaking creeper.

What the hell was I thinking coming here tonight? He's surrounded. He's *always* surrounded. He's amazing and popular and way out of my league. The blonde sitting beside him looks like she was born to be a cut-out advertisement propped in front of Abercrombie & Fitch. She's hot and girly and probably smells like fucking daffodils and . . . is standing up to leave.

The spot next to Shawn opens up, and before I can chicken out, I rush across the room and dive ass-first into it.

The cushion sinks beneath my sudden weight, and Shawn turns his head to check out the idiot who nearly slammed right into him. I should probably introduce myself, disclose my affinity for stalking and ass-diving, but instead I keep my mouth shut and force a nervous smile. A moment passes where I'm certain he's going to ask who the hell I am and what the hell I'm doing hijacking the seat beside him, but then his mouth just curves into a nice smile and he goes back to talking with the guys on his other side.

Oh, God. Now what? Now I'm just sitting awkwardly beside him for no apparent reason, and blondie is going to be back any second and order me to move, and then what? Then my shot is gone. Then I jumped out my bedroom window for no freaking reason.

"Hey," I say, tapping Shawn on the shoulder and trying not to do something humiliating like stutter or, you know, throw up all over him.

God, his T-shirt is so soft. Like seriously downy-soft. And warm. And—

"Hey," he says back, something between confusion and interest shading the way he looks at me. His eyes, glassy from drinks he's had, are a deep, deep green, and staring into them is like crossing the border into an enchanted forest at midnight. Terrifying and exhilarating. Like getting lost in a place that could swallow you whole.

"You sounded really good tonight," I offer, and Shawn smiles wider, giving the butterflies in my stomach a little puff of confidence.

"Thanks." He starts to turn away again, but I speak up to keep his attention.

"The riff you did in your last song," I blurt, blushing when he turns back toward me, "it's amazing. I can never quite get that one."

"You play?" Shawn's entire body shifts in my direction, his knees coming to rest against mine. Both of us have worn-through shreds at the knees, and I swear my skin tingles where his brushes against mine. He gives me his complete attention, and it's like every light in the room focuses its heat on me, like every word I say is being documented for the record.

A shadow falls over me, and the Abercrombie model from before glowers down at me, all blonde hair and demon eyes. "You're in my seat."

Shawn's hand lands on my knee to keep me from moving. "You play?" he asks again.

My eyes are glued to his hand—his *hand* on my *knee*—when Demon Eyes whines, "Shawn, she's in my seat."

"So find a new one," he counters, casting her a glance before returning his attention to me. When she finally walks away, my cheeks are burning bright red.

Shawn stares at me expectantly, and I stare back at him for a loserly amount of time before remembering I'm supposed to be answering a question. "Yeah," I finally say, my heart cartwheeling in my chest at the feel of his heavy hand still resting on my knee. "I watched you . . . at a middle-school talent show"—*please don't throw up, please don't throw up, please don't throw up*—"a few years ago, and"—*oh God, am I really doing this?*—"and it made me want to learn to play. Because you were so good. I mean, you ARE so good. Still, I mean"—*train wreck, train wreck, train wreck!*—"You're still really, really good . . ."

My attempt to salvage my heartfelt reasons are rewarded with a warm smile that makes all the embarrassment worth it. "You started playing because of me?"

"Yeah," I say, swallowing hard and resisting the urge to squeeze my eyes shut while I wait for his reaction.

"Really?" Shawn asks, and before I know what he's doing, he removes his fingers from my knee to take my hands in his. He studies the calluses on the pads of my fingers, rubbing his thumbs over them and melting me from the inside out. "You any good?"

A cocky smile curves his lips when he lifts his gaze, and I confess, "Not as good as you."

His smile softens, and he releases my hands. "You've been to a few of our shows, right? Normally wear glasses?"

Is that *me*? The girl in the freaking glasses? I've screamed from the front row for more than a few of the band's shows at the local rec center, but I never thought Shawn noticed me. And now when I think about how dorky I probably looked with my thick, square frames . . . I'm not sure I'm glad he did. "Yeah. I just got contacts last month—"

"They look good," he says, and the blush that's been creeping across my cheeks blooms to epic proportions. I can feel the heat in my face, my neck, my *bones*. "You have pretty eyes."

"Thanks."

Shawn smiles, and I smile back, but before either of us can say another word, Joel is pushing at his arm to get his attention. He's shouting and laughing about some joke Adam told, and Shawn shifts away from me to rejoin their conversation.

And just like that, the moment is over and I didn't even say anything close to what I came here to say. I didn't say thank you or tell him that he changed my life or express anything even *remotely* meaningful.

"Hey Shawn," I say, tapping at his shoulder again when Joel's laughter dies down.

Shawn turns a curious gaze on me. "Yeah?"

"I actually wanted to ask you something."

He turns his body back toward me, and I realize I have no fucking clue what to say next. *I came here to ask you something?* Of all the things that could have come out of my mouth, *that's* what my brain settled on? The desperate, girly part of me that I don't like to acknowledge wants to tell him that I love him and beg him not to move away. But then I'd have to go drown myself in the pool.

"Oh yeah?" Shawn asks, and to stall for time, I lean toward his ear. He leans forward to meet me, and as I breathe in the scent of his shower-fresh cologne, my mind goes completely blank. I've lost the ability to form words, even simple ones like *thank you*. He's moving away soon, and I'm blowing my last chance to tell him how I feel. With my cheek next to his, I turn my face, and then Shawn's eyes are right in front of mine and our noses are practically brushing and his lips are centimeters away—and my brain says *fuck it*. And I lean forward.

And I kiss him.

Not quickly, not slowly. With my eyes closed, I press a warm kiss against his soft bottom lip, which tastes like a million different things. Like beer, like a dream, like the way the clouds swept across the moon tonight. My brain is flickering between wanting to melt into him and needing to pull away when Shawn makes the decision for me.

When his lips open to mine and he deepens the kiss, my heart hammers in my chest and my trembling hands anchor themselves to his sides. His fingers bury in the thick of my hair, pulling me closer, and I'm far too lost to ever want to be found. My fingers fist in the loose fabric of his T-shirt, and Shawn breaks his lips from mine to purr low in my ear, "Come with me."

Acknowledgments

FIRST, LET ME just say: I am an unintentional method writer. When I write, my heroine possesses me, and living inside Dee's head was . . . an experience. Weekly melt-downs. Tons of attitude. Angst like nobody's business. Writing her was a challenge—for me and everyone who had to breathe the same air as me. So a HUGE thanks to the man who had to live with me: my husband, Mike. And thanks to the four ladies who were always there to talk me off the ledge: Rocky Allinger, Kim Mong, Kelleigh McHenry, and my mom, Claudia.

Thanks to my agent, Stacey Donaghy, for crying ugly tears over the same scenes I did. Thanks to my editor, Nicole Fischer, for spending time with Joel even in her sleep. Thanks to Jay Crownover for spoiling me with kick-ass blurbs. Thanks to everyone at HarperCollins who works their magic on my stories to put them in your hands. And last but not least, thanks to each and every one of YOU who are reading this right now. You mean the world to me, and it's because of you that I'm able to continue doing what I love. Thank you, thank you, thank you.

About the Author

Born and raised in South Central Pennsylvania, JAMIE SHAW earned her M.S. in Professional Writing from Towson University before realizing that the creative side of writing was her calling. An incurable night owl, she spends late hours crafting novels with relatable heroines and swoon-worthy leading men. She's a loyal drinker of white mochas, a fierce defender of emo music, and a passionate enthusiast of all things romance. She loves interacting with readers and always aims to add new names to their book-boyfriend lists.

www.authorjamieshaw.blogspot.com

www.facebook.com/jamieshawauthor

Discover great authors, exclusive offers, and more at hc.com.

Give in to your impulses . . .
Read on for a sneak peek at seven brand-new
e-book original tales of romance
from HarperCollins.
Available now wherever e-books are sold.

VARIOUS STATES OF UNDRESS: GEORGIA
By Laura Simcox

MAKE IT LAST
A BOWLER UNIVERSITY NOVEL
By Megan Erickson

HERO BY NIGHT
BOOK THREE: INDEPENDENCE FALLS
By Sara Jane Stone

MAYHEM
By Jamie Shaw

SINFUL REWARDS 1
A Billionaires and Bikers Novella
By Cynthia Sax

FORBIDDEN
An Under the Skin Novel
By Charlotte Stein

HER HIGHLAND FLING
A Novella
By Jennifer McQuiston

An Excerpt from

VARIOUS STATES OF UNDRESS: GEORGIA

by Laura Simcox

Laura Simcox concludes her fun, flirty
Various States of Undress series with a
presidential daughter, a hot baseball player,
and a tale of love at the ballgame.

"Uh. Hi."

Georgia splayed her hand over the front of her wet blouse and stared. The impossibly tanned guy standing just inside the doorway—wearing a tight T-shirt, jeans, and a smile—was as still as a statue. A statue with fathomless, unblinking chocolate brown eyes. She let her gaze drop from his face to his broad chest. "Oh. Hello. I was expecting someone else."

He didn't comment, but when she lifted her gaze again, past his wide shoulders and carved chin, she watched his smile turn into a grin, revealing way-too-sexy brackets at the corners of his mouth. He walked down the steps and onto the platform where she stood. He had to be at least 6'3", and testosterone poured off him like heat waves on the field below. She shouldn't stare at him, right? Damn. Her gaze flicked from him to the glass wall but moved right back again.

"Scared of heights?" he asked. His voice was a slow, deep Southern drawl. Sexy deep. "Maybe you oughta sit down."

"No, thanks. I was just . . . looking for something."

Looking for something? Like what—a tryst with a stranger in the press box? Her face heated, and she clutched the water bottle, the plastic making a snapping sound under her fingers. "So . . . how did you get past my agents?"

He smiled again. "They know who I am."

"And you are?"

"Brett Knox."

His name sounded familiar. "Okay. I'm Georgia Fulton. It's nice to meet you," she said, putting down her water.

He shook her hand briefly. "You, too. But I just came up here to let you know that I'm declining the interview. Too busy."

Georgia felt herself nodding in agreement, even as she realized *exactly* who Brett Knox was. He was the star catcher—and right in front of her, shooting her down before she'd even had a chance to ask. Such a typical jock.

"I'm busy, too, which is why I'd like to set up a time that's convenient for both of us," she said, even though she hoped it wouldn't be necessary. But she couldn't very well walk into the news station without accomplishing what she'd been tasked with—pinning him down. Georgia was a team player. So was Brett, literally.

"I don't want to disappoint my boss, and I'm betting you feel the same way about yours," she continued.

"Sure. I sign autographs, pose for photos, visit Little League teams. Like I said, I'm busy."

"That's nice." She nodded. "I'm flattered that you found the time to come all the way up to the press box and tell me, in person, that you don't have time for an interview. Thanks."

He smiled a little. "You're welcome." Then he stretched,

his broad chest expanding with the movement. He flexed his long fingers, braced a hand high on the post, and grinned at her again. Her heart flipped down into her stomach. Oh, no.

"I get it, you know. I've posed for photos and signed autographs, too. I've visited hospitals and ribbon cutting ceremonies, and I know it makes people happy. But public appearances can be draining, and it takes time away from work. Right?"

"Right." He gave her a curious look. "We have that in common, though it's not exactly the same. I may be semi-famous in Memphis, but I don't have paparazzi following me around, and I like it that way. You interviewing me would turn into a big hassle."

"I won't take much of your time. Just think of me as another reporter." She ventured a warm, inviting smile, and Brett's dark eyes widened. "The paparazzi don't follow me like they do my sisters. I'm the boring one."

"Really?" He folded his arms across his lean middle, and his gaze traveled slowly over her face.

She felt her heart speed up. "Yes, really."

"I beg to differ."

Before she could respond, he gave her another devastating smile and jogged up the steps. It was the best view she'd had all day. When Brett disappeared, she collapsed back against the post. He was right, of course. She wasn't just another reporter; she was the president's brainy daughter—who secretly lusted after athletes. And she'd just met a hell of an athlete.

Talk about a hot mess.

An Excerpt from

MAKE IT LAST
A Bowler University Novel
by Megan Erickson

The last installment in Megan Erickson's
daringly sexy Bowler University series
finds Cam Ruiz back in his hometown
of Paradise, where he comes face-to-
face with the only girl he ever loved.

CAM SIGHED, FEELING the weight of responsibility pressing down on his shoulders. But if he didn't help his mom, who would?

He jingled his keys in his pocket and turned to walk toward his truck. It was nice of Max and Lea to visit him on their road trip. College had been some of the best years of his life. Great friends, fun parties, hot girls.

But now it felt like a small blip, like a week vacation instead of three and a half years. And now he was right back where he started.

As he walked by the alley beside the restaurant, something flickered out of the corner of his eye.

He turned and spotted her legs first. One foot bent at the knee and braced on the brick wall, the other flat on the ground. Her head was bent, a curtain of hair blocking her face. But he knew those legs. He knew those hands. And he knew that hair, a light brown that held just a glint of strawberry in the sun. He knew by the end of August it'd be lighter and redder and she'd laugh about that time she put lemon juice in it. It'd backfired and turned her hair orange.

The light flickered again but it was something weird and artificial, not like the menthols she had smoked. Back when he knew her.

As she lowered her hand down to her side, he caught sight of the small white cylinder. It was an electronic cigarette. She'd quit.

She raised her head then, like she knew someone watched her, and he wanted to keep walking, avoid this awkward moment. Avoid those eyes he didn't think he'd ever see again and never thought he'd wanted to see again. But now that his eyes locked on her hazel eyes—the ones he knew began as green on the outside of her iris and darkened to brown by the time they met her pupil—he couldn't look away. His boots wouldn't move.

The small cigarette fell to the ground with a soft click and she straightened, both her feet on the ground.

And that was when he noticed the wedge shoes. And the black apron. What was she doing here?

"Camilo."

Other than his mom, she was the only one who used his full name. He'd heard her say it while laughing. He'd her moan it while he was inside her. He'd heard her sigh it with an eye roll when he made a bad joke. But he'd never heard it the way she said it now, with a little bit of fear and anxiety and . . . longing? He took a deep breath to steady his voice. "Tatum."

He hadn't spoken her name since that night Trevor called him and told him what she did. The night the future that he'd set out for himself and for her completely changed course.

She'd lost some weight in the four years since he'd last seen her. He'd always loved her curves. She had it all— thighs, ass and tits in abundance. Naked, she was a fucking vision.

Damn it, he wasn't going there.

But now her face looked thinner, her clothes hung a little loose and he didn't like this look as much. Not that she probably gave a fuck about his opinion anymore.

She still had her gorgeous hair, pinned up halfway with a bump in front, and a smattering of freckles across the bridge of her nose and on her cheekbones. And she still wore her makeup exactly the same—thickly mascaraed eyelashes, heavy eyeliner that stretched to a point on the outside of her eyes, like a modern-day Audrey Hepburn.

She was still beautiful. And she still took his breath away.

And his heart felt like it was breaking all over again.

And he hated her even more for that.

Her eyes were wide. "What are you doing here?"

Something in him bristled at that. Maybe it was because he didn't feel like he belonged here. But then, she didn't either. She never did. *They* never did.

But there was no longer a *they*.

An Excerpt from

HERO BY NIGHT
Book Three: Independence Falls
by Sara Jane Stone

Travel back to Independence Falls in Sara
Jane Stone's next thrilling read. Armed with
a golden retriever and a concealed weapons
permit, Lena Clark is fighting for normal. She
served her country, but the experience left her
afraid to be touched and estranged from her
career-military family. Staying in Independence
Falls, and finding a job, seems like the first
step to reclaiming her life and preparing for
the upcoming medal ceremony—until the
town playboy stumbles into her bed . . .

SOMETIMES BEAUTY KNOCKED a man on his ass, leaving him damn near desperate for a taste, a touch, and hopefully a round or two between the sheets—or tied up in them. The knockout blonde with the large golden retriever at her feet took the word "beautiful" to a new level.

Chad Summers stared at her, unable to look away or dim the smile on his face. He usually masked his interest better, stopping short of looking like he was begging for it before learning a woman's name. But this mysterious beauty had special written all over her.

She stared at him, her gaze open and wanting. For a heartbeat. Then she turned away, her back to the party as she stared out at Eric Moore's pond.

Her hair flowed in long waves down her back. One look left him wishing he could wrap his hand around her shiny locks and pull. His gaze traveled over her back, taking in the outline of gentle curves beneath her flowing, and oh-so-feminine, floor-length dress. The thought of the beauty's long skirt decorating her waist propelled him into motion. Chad headed in her direction, moving away from the easy, quiet conversation about God-knew-what on the patio.

The blonde, a mysterious stranger in a sea of familiar

faces, might be the spark this party needed. He was a few feet away when the dog abandoned his post at her side and cut Chad off. Either the golden retriever was protecting his owner, or the animal was in cahoots with the familiar voice calling his name.

"Chad Summers!"

The blonde turned at the sound, looking first at him, her blue eyes widening as if surprised at how close he stood, and then at her dog. From the other direction, a familiar face with short black hair—Susan maybe?—marched toward him.

Without a word, Maybe Susan stopped by his side and raised her glass. With a dog in front of him, trees to one side, and an angry woman on his other, there was no escape.

"Hi there." He left off her name just in case he'd guessed wrong, but offered a warm, inviting smile. Most women fell for that grin, but if Maybe Susan had at one time—and seeing her up close, she looked very familiar, though he could swear he'd never slept with her—she wasn't falling for it today.

She poured the cool beer over his head, her mouth set in a firm line. "That was for my sister. Susan Lewis? You spent the night with her six months ago and never called."

Chad nodded, silently grateful he hadn't addressed the pissed-off woman by her sister's name. "My apologies, ma'am."

"You're a dog," Susan's sister announced. The animal at his feet stepped forward as if affronted by the comparison.

"For the past six months, my little sister has talked

about you, saving every article about your family's company," the angry woman continued.

Whoa . . . Yes, he'd taken Susan Lewis out once and they'd ended the night back at his place, but he could have sworn they were on the same page. Hell, he'd heard her say the words, *I'm not looking for anything serious*, and he'd believed her. It was one freaking night. He didn't think he needed signed documents that spelled out his intentions and hers.

"She's practically built a shrine to you," she added, waving her empty beer cup. "Susan was ready to plan your wedding."

"Again, I'm sorry, but it sounds like there was a miscommunication." Chad withdrew a bandana from his back pocket, one that had belonged to his father, and wiped his brow. "But wedding bells are not in my future. At least not anytime soon."

The angry sister shook her head, spun on her heels, and marched off.

Chad turned to the blonde and offered a grin. She looked curious, but not ready to run for the hills. "I guess I made one helluva first impression."

"Hmm." She glanced down at her dog as if seeking comfort in the fact that he stood between them.

"I'm Chad Summers." He held out his hand—the one part of his body not covered in beer.

"You're Katie's brother." She glanced briefly at his extended hand, but didn't take it.

He lowered his arm, still smiling. "Guilty."

"Lena." She nodded to the dog. "That's Hero."

"Nice to meet you both." He looked up the hill. Country music drifted down from the house. Someone had finally added some life to the party. Couples moved to the beat on the blue stone patio, laughing and drinking under the clear Oregon night sky. In the corner, Liam Trulane tossed logs into a fire pit.

"After I dry off," Chad said, turning back to the blonde, "how about a dance?"

"No."

An Excerpt from

MAYHEM

by Jamie Shaw

**A straitlaced college freshman is drawn
to a sexy and charismatic rock star in this
fabulous debut New Adult novel for fans
of Jamie McGuire and Jay Crownover!**

"I can't believe I let you talk me into this." I tug at the black hem of the stretchy nylon skirt my best friend squeezed me into, but unless I want to show the top of my panties instead of the skin of my thighs, there's nothing I can do. After casting yet another uneasy glance at the long line of people stretched behind me on the sidewalk, I shift my eyes back to the sun-warmed fabric pinched between my fingers and grumble, "The least you could've done was let me wear some leggings."

I look like Dee's closet drank too much and threw up on me. She somehow talked me into wearing this miniskirt—which skintight doesn't even begin to describe—and a hot-pink top that shows more cleavage than should be legal. The front of it drapes all the way down to just above my navel, and the bottom exposes a pale sliver of skin between the hem of the shirt and the top of my skirt. The fabric matches my killer hot-pink heels.

Literally, killer. Because I know I'm going to fall on my face and die.

I'm fiddling with the skirt again when one of the guys near us in line leans in close, a jackass smile on his lips. "I think you look hot."

"I have a boyfriend," I counter, but Dee just scoffs at me.

"She means *thank you*," she shoots back, chastising me with her tone until the guy flashes us another arrogant smile—he's stuffed into an appallingly snug graphic-print tee that might as well say "douche bag" in its shiny metallic lettering, and even Dee can't help but make a face before we both turn away.

She and I are the first ones in line for the show tonight, standing by the doors to Mayhem under the red-orange glow of a setting summer sun. She's been looking forward to this night for weeks, but I was more excited about it before my boyfriend of three years had to back out.

"Brady is a jerk," she says, and all I can do is sigh because I wish those two could just get along. Deandra and I have been best friends since preschool, but Brady and I have been dating since my sophomore year of high school and living together for the past two months. "He should be here to appreciate how gorgeous you look tonight, but nooo, it's always work first with him."

"He moved all the way here to be with me, Dee. Cut him some slack, all right?"

She grumbles her frustration until she catches me touching my eyelids for the zillionth time tonight. Yanking my fingers away, she orders, "Stop messing with it. You'll smear."

I stare down at my shadowy fingertips and rub them together. "Tell me the truth," I say, flicking the clumped powder away. "Do I look like a clown?"

"You look smoking hot!" she assures me with a smile.

I finally feel like I'm beginning to loosen up when a guy walks right past us like he's going to cut in line. In dark shades and a baggy black knit cap that droops in the back, he flicks a cigarette to the ground, and my eyes narrow on him.

Dee and I have been waiting for way too long to let some self-entitled jerk cut in front of us, so when he knocks on the door to the club, I force myself to speak up.

"They're not letting people in yet," I say, hoping he takes the hint. Even with my skyscraper heels, I feel dwarfed standing next to him. He has to be at least six-foot-two, maybe taller.

He turns his head toward me and lowers his shades, smirking like something's funny. His wrist is covered with string bracelets and rubber bracelets and a thick leather cuff, and three of his fingernails on each hand are painted black. But his eyes are what steal the words from my lips—a greenish shade of light gray. They're stunning.

When the door opens, he turns back to it and locks hands with the bouncer.

"You're late," the bouncer says, and the guy in the shades laughs and slips inside. Once he disappears, Dee pushes my shoulders.

"Oh my GOD! Do you know who you were just talking to?!"

I shake my head.

"That was *Adam* EVEREST! He's the lead singer of the band we're here to see!"

An Excerpt from

SINFUL REWARDS 1
A Billionaires and Bikers Novella
by Cynthia Sax

Belinda "Bee" Carter is a good girl; at least,
that's what she tells herself. And a good girl
deserves a nice guy—just like the gorgeous
and moody billionaire Nicolas Rainer. Or
so she thinks, until she takes a look through
her telescope and sees a naked, tattooed man
on the balcony across the courtyard. He has
been watching her, and that makes him all
the more enticing. But when a mysterious
and anonymous text message dares her to
do something bad, she must decide if she is
really the good girl she has always claimed
to be, or if she's willing to risk everything
for her secret fantasy of being watched.

An Avon Red Impulse Novella

I'D TOLD CYNDI I'd never use it, that it was an instrument purchased by perverts to spy on their neighbors. She'd laughed and called me a prude, not knowing that I was one of those perverts, that I secretly yearned to watch and be watched, to care and be cared for.

If I'm cautious, and I'm always cautious, she'll never realize I used her telescope this morning. I swing the tube toward the bench and adjust the knob, bringing the mysterious object into focus.

It's a phone. Nicolas's phone. I bounce on the balls of my feet. This is a sign, another declaration from fate that we belong together. I'll return Nicolas's much-needed device to him. As a thank you, he'll invite me to dinner. We'll talk. He'll realize how perfect I am for him, fall in love with me, marry me.

Cyndi will find a fiancé also—everyone loves her—and we'll have a double wedding, as sisters of the heart often do. It'll be the first wedding my family has had in generations.

Everyone will watch us as we walk down the aisle. I'll wear a strapless white Vera Wang mermaid gown with organza and lace details, crystal and pearl embroidery accents, the bodice fitted, and the skirt hemmed for my shorter height. My hair will be swept up. My shoes—

Voices murmur outside the condo's door, the sound piercing my delightful daydream. I swing the telescope upward, not wanting to be caught using it. The snippets of conversation drift away.

I don't relax. If the telescope isn't positioned in the same way as it was last night, Cyndi will realize I've been using it. She'll tease me about being a fellow pervert, sharing the story, embellished for dramatic effect, with her stern, serious dad—or, worse, with Angel, that snobby friend of hers.

I'll die. It'll be worse than being the butt of jokes in high school because that ridicule was about my clothes and this will center on the part of my soul I've always kept hidden. It'll also be the truth, and I won't be able to deny it. I am a pervert.

I have to return the telescope to its original position. This is the only acceptable solution. I tap the metal tube.

Last night, my man-crazy roommate was giggling over the new guy in three-eleven north. The previous occupant was a gray-haired, bowtie-wearing tax auditor, his luxurious accommodations supplied by Nicolas. The most exciting thing he ever did was drink his tea on the balcony.

According to Cyndi, the new occupant is a delicious piece of man candy—tattooed, buff, and head-to-toe lickable. He was completing armcurls outside, and she enthusiastically counted his reps, oohing and aahing over his bulging biceps, calling to me to take a look.

I resisted that temptation, focusing on making macaroni and cheese for the two of us, the recipe snagged from the diner my mom works in. After we scarfed down dinner, Cyndi licking her plate clean, she left for the club and hasn't returned.

Three-eleven north is the mirror condo to ours. I straighten the telescope. That position looks about right, but then, the imitation UGGs I bought in my second year of college looked about right also. The first time I wore the boots in the rain, the sheepskin fell apart, leaving me barefoot in Economics 201.

Unwilling to risk Cyndi's friendship on "about right," I gaze through the eyepiece. The view consists of rippling golden planes, almost like . . .

Tanned skin pulled over defined abs.

I blink. It can't be. I take another look. A perfect pearl of perspiration clings to a puckered scar. The drop elongates more and more, stretching, snapping. It trickles downward, navigating the swells and valleys of a man's honed torso.

No. I straighten. This is wrong. I shouldn't watch our sexy neighbor as he stands on his balcony. If anyone catches me . . .

Parts 1 – 7 available now!

An Excerpt from

FORBIDDEN
An Under the Skin Novel
by Charlotte Stein

Killian is on the verge of making his final vows
for the priesthood when he saves Dorothy from a
puritanical and oppressive home. The attraction
between them is swift and undeniable, but every
touch, every glance, every moment of connection
between them is completely forbidden . . .

An Avon Red Impulse Novel

WE GET OUT of the car at this swanky-looking place called Marriott, with a big promise next to the door about all-day breakfasts and internet and other stuff I've never had in my whole life, all these nice cars in the parking lot gleaming in the dimming light and a dozen windows lit up like some Christmas card, and then it just happens. My excitement suddenly bursts out of my chest, and before I can haul it back in, it runs right down the length of my arm, all the way to my hand.

Which grabs hold of his, so tight it could never be mistaken for anything else.

Course I want it to be mistaken for anything else, as soon as he looks at me. His eyes snap to my face like I poked him in the ribs with a rattler snake, and just in case I'm in any doubt, he glances down at the thing I'm doing. He sees me touching him as though he's not nearly a priest and I'm not under his care, and instead we're just two people having some kind of happy honeymoon.

In a second we're going inside to have all the sex.

That's what it seems like—like a sex thing.

I can't even explain it away as just being friendly, because somehow it doesn't feel friendly at all. My palm has been laced with electricity, and it just shot ten thousand volts into him. His whole body has gone tense, and so my body goes tense, but the worst part about it is:

For some ungodly reason he doesn't take his hand away.

Maybe he thinks if he does it will look bad, like admitting to a guilty thing that neither of us has done. Or at least that he hasn't done. He didn't ask to have his hand grabbed. His hand is totally innocent in all of this. My hand is the evil one. It keeps right on grasping him even after I tell it to stop. I don't even care if it makes me look worse—*just let go*, I think at it.

But the hand refuses.

It still has him in its evil clutches when we go inside the motel. My fingers are starting to sweat, and the guy behind the counter is noticing, yet I can't seem to do a single thing about it. Could be we have to spend the rest of our lives like this, out of sheer terror at drawing any attention to the thing I have done.

Unless he's just carrying on because he thinks I'm scared of this place. Maybe he thinks I need comfort, in which case all of this might be okay. I am just a girl with her friendly, good-looking priest, getting a motel room in a real honest and platonic way so I can wash my lank hair and secretly watch television about spaceships.

Nothing is going to happen—a fact that I communicate to the counter guy with my eyes. I don't know why I'm doing it, however. He doesn't know Killian is a priest. He has no clue that I'm some beat-up kid who needs help and protection rather than sordid hand-holding. He probably thinks we're married, just like I thought before, and the only thing that makes that idea kind of off is how I look in comparison.

I could pass for a stripe of beige paint next to him. In here his black hair is like someone took a slice out of the night sky. His cheekbones are so big and manly I could bludgeon the counter guy with them, and I'm liable to do it. He keeps staring, even after Killian says "two rooms please." He's still staring as we go down the carpeted hallway, to the point where I have to ask.

"Why was he looking like that?" I whisper as Killian fits a key that is not really a key but a gosh darn credit card into a room door. So of course I'm looking at that when he answers me, and not at his face.

But I wish I had been. I wish I'd seen his expression when he spoke, because when he did he said the single most startling thing I ever heard in my whole life.

"He was looking because you're lovely."

An Excerpt from

HER HIGHLAND FLING
A Novella

by Jennifer McQuiston

When his little Scottish town is in desperate
straits, William MacKenzie decides to resurrect
the Highland Games in an effort to take
advantage of the new tourism boom and invites
a London newspaper to report on the events.
He's prepared to show off for the sake of the
town, but the one thing William never expects
is for this intrepid reporter to be a she . . .

WILLIAM SCOWLED. MORAIG'S future was at stake. The town's economy was hardly prospering, and its weathered residents couldn't depend on fishing and gossip to sustain them forever. They needed a new direction, and as the Earl of Kilmartie's heir, he felt obligated to sort out a solution. He'd spent months organizing the upcoming Highland Games. It was a calculated risk that, if properly orchestrated, would ensure the betterment of every life in town. It had seemed a brilliant opportunity to reach those very tourists they were aiming to attract.

But with the sweat now pooling in places best left unmentioned and the minutes ticking slowly by, that brilliance was beginning to tarnish.

William peered down the road that led into town, imagining he could see a cloud of dust implying the arrival of the afternoon coach. The very *late* afternoon coach. But all he saw was the delicate shimmer of heat reflecting the nature of the devilishly hot day.

"Bugger it all," he muttered. "How late can a coach be? There's only one route from Inverness." He plucked at the damp collar of his shirt, wondering where the coachman could be. "Mr. Jeffers knew the importance of being on time today. We need to make a ripping first impression on this reporter."

James's gaze dropped once more to William's bare legs. "Oh, I don't think there's any doubt of it." He leaned against the posthouse wall and crossed his arms. "If I might ask the question . . . why turn it into such a circus? Why these Games instead of, say, a well-placed rumor of a beastie living in Loch Moraig? You've got the entire town in an uproar preparing for it."

William could allow that James was perhaps a bit distracted by his pretty wife and new baby—and understandably so. But given that his brother was raising his bairns here, shouldn't he want to ensure Moraig's future success more than anyone?

James looked up suddenly, shading his eyes with a hand. "Well, best get those knees polished to a shine. There's your coach now. Half hour late, as per usual."

With a near-groan of relief, William stood at attention on the posthouse steps as the mail coach roared up in a choking cloud of dust and hot wind.

A half hour off schedule. Perhaps it wasn't the tragedy he'd feared. They could skip the initial stroll down Main Street he'd planned and head straight to the inn. He could point out some of the pertinent sights later, when he showed the man the competition field that had been prepared on the east side of town.

"And dinna tell the reporter I'm the heir," William warned as an afterthought. "We want him to think of Moraig as a charming and rustic retreat from London." If the town was to have a future, it needed to be seen as a welcome escape from titles and peers and such, and he did not want this turning into a circus where he stood at the center of the ring.

As the coach groaned to a stop, James clapped William on the shoulder with mock sympathy. "Don't worry. With those bare legs, I suspect your reporter will have enough to write about without nosing about the details of your inheritance."

The coachman secured the reins and jumped down from his perch. A smile of amusement broke across Mr. Jeffers's broad features. "Wore the plaid today, did we?"

Bloody hell. Not Jeffers, too.

"You're late." William scowled. "Were there any problems fetching the chap from Inverness?" He was anxious to greet the reporter, get the man properly situated in the Blue Gander, and then go home to change into something less . . . *Scottish.* And God knew he could also use a pint or three, though preferably ones not raised at his expense.

Mr. Jeffers pushed the brim of his hat up an inch and scratched his head. "Well, see, here's the thing. I dinna exactly fetch a chap, as it were."

This time William couldn't suppress the growl that erupted from his throat. "Mr. Jeffers, don't tell me you *left* him there!" It would be a nightmare if he had. The entire thing was carefully orchestrated, down to a reservation for the best room the Blue Gander had to offer. The goal had been to install the reporter safely in Moraig and give him a taste of the town's charms *before* the Games commenced on Saturday.

"Well, I . . . that is . . ." Mr. Jeffers's gaze swung between them, and he finally shrugged. "Well, I suppose you'll see well enough for yourself."

He turned the handle, then swung the coach door open.

A gloved hand clasped Mr. Jeffers's palm, and then a high, elegant boot flashed into sight.

"What in the blazes—" William started to say, only to choke on his surprise as a blonde head dipped into view. A body soon followed, stepping down in a froth of blue skirts. She dropped Jeffers's hand and looked around with bright interest.

"Your chap's a lass," explained a bemused Mr. Jeffers.

"A lass?" echoed William stupidly.

And not only a lass . . . a very pretty lass.

She smiled at them, and it was like the sun cresting over the hills that rimmed Loch Moraig, warming all who were fortunate enough to fall in its path. He was suddenly and inexplicably consumed by the desire to recite poetry to the sound of twittering birds. That alone might have been manageable, but as her eyes met his, he was also consumed by an unfortunate jolt of lustful awareness that left no inch of him unscathed—and there were quite a few inches to cover.

"Miss Penelope Tolbertson," she said, extending her gloved hand as though she were a man. "R-reporter for the *London Times*."

He stared at her hand, unsure of whether to shake it or kiss it. Her manners might be bold, but her voice was like butter, flowing over his body until it didn't know which end was up. His tongue seemed wrapped in cotton, muffling even the merest hope of a proper greeting.

The reporter was female?

And not only female . . . a veritable goddess, with eyes the color of a fair Highland sky?

He raised his eyes to meet hers, giving himself up to the sense of falling.

Or perhaps more aptly put, a sense of flailing.

"W-welcome to Moraig, Miss Tolbertson."